To Win a Highland Scot

A TIME-TRAVELER'S HIGHLAND LOVE, BOOK 3

COPYRIGHT

To Win a Highland Scot
A Time-Traveler's Highland Love, Book 3

Cover Art by Wicked Smart Designs
Editor Grace Bradley Editing

ISBN: 978-0-6451138-7-7

PROLOGUE

Druiminn Castle 1410, Scotland

Boyd Macleod, chief of the Macleod clan, stood before his stronghold, staring down the Fae who threatened him and those he loved. "You will not take her!" he roared, fear and panic threatening his control. The Fae Queen smirked to his outburst.

His wife stood behind him. He could not see her, but knew she would be as defiant as he, standing tall and proud, a sword in her hand and ready to die this day if it meant that they would be separated.

He would not let them take her. Never.

The Fae Queen gestured to Sorcha. "Mayhap, I have not been clear enough, Chief Macleod. Sorcha's mother, a Fae Princess, was granted the child's life on the condition that she would be returned to us on her five and twentieth year. She is half-Fae, after all, and does not belong in your dirty, ancient world." The Fae Queen cast a scathing look about his land, disdain on her face as she gazed up to the castle itself, the curtain wall protecting his four-story tower castle that his father finished building late last century. It was one of the best fortresses in Scotland, and she dared to mock it. Ridicule him and his people.

"I doona care what deal you had. Sorcha doona belong to you. She belongs here with me. With our people."

"No, she does not," the queen said, her tone bored. "No matter what iron you wield toward me, it will make no difference here. I could strike you down with a flick of my hand and take her anyway, take you and your men's life away." The queen's eyes seemed to glow, and for a moment, Boyd thought she may do what she threatened before seemingly thinking otherwise.

"If I do not take Sorcha, she will die here this day. I always collect on what is due to my kind, but I shall gift you something in return, Chief Macleod."

"I doona want anything from you. No more deals will be made here. Not today or ever."

The queen smiled. She was a beautiful woman, her long, flowing white hair sparkled as if the precious metal of silver was threaded into her locks. Her eyes were fiercely blue, as ancient as his land, and all-knowing. A powerful being that, although standing in long, white robes that appeared angelic to anyone who viewed her, the being was as cold as ice and her soul as hard as rock.

"Boyd," Sorcha whispered behind him, clutching his arm and showing the first signs she was scared. Hell, he was afraid, not that he'd ever admit to such a fault, but he was. Sorcha was everything to him. He could not lose her.

"Aye." He turned, clasping Sorcha's arms. "'Tis alright, lass. I'll not let them harm you."

Tears welled in her eyes, and she cast a glance in the queen's direction. "I doona want to go. I'm not a Fae. The tales are untrue," his wife declared, her voice breaking on her last words.

Boyd pulled her against him, stroking her long, white locks, so similar to the Fae before them, and he knew that statement to be a lie. She had come to him as a young woman looking for a husband, her parents seeking an alliance. Sorcha was small-boned with striking features, otherworldly, and he had been captured by her beauty. He had fallen in love with her the moment he'd seen her. His only regret in their marriage was the absence of a bairn. No matter how much they had tried, they had not been blessed by children of their own.

Keeping hold of Sorcha, he unsheathed his sword, holding it at his side. His men, armed and behind him, did the same, and the sound of metal sliding against metal rent the air. A fog descended over the land, and a biting wind accompanied it. An ominous sight, and he could feel his men's alarm, their fear of the change of the elements.

"Do not disappoint me, Macleod. A deal is a deal. If you do not obey my decree, Sorcha will be no more. If she does not come with us now, she will die. The choice is yours."

There was no choice in such a decree. His mind roared with alarm, with hate and anger. How dare the Fae Queen do this to him and his people? If she chose, she could leave Sorcha alone, let her live out her life here with him. He knew the Fae to be fickle, untrustworthy, and cruel when they wanted to be, but this… This was beyond evil. There were no words for such an act.

"Sorcha is mortal. To take her makes no sense. Leave her be. Mayhap we can exchange something else, coin or land."

The queen laughed, the sound echoing through the

land, mocking his words. "I have no need for your riches, Chief Macleod. The child is to be returned to us. Her mother has paid for her crimes of siring a child with a mortal. Now that child is grown and can return to the people she should always have known."

"This is my family. I doona want anything to do with the Fae," Sorcha yelled out over the wind.

But it was no use. No matter how they pleaded or what they offered, nothing but Sorcha would satisfy them. They would take his wife and his life along with it. For to live without her was equivalent to death itself.

The queen raised her hand, sweeping it over his armed men. The sound of clanging metal, of bodies falling onto one another, met his ears, and Boyd turned to see his men still as death.

"Do not be alarmed. They are not dead, merely sleeping. Once Sorcha is with us, they will wake." The queen held out her hand toward Sorcha, her confidence that his wife would go with them spiking a fury inside Boyd he had held dormant.

But no more.

He charged forward, raising his sword. The queen's eyes flared as he came within striking distance, but then he was floating above his lands, his ability to move stripped from him.

The queen's face morphed into something angry and displeased. She no longer radiated light and calm, but darkness, her gown changing to black instead of white, the silks swirling like an angry sea.

"That was uncalled for, Macleod, and I cannot stand for such insolence. Come." She reached for Sorcha. His wife fought the command, turned, and tried to hold on to the men lying at her feet, but like an unknown force, she was pulled toward the queen.

Panic tore through Boyd, and he struggled in his invisible chains, the movement like swimming through a fast-moving current, heavy and impossible to gain traction. "Stop, please, doona take her." He would beg if he had to. This was his wife, his love. He could not have her stolen from him.

"Say your goodbyes. You will not see her again." The queen took Sorcha's hand, and with horror, Boyd watched as his wife seemed to lose all her fear, anger, and panic. Her face relaxed to the beautiful curves he knew so well, that he had traced with his fingers, had kissed when they made love. Her woolen gown made of the clan's red, blue, and green colors fell from her body and was replaced by a long, white, flowing robe, barely appropriate to retain honor.

"Sorcha will be happier with us, Macleod, but we thank you for your care toward our princess."

Sorcha looked up at him, a small frown between her brow. "I love you, Boyd." Her whispered words carried off into the wind.

"No," he roared, "doona take her. No!" Boyd fought against his bonds, but it was no use. He was captured, held above the ground, and as useless as the Campbells.

The Fae and Sorcha disappeared. The queen remained, stared up at him, a smirk marring her lips. "She will be happy with us and live forever, but you'll never see her again. But do not despair, Macleod, for I have something for you too, just as I promised."

"I doona want your doaty gift, shrew," he seethed, conceiving a hundred different ways he'd like to lob off her head.

"Had you cooperated, I would not need to bestow upon you anything, but now I must. You defied our laws. You loved a Fae and sought to keep her here in the human world where she did not belong. Punishment must be served," she said, her eyes glowing alarmingly bright. "I curse you with immortality. You shall live as long as the Fae you valued so dearly. An eternity without the one you love until your heart is full of another. The people you love, your clan and family shall grow old and die, while you, Macleod will be forced to watch. No strike against you will save you from this curse. Not even one against yourself."

He would never love again. No woman could compare to his wife. Sorcha was his heart and soul. "I welcome the curse, for if only to give me time to seek justice upon you." Boyd gained pleasure at the queen being taken aback by his words. Good, he wanted to insult her, scare her, let her know that one day, may it be a week or a thousand years from now, he would have his vengeance.

The queen shrugged one delicate shoulder. "Well then, I suppose you shall live forever. Open your heart, Macleod, and your pain will be over. Fight me on this, and you shall forever dwell in your darkness, your anguish and resentment." And then she was gone.

Boyd dropped like a stone to the ground, making an *oomph* sound when his gut landed against a rock. He stared at where he'd seen Sorcha last, the sound of his men gaining their wits behind him.

He stood, turned to face his men, despair swamping him. He'd lost the only woman he had ever loved. His life. He raised his eyes and found his men, some still on the ground, staring at him as if they'd seen a ghoul.

"Chief," Corey, one of his guardsmen gasped, pointing at Boyd's head. "Your hair, 'tis white."

Boyd grabbed a lock of his hair and started at the sight of it. Gone was his dark-red brown hair, and in its place was the coloring of the Fae. He could not speak, did not know what the change meant. Or if it were simply the marking of the curse now in place.

The sound of laughter floated through the trees, and he turned, glaring at the woods, knowing the Fae Queen was watching, enjoying her foolery.

"Laugh all you like, but know that one day I shall have my revenge on you. I promise on my own heart's blood," he yelled, slicing across his hand with his dirk. Blood pooled in his palm and slid down his arm. He fisted his hand, raising it to the sky. "I will not die until I see your head upon the ground. See who is laughing then."

The laughter stopped, and he turned, striding back to Castle Druiminn, past his startled men's faces and his staff who went about their chores.

Today, he may have lost everything, but tomorrow was a new dawn. A new day to plan, plot, and ultimately act. He would get Sorcha back, and he would kill the Faery Queen, and he would not die until he had done so.

CHAPTER 1

Druiminn Castle 2021, Scotland

Maya Harris stood at the gates of Druiminn Castle and watched as bus after bus unloaded its many tourists, all eager and excited for their tour of the old Scottish stronghold. Maya shaded her eyes and glanced up at the castle, forever in awe of this estate and still home to the Laird Macleod.

How lucky she was to be working here for the summer and helping out in the kitchens when they needed more staff. With the multitude of tours every day, she was constantly cleaning up after the sightseers. Yet, she loved every minute of her work. Just to be within the ancient walls, looking up at the magnificent portraits of past lairds, the tapestries, the oldest dating back to the 15th century was one that had always captured her notice.

Her employer and head housekeeper, Mrs. Holmes, had stated it depicted a standoff between Chief Boyd Macleod and the Fae Queen in the early fifteenth century. Maya had inwardly scoffed at the old folk tale, as an

English woman, born and raised in Kent, she never believed in the Scottish superstitions. Still, the tapestry was unbelievably well kept and lifelike. Not that she could touch it to see how perfect it really was since it sat behind a wall of Perspex to stop grubby, oily hands from feeling it.

Hers included.

She strolled around the side of the castle, entering through the kitchen that also served as the staff entrance. Maya greeted the chef Samuel, Molly, and Heidi, her two closest friends she'd made in Scotland, who were eating their lunch.

"Oh, Maya, you'll be so excited to hear what we have to tell you today. Mrs. Holmes was stating this morning that she needs to clean the Perspex covering the tapestries in the great hall this afternoon," Molly said, her eyes bright with excitement.

"If you're sneaky and quick enough, you may be able to feel one for the first time. We all know you're a little obsessed, just like the rest of us who want to touch things we're not supposed to," Heidi joked.

Samuel, who had been standing kneading dough, scoffed, didn't comment on Heidi's words.

"I wouldn't dare touch it. Mrs. Holmes would sack me on the spot, and I would hate to lose this job. I love it here." Maya pulled off her coat and hung it in a small closet before sitting down at the table. "Have you just finished your morning shift? Are we still on for drinks down in Druiminn tonight?"

Every Friday night, the staff would get together and have a few wines or beers at the local pub. The week had been extremely busy, what with the height of the tourist season, and they would all have earned their night of relaxing and partying before another busload of people arrived tomorrow.

"I can't make it tonight," Molly said, her tone dejected. "I'm training for my night job at the petrol station. It's only from eight to eleven every night, so I'll still be able to work here, but it'll mean more money for me, and I'll get to Dubai for my holiday even more quickly."

Maya smiled at the thought of a holiday in Dubai. All that warm, hot air, the beaches, the amazing architecture, and the people. "I would love to travel there. What an amazing place it would be." One day, Maya promised herself.

She had very few holidays in her life. As an orphan, she never knew her parents, didn't even know who they were. From what she could find out from Child Services, they had left her on the doorstep of a hospital in Kent and never returned.

Her life hadn't been too terrible, however. Not like what so many other children had to endure when in foster care. She had been put with kind people, if not a little distracted and not too involved, but at least they never hurt her.

She had finished high school, attended university, and earned a degree in media studies, but found after she left that gaining employment in that field was a hard gig to score. With her money running out, she had seen the advertisement for cleaning work required on a Highland estate during busy tourist seasons and had applied.

The moment she had walked up from Druiminn toward the castle, watching as it slowly revealed itself through the trees, she had fallen instantly in love and under its spell. When summer was over, she would ask to be kept on or seek employment locally. There was something about

Scotland that pulled at her heartstrings and made her feel at home.

"She's only going because she has fantasies of marrying a rich sheik," Heidi teased, grinning. "If you do happen to land one, see if he has any brothers. I could endure quite well a life of luxury."

Molly laughed, sipping her can of soft drink. "Oh, I will, and I can find one for you too, Maya. If you like."

Maya chuckled, pushing back her chair when she noticed the time. "If you find a sheik, it'll be enough for me that you'll be happy." She went over to the uniforms closet and pulled out a clean apron. "I better get going, the morning tour will be gone by now, but I'll see you tonight, Heidi?"

Heidi saluted, grinning. "Oh, yes, you'll see me for sure. I'll probably beat you there since you're working this afternoon, but I'll have a wine waiting for you."

"Thank you. Seeya, ladies," she said, striding out into a passage that led toward the great hall. Maya found Mrs. Holmes ordering a bevy of men to remove the Perspex from several tapestries in the great hall, her deep frown showing her concern, not to mention she was hovering over the men's work like a panicked mother hen.

"Do you need any help?" Maya asked, coming to stand beside Mrs. Holmes and watching as three men worked on the Fae tapestry she loved so much.

"Oh, Maya, just the girl I wanted to see. You'll be with me today. We've roped off the Great Hall, the tourists can walk past the hall, but they canna enter. I'm sure they will not mind since they'll see the restoration of sorts that we're doing. No point in looking at the tapestries when you can't see the actual needlework."

"I would love to help you. What would you like me to do?"

Mrs. Holmes pointed toward several buckets and cleaning items. "Once the Perspex is down, we'll need to clean and dry them thoroughly. The men will come back later today to put the Perspex back up, so we won't have them waiting around for us to finish, but we'll try and get this done today."

"Of course," Maya said, inspecting the cleaning items before turning to watch as another group of men had the first Perspex down. It was not her favorite tapestry, but another work that depicted a lady looking out over the ocean from Druiminn's Castle walls, but she was turned toward the artist, a cheeky grin on her face as if she was laughing at something that was said behind her.

"I know you love the Fae tapestry, but this is my favorite," Mrs. Holmes said, staring up at the work now free from its plastic bonds. It had faded of course, they all had over the hundreds of years since they had been sewn, but they were all still so beautiful.

"Who is this of?" Maya asked, unable to look away from the striking woman grinning back at them all from the tapestry.

"Her name was Abigail, but everyone from historical records called her Abby. She married Aedan Macleod, laird here in 1601. It is rumored she was from foreign shores, but nobody really knew for certain which ones. I've always thought she has an air of mischief and knowledge about her that you doona often see in paintings or tapestries. Like she knows something we do not."

Maya had to agree. The woman looked so happy, like the tapestry had caught a moment in time, similar to a photo today. "She's very beautiful. Is this the same woman in the painting in the upstairs gallery? The large one, over the fireplace?"

"Oh aye, the very same. Laird Macleod and Abigail were a love match. Devoted to each other to their very last days. He had many portraits commissioned of her."

How lovely to have found a love such as they had and in 1601. Not the easiest time in history to be a woman or wife to a man with such responsibilities. Scotland's history was as savage and as rough as the highland mountains.

"Right now," Mrs. Holmes said, cutting into her thoughts. "Enough of the past, let us finish our jobs so we may enjoy our weekend. I know you wish to get to the tavern and enjoy a night out with your friends."

"Are you doing anything this weekend, Mrs. Holmes?"

"Nay, just a spot of gardening and cleaning up around the yard. The usual."

Maya smiled at the older woman before rinsing out her cloth and wiping the Perspex, ensuring it was spotless and free from any smears. They worked for several hours. The large, rectangular-shaped Perspex covers were dustier than Maya had assumed them to be when they were on the wall. They placed the ones that were finished in front of the tapestries they belonged to before Maya turned to the last Perspex that needed to be cleaned.

Mrs. Holmes stood, clutching her back as she came into a standing position. The older woman looked tired and pained from the day's work. Maya took pity on her. "I can finish this one, Mrs. Holmes, if you wish to head home. I'll let the laird's staff know that I'm leaving, and they can lock up the rooms they have open to the public."

Mrs. Homes didn't look sure, and Maya smiled, trying to put her at ease. "Truly, I'm more than happy to finish this one alone. It'll only take me an hour at most, and I'll be done. You head off, enjoy your weekend, and I'll see you on Monday."

"You're rostered on for tomorrow. Are you sure you doona want me to stay and finish this one? I doona have to be back here until Monday."

Maya waved her concerns away, rinsing out her cloth. "It's no trouble at all. I love being here, and at this time of the evening, it's lovely and quiet. I can almost picture myself as the lady of the manor, going about her chores in the house."

Mrs. Holmes chuckled, stretching out her back yet again before throwing her cleaning rag into the bucket beside her. "I am aching a little, so if you're sure? I doona want to leave you in the lurch."

Maya shook her head. If she showed she was willing to go the extra mile while working for the laird during their busy season, perhaps it would lead to a full-time position. She would love to live and work here full time. One of the most beautiful places in the world, without a doubt. "Not at all. You go. I'll finish soon enough. You enjoy your weekend."

Without further prompting, Mrs. Holmes picked up her bucket and started for the door. "Thank you, Maya. You're a real asset to this estate. I canna thank you enough."

Maya smiled, bidding Mrs. Holmes goodnight before turning the Perspex and scrubbing it. She finished the last cover within the hour, placing it before the tapestry for the men to rehang tomorrow. It took her minutes only to empty her bucket and pack away the cleaning products they had used.

She entered the Great Hall, tidied up the chairs, a few display items that were moved during the day's work, and put the room back to rights before leaving. Standing in the central hall, she was amazed as she looked up at the tall stone walls, the dais at the end of the room that so many lairds had sat, ate, and laughed with their people. It was a magical feeling. It wasn't hard to imagine times of old, the people, the music, and laughter that must have passed within these walls.

Maya wasn't sure what it was about this place, but she felt like she was coming home the moment she had arrived at Druiminn Castle. That this was where she was supposed to have always been. Not Kent. Not England. But here, the Isle of Sky, the Highlands. Scotland.

She walked over to her favorite tapestry, studying the masterpiece yet again. This one was lifelike, almost like a photo, and the laird in this time was so handsome with his cutting features, his build worthy of a romance book. They rarely made men like that in her time. Not that she had been looking much these days. Men, in general, had been a disappointment, and so she had decided to concentrate on herself and no one else. Make herself happy before attempting to make others so.

The castle was quiet, not a breath of wind or a creak to be heard. Maya frowned, looking about the hall when a shiver stole down her spine. The sense that the castle was waiting for something, someone, trembled through her.

She crossed her arms, hugging herself and looking again to see if anyone was about. There was no one there, and she shook her head, disregarding her silly notions. Not that it would surprise her to find the castle to be haunted, but she didn't believe in those sorts of things.

With a sigh, she turned back to the tapestry, the urge to feel it, just once, overwhelming. If the laird found out, she would be sacked on the spot, her dream of living and working here full time over.

And yet, she was alone, there were no security cameras...

A voice in her head taunted her, told her to touch it. That this was her only chance. It could be years before they took the covers off again. With a need, a yearning that burned through her body, she reached out, wanting to touch the handsome laird.

With a will of its own, her hand would not stop, and then, finally, the pad of her finger touched the tapestry, the silk thread soft and smooth to the touch. "Beautiful," she gasped on a breath. And then everything changed.

The room spun, voices echoed, faces she could not recognize came in and out of view.

What is happening to me?

Fear froze her to the spot. She tried to run toward the door, but the room turned at an increasing rate, making it impossible to flee. Something bad was happening—something she couldn't control.

She screamed for help, but even though her mouth was open, and her mind shouted the words, no sound emerged. What had she done! Why did she touch the tapestry!

So, this was how she would die, her final thought before the blackness enfolded her, and there was nothing.

Nothing at all.

CHAPTER 2

Druiminn Castle 1510, Scotland

Maya scrunched up her face as the odor of wet dog woke her, along with the stench of rotten breath. She cracked her eyes open the smallest bit to see where she was. What met her vision wasn't at all what she expected.

A large wolfhound, panting before her face, stared and sniffed her head. She didn't move for fear of frightening the dog and causing it to react.

Gone were the stone flagstone floors with soft Aubusson rugs upon them, and in their place were hard, musty-smelling rushes. She sat up, looking about the room, her mind telling her it was the same place she worked, the same walls, dais, and fireplace, but there were so many things different about it too.

The fine furniture she polished was no more. Rough, handmade benches ran up and down the length of the room. The dais, a polished, darker wooden table, sat before the fire at one end. Two large high-back chairs lined up behind it.

Voices met her ears, men's voices in particular, and fear prickled down her spine, but when she went to move, she could not. Her limbs, buttery and weak, refused to work.

Like a nightmare, she watched as men and women entered the hall, some ignoring her presence altogether while others gave her a curious stare before seating themselves.

A woman in a gray, woolen dress bustled into the room, a bevy of women behind her, all carrying trays with a profuse amount of food. They set them on each table, another group of servants following those carrying trays and laying down wooden plates and spoons.

One of the servants whispered something in the older woman's ear, and she turned, her eyes widening at the sight of Maya.

"Och, and who are you, may I ask?" The woman came to stand before her, her hands settling on her wide hips.

"I, ah," Maya croaked, her mind not wanting to believe what she was starting to think had happened to her, but there was nothing else for it. No other explanation. Had she just time traveled? There wasn't any way in hell Mrs. Holmes could pull off such a trick and so quickly unless they drugged her in some way, and she'd been out of it for days. That was unlikely. Mrs. Holmes was a kind woman, no prankster.

"I'm Maya Harris."

At hearing her voice, the occupants of the hall stopped and turned, looking at her with something akin to disdain. Maya shut her mouth, pushing herself back against the wall and wishing it would open up and swallow her whole. Or better yet, return her home.

Why had she touched the tapestry? Stupid, curious fool.

The tapestry must have been what sent her here. Could it return her home? She looked up at the wall where it hung, but found nothing but bare stone staring back at her. No tapestry, no nothing that could help her return to her time. There were several large spikes and swords. Maybe they could at least keep her safe if these people turned on her.

"You are English. What are you doing in Druiminn Castle? I doona think I hired you as help, so I'm curious to know what you are seeking here, lass?"

Maya thought over her reply. She had to be careful. If she were kicked out, then where would she go? What would she do? The castle must hold the key in getting her back to her time, and she had to stay here to enable that.

"I fell and hit my head when I entered the hall. I traveled here from England. I'm looking for work." It was all she could think of to say, and absurd as it sounded when speaking it aloud, there was little she could do to change her fate. "I'm sorry I'm a little confused." Maya leaned forward, electing the same response from the older lady who seemed to be in charge. "May I ask what year this is?"

The woman's demeanor changed, and then everything happened quickly after her words. The older woman reached down, clasping her arm and dragging her up and out of the hall. She took her into a small room that sat alongside the Great Hall, shutting them both inside. This was used as a small linen closet in her time. Now, however, it held a different purpose. The room had a window and a small desk, a lone candle burning on the bureau with a few papers scattered about.

"You are a time walker then. Well, 'tis good to meet

you, Maya Harris. We have been waiting a long time for your arrival."

Maya frowned, her stomach roiling at the absurdness of what the older woman had said. The past fifteen minutes were the most impossible of her life. "A what? What is a time walker?" She had never heard of such a thing, and she was certainly not one. Nothing so impossible had happened to her in the past. Nothing ever happened to her at all.

Nothing exciting anyway.

"You are not from our time, if I have that correct. Your clothing states as much, and your hair. Mayhap your skin is as clean and fresh as the day you were born, I imagine. Had you lived in our time, traveled from England as you state, no such thing would be possible." The woman stepped back, studying her. "What time have you traveled from, lass? What brought you here?"

Maya chewed her bottom lip while her mind frantically fought to calm down. "I'm from the twenty-first century. I was working at Druiminn, but in my time. I…" She rubbed her head, her thoughts a jumble. "I touched a tapestry and then I woke up in the hall below. That's all I remember."

"Hmm," the woman said, nodding slowly. "Well, that you were gifted with such a journey tells me that you are the one whom the laird has been waiting for. Even if the stubborn lad doona know it." She smiled at Maya and a little of Maya's concern dissipated. She seemed like a nice woman, and looked to be trying to help her.

"What am I going to do? The tapestry that I touched isn't in the hall. I thought if I touched it again it may send me back. Do you know of any in the castle?" Maya looked about, not seeing any wall hangings in this room either.

"Nay, there are several paintings, but no tapestries, not as yet in any case. I do believe the laird has one being made, but that is several months from completion."

Maya let out a frustrated breath. This was hopeless. What if this laird was cruel and unkind? What if he did not trust her and killed her on the spot? She was too young to die. And she certainly didn't want to die via a sword or hanging. Oh dear God, did they hang people in Scotland in this time?

"All will be well, lass. You doona need to look so frightened. We must have your attire changed and come up with a story for your past before the laird meets you." The older woman frowned, studying Maya as if she were some kind of otherworldly being. "I'm Mrs. Fletcher, the head housekeeper here at Druiminn Castle. I've worked for the family for many years since I was a lass of your age or younger. A position that has been passed down through my family since the laird lost his wife many years ago."

"What is the year, Mrs. Fletcher?" Maya pressed, needing to know as much as she needed air to breathe.

"It is the year of our Lord, fifteen hundred and ten, Maya lass. Tell me what year it is that you have traveled from?"

She slumped down on a nearby chair, her legs refusing to hold her upright any longer. "How do you know that I have traveled from anywhere, except England as I said? Is it so obvious that I'm not a local?"

"Oh, I've seen and heard many a tale about time walkers, the Fae, superstitions that would keep your pretty head awake forever and a day. I know a time walker when I see one, and I believe you are one of those. Now, no more nonsense. Tell me what year, and then we can decide what to do about it, if anything. Or at least try to work out what you being here means."

"Does it have to mean anything?" Maya asked, her stomach roiling with nerves. Would she ever be able to travel home? Would she ever see her friends again? Experience indoor plumbing? Dear Lord, what would she do without a toilet!

She took in the room. There was no overhanging light, no light switch, all the modern conveniences the castle had in her time were stripped and gone. Surely this sort of thing, time travel, wasn't possible. And certainly not something that happened to people such as herself. Nothing ever happened to her that was remarkable.

"It's 2021 where I'm from. As I said, I work at Druiminn Castle as a cleaner during the holiday season. The current laird, Richard Macleod opens up his estate and grounds to the public for them to tour." The truth bubbled out of her, no matter that Mrs. Fletcher's face had paled to a deathly gray. "I came up to Scotland to work. I've seen the laird from afar, but I have yet to meet him. He's happily married with children."

"There is a laird still in your time? Five hundred years from now, there is a Laird Macleod?" the older woman squeaked, clapping her hands, a smile breaking out on her face. "Och, 'tis good news, lass. It means our laird, Boyd Macleod, breaks the curse that has ailed him these hundred years."

"What?" Maya stood, stepping away from the older lady. "He's cursed and been living for over a hundred years?" How old was this laird? If he were over a hundred years, he must look like a walking corpse by now. Maybe she had hit her head harder than she thought. Or the housekeeper had. Who believed in curses? Only crazy people, right? But then, she was standing in a room, had seen people already with her own eyes who defied reality, so who really was the crazy person…

Mrs. Fletcher held out her hand in a placating kind of way, trying to stem her fears. "Boyd Macleod's age has been frozen in time since the Fae Queen cursed him to find a love greater than the one he had with his wife. The woman they took from him. Of course, our laird loved dearly and has never found another, nor would he, since he's sworn himself to revenge, not life. Not a life with another that is."

The tapestry, of course. The day Boyd Macleod, Chief of the Macleod clan, faced the Fae Queen and lost everything he had ever loved. "The tapestry you mention that the laird is having made and is due in several months… Does this by any chance depict the day he lost his wife?" If such a thing could be confirmed, and she had access to it when it was delivered, maybe it would send her home, and this nightmare would be over.

"I believe that is the case, Maya. 'Tis not ready yet, has been years in the making, but we hope to have it here by Samhain." Mrs. Fletcher studied her a moment before she said, "You believe the tapestry will send you home should you touch it again?"

"I do," she said, but a little of her hope fled at the woman's statement. Samhain was months away, that's if the time lined up the same. It had been June when she was in her time. Maybe it was closer to Samhain than she thought.

"What month are we in?" she queried, praying the woman said late October, which would place her right near the time the tapestry may be ready.

"'Tis June, lass."

Maya swallowed the lump that wedged in her throat. It would be no use to anyone to fall into a heap of tears. There was little she could do until the tapestry was ready. Other than the Fae turning up again and sending her home.

She pulled herself out of her dejected musings and looked over to the older woman. She supposed she had to thank her lucky stars that Mrs. Fletcher seemed like a nice lady. One with an open mind who wouldn't tie her to a pole and burn her as a witch simply because she appeared one night in the Great Hall. "My only chance of returning home is to remain here until the tapestry returns. I can only pray that it sends me back home. I do not belong in this time. I have friends who'll worry about me. They'll think something awful has happened."

Mrs. Fletcher nodded, taking in Maya's words and finding merit in them. "While I doona know all the particulars of time travel, I do believe this to be true. You touching the tapestry and that it sent you here can only mean one thing. You are the key to the clan's future. You are the way in which our laird will find love and peace."

"Me?" Maya said, her word coming out as a squeak. She didn't want to be any laird's great love and certainly not one who was over a hundred years old. Eww. Her lip curled up in disgust at the thought of trying to win his affections. She was only twenty-seven. If he had been cursed a hundred years already and had been married before that, he would be at least 120 years old. "The laird will not be interested in me, and I'm certainly not interested in playing this game. I'm sure other Scottish lasses could warm his bed."

Mrs. Fletcher's brow furrowed in a confused frown. "The laird may be 127 years old, but he doona look a day over twenty-five. Meet the laird first and then see what you think. He's used to me throwing women in his path, but none have ever captured his heart. You, however, my dear, I think may be different. The Fae Queen cursed him until he found a love greater than the one he had with his wife. We have tried many women of his time, all of them sent home without harm or husband. But the Fae doona think about a woman out of time that may be sent back to claim the laird's heart. You may be just the woman to break this curse and find love while you are here."

Maya stared at Mrs. Fletcher, wondering if the older woman had lost her mind. She had touched a stupid tapestry, that was all. That did not mean she was destined to break an ancient curse in a bygone time.

"Come, lass, we'll get you settled in your room and dressed. Canna have you walking around in those clothes," she said, distaste crossing her features as if her uniform offended her in some way.

Maya glanced down at her black trousers and shirt, the white apron she still had tied over the front. She debated making a run for it, bolting out the castle and grounds, but then where would she go? She knew no one, and if she really was in 1510, then the time would not be safe for a woman wandering about Scotland.

No, Druiminn Castle held the key to her returning home, or at least when the tapestry was finished and was finally hung on the walls, it would. She would touch the silk thread again and pray it threw her back into her time. Until then, she would bide her time and her tongue and pray that she would be home soon, and all this would be nothing but a nightmare to forget.

CHAPTER 3

Boyd strode into the Great Hall and started for the dais. His clansmen were enjoying the nightly feast already. The hum of conversation, laughter, and jesting soothed a part of his soul and made his long life worth something, knowing his people were well cared for and content.

He slumped down into his chair, nodding for a serving wench to pour him ale.

He'd spent the day out in the fields, looking over the harvest, the crops, and discussing the good yields they should gain this year.

A bowl of stew, the smell of game, onions, and garlic wafted up to him, and his stomach rumbled, reminding him he'd not eaten since breaking his fast at dawn.

Boyd ripped some bread apart and dipped it into the steaming hot meal, engrossed himself for a moment with the food's deliciousness when the hairs on the back of his neck rose.

He wiped his mouth with the back of his hand, looking out over the hall. His people sat staring at the archway that led to the spiraling stone staircase leading to the upstairs bedchambers. Boyd frowned, dread coiling in his gut that the Fae had returned, that the queen herself had shown her fickle human form again to his people after all these years.

But it was not the Fae Queen. It was his housekeeper and another lass, one whom he did not recognize. He shut his eyes a moment, sighing at the sight of the lass who looked as startled as his people.

It seemed Mrs. Fletcher had found another woman to parade before him like a peahen, ruffling their tail feathers and trying to gain the peacock's attention.

Well, he had enough of his housekeeper's infuriating meddling, and he'd not put up with it a moment longer. The lass could stay, of course. To send her home to her family without housing her for a time would be a great insult, but he'd not do much else to make her stay here worthwhile.

He had long given up any hope of having another woman in his life. His wife was lost to him, had never tried to visit with him or give him hope.

A little part of him hated her for that. Sorcha had meant everything to him, and yet she had never once defied the Fae to try to see him. If only to say a proper goodbye.

He would never forgive her for that.

Out the corner of his eye, he could see Mrs. Fletcher walking the woman toward him, and he supposed she would be deposited at the dais to eat dinner.

He stared out over the hall, glaring at his people when they continued to watch him and his reaction to the intrusion. Understanding dawned on their features, and they turned back to their meals, pretending at least not to be taking notice of what was happening at their laird's table.

Mrs. Fletcher cleared her throat, coming to stand before him. "This is our clan chief, Boyd Macleod. Laird, this is Maya Harris. She will be staying with us for a time."

Boyd threw a displeased glance at Mrs. Fletcher before he recommenced eating. "A pleasure," he mumbled, not bothering to look at the lass. He had seen hundreds of them over the years, Mrs. Fletcher's ancestors as nosy and infuriating as the woman before him. Throughout the hundred years his housekeeper's family had served him, they had also tried to serve up women as often as meals. He was tired of it all.

"Sit down here, lass. I'll fetch you some food."

Boyd chewed his meal, ignoring the sweet-smelling scent that wafted over to him when she sat. Citrus, he mused, downing his ale.

He hoped she could not smell his odor. After the hard day's work, he knew he would stink. He should have bathed before dinner, but he had not expected his housekeeper to produce another lass for him to ignore.

Mrs. Fletcher brought a bowl of stew and a cup of wine. The lass did not delve into her food straightaway but went for the wine itself. She drank continuously, and when she placed the cup down upon the table, the hollowness of the sound told Boyd the goblet was empty.

His lips twitched at the notion she liked her wine, but he frowned instead, making a point to eat, to finish his meal so he could escape and get the hell out of the hall and away from the lass beside him.

"You're cursed, Mrs. Fletcher said."

Boyd spat out his ale, turning to face her, and the moment he did, he knew it to be a mistake. Dark-blue eyes looked up at him expectantly, long, dark lashes fanned across her cheeks each time she blinked. He'd never seen the like before. He wanted to reach out and touch them to see if they were real, for never had he ever seen lashes as long as the woman's beside him.

Her lips were full, a little too pouty for his liking, and yet his groin flexed at the sight of her luscious lips. He wiped his mouth, staring at her. He knew he had not answered, and yet, the words would not come. He cleared his throat, reminding himself he never dallied with the lasses Mrs. Fletcher brought before him to inspect.

He wasn't a man who needed a woman in his life. He had a wife, and no matter how bitter he may be at Sorcha for leaving him, he was a patient man. To wait another hundred years to have her in his arms would be a hardship, but one he would bear. He would not touch another female unless it were the woman he had promised to love for all time.

"Aye, I'm cursed, and if you are a smart lass, you will hie yourself back to your family and never look back toward Macleod land again."

She shrugged, and his eyes dipped to the blue velvet gown she wore. He clenched his jaw at the sight of her breasts, rising and falling with each breath. She was a comely wench, and yet she wasn't for him.

No one was.

"I'm unable to return home at present. Otherwise, I would. I assure you."

"You are English. Whatever made you think to travel to the Highlands to gain a husband? Are there none in England who will do you very well?"

She chuckled, poking at her food with a spoon. Had the lass never seen stew before? Was she daft of mind, and that's why her family had sent her here? It was well known in the Highlands that he was cursed, a man not to be crossed. All thanks to the Fae and their shrew queen who ruined his life, his legacy. However, the lasses didn't seem to mind his past and continued to parade through his doors when their family allowed.

She pinned him with her stare. "No matter what Mrs. Fletcher may have said to you, Macleod, I do not want a husband, but I do need you to allow me to stay here for a few months at least before I return home. If you permit me to stay, I promise not to harass you with the possibility of marriage."

He turned, staring at her. Was this some kind of game she was playing? Was she trying to fool him into a false sense of salvation? "You doona want to marry me? Am I not good enough for you then?" Boyd wasn't sure why he was so displeased with the notion that the comely lass beside him didn't want his hand in marriage, but it grated on his nerves. Every lass wished to win the heart of the cursed Laird Boyd Macleod. Over the years, it had become somewhat of a living legend, a game for those who wished to play, not that anyone ever won.

Only the Fae won this war, and he and Sorcha were the losers.

But this English lass did not want to win his heart. What the devil? "A Scottish lad not good enough for your pure, sweet, English blood?" Even to Boyd, his tone reeked of sarcasm and annoyance.

"Nothing of the kind, I promise you. But I do not know you, and I don't particularly like being thrown into situations not of my own making. I don't know about you, but I feel extremely uncomfortable knowing your people think

I'm here to win your heart. I would prefer that we could be friends until it is time that I leave."

The pleading note in her voice pulled at a part of him he'd thought long obsolete. He rubbed his chest, shrugging. What did it matter what this lass wanted to do or not? He had no intention of trying to get her to warm his bed. To occupy his heart. "You may stay, and I promise you in return that I shall not try to molest you in any way either. I doona want to marry you any more than you want to marry me."

She smiled, sighing in relief, and Boyd stilled. For an English lass, she was comely, more so than any of the women paraded before him in the past hundred years. What was a woman of such beauty doing unmarried? Somebody surely should have handfasted her years ago.

"It's settled then. We're to be friends and nothing more."

He stared at her, unsure if the lass was sound. What woman doona want Laird Boyd Macleod to be her husband? Mrs. Fletcher had brought him the only one in England and Scotland who did not.

His housekeeper must be losing her touch.

This wee English lass was different. He wasn't sure how he felt about that right now, nor did he care to dwell on the facts. He merely wished to eat his dinner, drink his good ale, and be left alone. He'd been isolated for a hundred years. Of all the women who could accost him now and ruin his dinner, it was this English one. The idea dinna bear thinking over.

As if his life couldn't get any worse.

But it just had.

CHAPTER 4

The following day Maya found herself standing out the front of Druiminn Castle, staring back at a building she hardly recognized. Gone was the second tower, the great front doors that joined the original part of the castle with the newer build that still stood today in her time. The bridge that crossed over the slow-flowing river was there, but less ornate than the one that stood today. There was a stone wall that surrounded the castle, kept those who looked out over the ocean safe from falling in.

The ocean that crashed against the back of the castle's fortifications remained unchanged, as did the forest that lay past the river. Would the small town of Druiminn still be there? Would it be as quaint and welcoming as it always appeared?

A group of guards strode past her, their Scottish dialect thick and hard to decipher, and yet some words were easy to separate.

Sassenach. English wench after a rich husband. The laird's future bride.

She stared after them, hoping that none of those things became truth.

She didn't want to marry Boyd Macleod any more than he wished to marry her, even if he was one of the most handsome men she'd ever met in her life.

The tapestry in her time did not do him justice. When he'd stood after finishing his hastily eaten meal the night before, she'd been shocked mute by his height.

The size of his pecs was enough to distract her, and she'd drank way too much red wine by then to stop her ogling. Worse was the fact she'd dreamed of him, not a sweet-natured one either. But a hot, dirty dream that made her curious about the man more than she ought to be.

He was a medieval laird. He was used to getting his way with his servants, his people, and his women. She didn't want to be part of his adoring pets.

Maya turned to look out over the forest, thinking of her dream. Macleod had stormed her room, finding her in bed, groggy and a little unsure from having been woken up. He had yanked the covers off her naked form before he'd come over her, laying claim to her body and doing so many naughty and delicious things that she'd woken up hot, wet, and bothered. Even now, her skin shivered at the thought of his touch. He'd been magnificent and more satisfying than any of her lovers in the past.

She could only thank the Lord she'd not come across him at breakfast. She wasn't sure how she would ever look at him again after what she'd allowed him to do to her in her dreams. What he had allowed her to do to him.

Maya wiped her brow, blowing out a frustrated breath. 1510 Druiminn Castle would be her home, at least until the tapestry was finished. As soon as it was hanging back on the castle walls, she would return to her time, and all of this life would be over.

She hoped her friends were not too worried about her, not that she didn't think they wouldn't be. They would've already called the police, and she would've been presumed missing, dead even. However, how would she explain her disappearance when she returned? No one would believe this tall story if she were to tell them the truth.

A chill ran down her spine at the thought of the tapestry not working. That even with it finished, it may not be the key that sent her here. Whatever would she do then?

The laird would not let her stay here forever. Would she be sent off the lands to face life in medieval Scotland? There was little doubt in Maya's mind that she'd be dead within a month. She wasn't made for this time, and she didn't know a thing about survival in the outdoors.

"Something troubling you, lass?"

The deep, gravelly voice pulled her from her thoughts. Maya turned to see Macleod striding toward her, the handle of a sword poking up from behind his shoulder. She swallowed. He was everything anyone would want from a Scottish highlander—tunic, plaid shawl over one shoulder, dagger, sporran. Holy shit, trews that hugged his muscular thighs. Damn, he was hot.

"Nothing at all. Why do you ask?" Maya turned to look back at the forest, hoping he didn't notice her face had turned hot and was no doubt blotchy and red.

"You are chewing you bottom lip, and you had a pensive frown upon your brow." He reached out, sliding his thumb over her brow and seemingly trying to smooth out her skin.

She stilled. The breath in her lungs expired. The pad of his thumb was course and rough from manual labor, and yet she knew to her very core she liked what she felt. Liked his hands on her as much now as she enjoyed them in her dream the night before.

The remembrance of her dirty dream made her skin burn even more. Damn it all to hell. He would ask her about her blushing next, and then she'd be really stuffed.

"Well," she started, her mind whirling with what to say to him. How to explain her fear without telling him where she was from? Mrs. Fletcher didn't think it a good idea that he know, and the woman would know the laird and how he would react better than Maya would.

"I cannot sit around your castle for the next few months without anything to do. I've never been a person who sits around and sews all day." Because she was pretty certain from the few history books she had read in the past, this was at least one pastime women partook in to fill the time. "I need employment. Maybe I could help you with the castle upkeep? Or in the gardens?" She would do anything if it kept her occupied, stopped her mind from dwelling on the thought she was hundreds of years from her time and with no possibility of returning there any time soon.

He crossed his arms, legs spread, staring down at her. "You wish to have employment at the castle like one of my servants. You are my guest. I coudna use you in that way. Your family would have my head if they heard of it."

"They will not hear of it, I promise. But I cannot be idle for so long. I shall go mad. Please, Macleod. Give me something to do."

. . .

Boyd narrowed his eyes, looking at the lass dressed today in a green velvet gown that was as comely as the blue of last evening, and he could think of many ways in which to keep the lass occupied.

He'd had the most dreadful nightmare last eve. He'd stormed the lass's bedchamber, had his way with her, with her approval, he might add. A night of enjoyment, of pleasure, something he had not known he'd missed until now.

Her mouth had been as maddening as he'd imagined it, and the things she had done with her pretty lips left his cock as hard as a rock. He'd woken spent on his sheets. His body breathing hard and fast from tupping her with a ferocious need that had left him reeling.

He'd ridden out on the lands early, not bothering to break his fast, but to see the lass standing just beyond his castle gates, pensive, a worried frown across her brow left him uncomfortable.

He put it down to not wanting any of his guests uncomfortable, no matter that he couldn't care less in the past about their comfort, but this lass did not want his hand in marriage. He could attend for her a little and remain safe from her family, demanding a handfasting.

"I canna have you cleaning the castle. 'Twould be an insult. Mayhap you could accompany me on a ride on Macleod lands once or twice a week. I know there is sewing that needs attending. Mrs. Fletcher is forever scolding me over the growing pile."

The lass let out an annoyed groan, and his lips twitched. Was she non-verbally telling him his ideas were not to her standard? "You doona like my suggestion?" he asked, raising his brow.

"I cannot sew, so to repair your shirts or pants or whatever it is that you wear," she stated, waving at his tunic, "will have to wait for a servant who can fix them. A ride would be nice, but maybe I could work with the horses, muck out the stables, or exercise your horses. I took riding lessons when I was in college."

College? Riding lessons? What the hell was wrong with the lass? "I doona know what college or riding lessons are that you 'took,'" he accentuated with his fingers, "but I canna have you mucking out the stables or working the horses. You are a lady." Boyd lost patience with the woman and started for the castle. "You will have to bide you time like a proper lady, sit about and look pretty. That is good enough."

Footsteps chased him toward the bailey walls. "Sit about and look pretty. You have got to be kidding. I'm not going to do that. I'm not a bimbo."

Boyd turned, and she crashed into him, having not expected him to stop. He reached out, preventing her from falling on her ass. Although the sight of her landing on her pretty rump would be sweet.

In his dream, he'd clasped her small, plump ass as he took his fill. Flexed his fingers into her soft skin with each thrust. He closed his eyes a moment, pushing her away and settling her from him less he hoist her up against the castle wall and sate a newfound need for female companionship.

"I doona know what bimbo is. Speak English, woman. You are English after all." He left her standing after him before her footsteps chased him down once again. He groaned.

"Macleod, I need something to do. Please don't make me beg."

He stopped walking, cringing at the pleading note in her voice. What was wrong with the lass? No woman wanted employment, certainly not the type from good families who were sent about the countries looking for husbands.

Maya Harris did not seem to fit that mold. In fact, he was certain they broke it the moment she was born.

"Very well, you can work the vegetable gardens on the other side of the castle. You'll be safe there within the bailey walls, and when you are tired, you can sit and enjoy the view out over the sea. You can do no harm there."

She walked around him, the smile on her face maddeningly sweet. Then, before he could leave her standing there like the crazy woman she was, she had thrown her arms about him and was hugging him with a strength he did not think she possessed.

He stilled, his arms caught beneath hers. Boyd looked about, glaring at any of his clansmen who smirked or chuckled at the crazy Englishwoman hugging him with thanks.

He shook her free, stepping toward the castle. "Right, that's enough, lass. Go about your day."

Boyd walked into the castle, making his way to his solar. He shook off the feel of her against him, not particularly fond of the sensation of having a woman so close to him.

Not Maya Harris in any case. His body, love, and affection were promised to another, and he would not break his vows to Sorcha, no matter how tempting the thought of Maya would be in his bed or that his wife had seemed to forget she was married to him at all.

Maya was not for him. No one was.

CHAPTER 5

Maya found life at Castle Druiminn interesting, to say the least. Her bedchamber was opulent, more comfortable than she assumed it to be, considering the time she had landed herself in. Although the garderobe was one household fixture she'd never get used to, and she could not wait to return home to normal, modern bathroom amenities.

She was allowed to bathe several times a week, even though some of the house staff thought her highly odd for doing so. Her working in the gardens was a pleasant way to pass the hours. Just in the last few days, she had weeded and managed to get the vegetables already growing in the plot to look a lot healthier than they were when she'd first started. It was fortunate that the castle had access to fresh water, even with the ocean being so close.

As for the laird, he was as elusive and distant as ever. Over the past week, she had dined with him every night, and yet he rarely spoke, and she could count on one hand the number of times he'd bothered to look at her.

It didn't bode well for the friendship that she hoped to

have with him during her stay. She was stuck here, after all, for several months. As the guest of the laird, very few servants spoke to her. Mrs. Fletcher being the only one who did regularly.

Maya wouldn't give in to loneliness, but she was certainly starting to feel isolated and without support. With no one to talk to, one did tend to dwell on things in life, and she had many hours through the day that were unoccupied with work.

Today, instead of going out to water the vegetables, she strode through the castle door and started for the stables where several riding horses were kept.

Surely one of them would be suitable for her, not too flighty or dangerous to get on the back of. She was a competent rider, but even she could grow nervous if the horse was high-strung.

She knocked on the open wooden doors leading into the stables, and an older man, a long, gray beard covering most of his face, came out to greet her. She could not tell if he was smiling or not due to his facial hair, but his eyes were not unkind, and she hoped he would help her.

"Hello, sir, I was hoping to go for a ride. Is there a horse that you can have saddled for me?"

He pulled at his beard, his eyes taking in her gown. She was wearing a dress, but she had also been fortunate enough to find a pair of trews left drying near the kitchen. She would have to apologize to Mrs. Fletcher on her return for stealing them.

"You wish to ride about the countryside, lass? 'Tis not safe."

"I will keep the castle within view at all times. I promise. I shall not go far." When he didn't look convinced, she bit her lip in thought. "Can one of your stable hands accompany me? Or a guard?" she said, looking behind him to see several men watching their exchange.

He raised his brow, looking past her in thought. "Thomas," he yelled, signaling for a tall, strapping lad to come over to them. Maya turned and felt her eyes widen at the sight of the young Scotsman. Were all the men in this time, in this country, made from the cast of romantic stories? Of course, she'd seen a few men who didn't fit her notion of what was hot, but she'd certainly knew some of the men here in this clan would make her friends Molly and Heidi sit up and take notice.

"Will you take Miss Harris for a ride? Keep her close and safe. Take your sword, and doona be afraid to use it."

Maya frowned, her attention snapping to the Thomas lad and seeing he too held a sword behind his back like the laird had the previous week. Surely this time wasn't so very dangerous that people had to ride about with such weaponry. This was Macleod land. How unsafe could it be?

"I'll keep by the river," Thomas said, striding past her and ordering the stable lads to saddle two horses.

Within only a few minutes, they were trotting away from the castle, heading down along the river, the castle a giant pillar of power behind them.

Maya studied the man, realizing he was perhaps only in his late teens. "Are you a Macleod?" she asked, wanting to break the silence and desperate for anyone to speak to her. Not just look at her as if she were some weird English invader.

"I'm Thomas Beaton, Miss Harris, but we're loyal to Clan Macleod."

"Have you lived here all your life?" She wanted to know anything really, so long as she didn't have to hear any more silence. She'd had a week of practically zero conversation. Maya wasn't sure she could stand much more of that.

He nodded, his attention snapping from side to side as if he were expecting an ambush of some kind. Gosh, Maya hoped that wasn't the case. This ride was supposed to be relaxing and already she felt on edge as if she should have eyes in the back of her head.

She reached down and patted her brown mare, pleased that at least her horse didn't seem frightened.

"Aye, I was born on the land."

"Are your parents living here?" she queried when he said nothing more.

He nodded yet again but didn't bother to answer her this time, and Maya didn't press him. It was obvious the guard was not interested in talking, and she refused to come across as desperate.

They rode for several minutes, wandering along the banks of the slow-flowing but deep river. The water was so clear that Maya could almost see to its bottom, even in the deepest parts, the grasses flowing like ribbons in the wind.

Thomas started them up the hill, and she knew he was turning them about to head back to the castle. They had to pass through dense forest trees, and so focused on his course, Thomas didn't seem to notice the three men that she spied through the trees and into a clearing.

Nor did they seem to notice them, and Maya was certainly not going to say anything this close, and with three burly men against her and a boy, they would have little chance of survival if they happened to be enemies to Clan Macleod.

Thankfully the horses did not nicker or step on any twigs and they passed them without their knowledge. So determined to give her the silent treatment, Thomas did not bother to seek out her conversation, alerting those nearby that they were near.

Perhaps the men were Macleod clansmen anyway. Maybe Thomas had seen them but did not deem notifying them of their presence necessary.

They returned to the castle without incident. Although the ride was embarrassingly short, at least it had got her out of the castle for five minutes.

Thomas jumped down and held her reins, waiting for her to follow his lead. She slid off the horse, thanking him before returning indoors. Mrs. Fletcher greeted her in the Great Hall, her eyes bright and clear.

"Miss Harris, 'tis good to see that you have had your outing. Will you be wishing to rest before supper this evening?"

Maya noted the maids were working about in the Great Hall, and she started off toward the stairs. "I'll rest for a little while. I'll only get in the way here."

"I'll send up a plate of cheese and bread for you. It doona escape my notice that you did not eat much at lunch."

Maya reached out, clasping Mrs. Fletcher's arm. "I was merely eager for my ride. I stole a pair of trews you had drying near the kitchen door. I'm sorry, but I didn't feel comfortable riding in only a gown."

"Aye, I knew that you had done so, lass. Doona flash yourself, I doona mind." Mrs. Fletcher scooted her toward the stairs. "Now off you go. I'll see you in a moment."

Maya started up the stairs, her feet heavy, her progress slow. Every so often, a narrow window opened up over the grounds. Hearing the shouts of men below, she stopped to look out of one, wondering who was yelling outside.

The breath in her lungs tightened, her ability to breathe difficult at the sight of Boyd Macleod, his chilling, white hair blowing in the breeze, the tops of his muscular legs revealing themselves as he jumped down from his horse.

What a magnificent man he was to behold. What a shame it was that his wife had been forced to leave all those years before. She could imagine he missed her. If she were his wife, she would miss having that large, muscular body beside her every night. Hers to do with as she pleased.

Maya bit her lip. It was not difficult to imagine having delicious, hot, hungry sex with him. She bet he never suffered from lack of bed partners.

A feminine laugh in the hall below reminded her she was supposed to be going back to her room to rest.

Soon she would be seated next to the god of a man, Boyd Macleod, and again he would eat, drink, and stride off without a backward glance. Well, not anymore. She could not stay here, months on end, and not have anyone to speak to. So tonight, the laird would talk to her, engage as a host should, or he would find his medieval sweet ass chastised by a twenty-first-century Englishwoman.

Even medieval Highlanders had to have some manners, surely.

CHAPTER 6

The Sassenach pulled everyone's attention as she walked into the hall for the evening meal. Boyd stared, unable to tear his eyes away from the sight she made. Never in his long life had any woman, mayhap not even Sorcha, looked so beautiful, and she was half-Fae, nothing but beauty and light.

Maya Harris walked along the edge of the room, Mrs. Fletcher standing at the base of the stairs, a proud, motherly type of smile on her lips before she noted Boyd's stare and hustled back out of the room to the kitchens.

What was the woman up to? Was she trying to make Maya more alluring to him?

If she were trying such wiles, she was winning the war. He could not tear his eyes from her, the sway of her hips as she walked, her straight back and perfectly clear skin. Not marked by the sun, nor a childhood disease. Not to mention her dark, long locks were half-up and curled this evening, making her neck seem more swanlike and certainly more kissable.

He shifted in his chair, forcing his attention back on the

gamebird they were eating for dinner. All the while, he knew Maya's every step, his heart beating a rhythm faster each time her footsteps brought her closer to him.

She sat, and the scent of jasmine engulfed him. Boyd shut his eyes and forced himself not to breathe deep like some desperate lout who had not had female company for years.

He had not, but that did not mean he did not know how to control his urges, desires, and needs as a man. Gods blood, he'd spent a century denying himself out of honor and loyalty to a woman who remained his wife. He would be able to survive another dinner.

"Good evening, Macleod," she said in that maddening, yet sweet English voice she had.

"Good evening, lass. I hope you had a pleasant day?" There, his host requirements were complete, no need for any more interchange between the two of them. He picked up a roll of bread, ripping it in half and dipping it into the gravy left from his meal.

"I did, thank you. I was hoping that we may be able to converse a little more tonight. I know that you're busy, but I'm alone here, and I'm not ashamed to admit I'm feeling a little isolated."

Her words pulled at a part of him he'd thought long dead. Boyd turned to her and almost swallowed his tongue at the hope, the pleading light in her eyes.

Damn it. He had never been the type of man who could hurt a woman or deny her an honest request. He inwardly cursed, but the words that escaped his mouth were nothing of the kind.

"Aye, of course, lass. What do you wish to speak of? I'm more than happy to oblige."

She smiled at him, relief easy to read on her features.

"Anything, really. I've not had anyone talk to me at all the past week, besides Mrs. Fletcher, but that's when she hands me a new gown to wear or chastises me when she finds me working in the vegetable garden."

Of course, the vegetable garden. He'd seen her bent over the plants and had decided to avoid that part of the castle grounds until she traveled back to England.

"Do you wish for me to hire a companion for you? I have a distant cousin who lives on Macleod land who can come in and keep you company."

Her eyes widened. "Really? You would do that for me? I would like that very much, but only if it doesn't take her away from her responsibilities. I can survive if I have to. I don't want to be any trouble."

Boyd shrugged, knowing Jeane would welcome a stay at Druiminn. After losing her husband in a skirmish with Clan O'Cain the previous winter, she would enjoy her role here with Maya. There was little doubt in Boyd's mind that she would have already heard of his new houseguest and would be eager to meet her.

"She will not mind. I'll send for her tomorrow."

The double doors leading into the great hall pushed open, startling Maya. Boyd frowned at the intrusion, but his senses went on guard at the sight of Douglas Albany, his head guardsman and a trusted ally these past twenty years.

"Laird," Douglas said, bowing his head in acknowledgement. "There has been a sighting of three men wearing O'Cain colors near where the Macleod and Mackinnon lands cross. They had several heads of cattle.

Boyd felt his temper rise at the blasted O'Cain clan. Could they never be anything but a thorn in his side? He picked up his ale, downing his drink. "Did the cattle have Macleod markings?"

"Aye, they did," Douglas confirmed. "'Twould look as if they have availed themselves of sheep as well."

"I wonder if it was the same three men I saw on my ride this afternoon. Although I wouldn't think they could travel that distance so quickly."

The English lass's words caught Boyd's attention, and he turned to her, something very akin to alarm curdling in his gut. "You went out on a horse today?" Boyd stood. "Who took Maya lass out on a ride this afternoon? Doona think to keep your tongue quiet, or you'll find yourself out on your ass." Although he had not stated they should not take her away from the safety of the castle wall, to do so without his approval was not acceptable. She could have been killed. Fallen off her horse, anything. The thought of her mangled, dead body cold in the grave sent a chill down his spine. He could not bear that. Not even for a woman he cared little to nothing for.

One of his promising guardsmen stood, wiping his mouth. "I took her for a ride along the river. She wished to go, and we couldna allow her to go unaccompanied."

Boyd turned to her, pinning her with a glare. The stupid lass was going to get herself killed. As for his men, he would deal with them on the morrow. "You wanted to go out for a ride about the estate. This isn't England, Sassenach. Here, you'll end up spiked on the end of a sword, or that of a man's, when he's taking your innocence from you."

She gasped, standing to face him. "How dare you say that to me. I was perfectly safe. Thomas had a sword, and the castle was never out of my sight. God forbid that I enjoy some time out of the castle walls. I don't know how anyone can live here, locked away like sacred relics."

Boyd had to agree somewhat. They were locked away most of the time, but it was only for his people's safety. The clan, wide-eyed and quiet watched their interaction. Boyd glared at them before turning back to her. "You are not to leave the castle grounds again. 'Tis not safe. Not even for guests of the Macleod."

She snorted at his reply. Snorted! Then sat back down, shrugging one of her delicate shoulders and making Boyd see red. The lass would end up over his lap with a tanned hide if she did not respect his rules.

"I cannot live here for months and only walk in the vegetable garden or look out over the ocean. I asked you if you would take me out to visit the fields, but you never do. I will not be a prisoner here."

"You can always leave."

Her mouth opened, a perfect O, and Boyd pushed down the need to cover her sweet lips with his own. It would serve at least in one way in shutting her up. Blast the lass for making his blood run hot, his temper soar. "'Tis not safe for you here. You are not to go out again without my knowing or my accompanying you." He turned back to his clansmen. "Doona have me hearing of you taking Maya lass out of these grounds again. She's under house arrest."

"The hell I am," she said, standing again, placing herself up close to his face. Her attempt at authority was lost somewhat since the top of her head only came up to his chin.

"The hell you are not. Doona fight me on this, lass, or I'll lock you in your room."

"You wouldn't dare," she hissed, her sweet breath kissing his lips.

Oh, yes, he would dare. The English lass was foolish to think otherwise. Boyd bent down, scooping her up and over his shoulder before starting for the staircase. She squealed, ranted against his back, and he slapped her on her ass in warning.

He may have allowed his hand to dwell there a little longer than what was wise, but what was he to do? To have her in his arms, or at least over his shoulder, was a pleasant turn of events. She punished his back with multiple punches, several that were not a bad effort with her limited strength.

His clansmen laughed and shouted their approval as he started up the stone staircase. The lass swore at his people, words that even he had never heard before. He chuckled, enjoying himself immensely.

"Stop your hissing, lass. Were you not taught manners when you were growing up?"

She growled, and he grinned. "This is manhandling, and I'll not stop 'hissing' at your treatment of me. Now put me down!"

"Nay," he said, reaching the second floor. He strode down the hall toward Maya's room, entering her private space.

He strode over to her bed, glad to see her room was well kept. Her needs, at least indoors, were cared for to his standard. An abundance of animal furs lay on her bed, which would keep her warm at night.

Boyd threw her onto the bed, and she bounced. Her gown rode a little high on her leg. He could see her knees, the sweep of her leg, the gateway to pleasure that lay between them. If she noticed her lack of decency for the moment, she did not say, merely glared up at him, color riding high on her cheeks.

The sight of her on the bed, as if she were waiting for him to join her, crawl over the many furs, push her legs apart and settle there made his cock twitch.

"You will stay here," he said, forcing his attention away from her alluring legs, "until you can behave yourself and not gallivant about Scotland as if you have not a care in the world. I doona want to have to bury you, lass. Or explain to your English family how you died in Scotland under my watch."

Her breasts rose and fell with her labored breaths. Boyd clamped his jaw, turning away from her and striding from the room, slamming the door shut and throwing the bolt across to keep her locked in.

He could hear her rants muffled behind the wood, and he stood there a moment, taking deep, calming breaths.

He'd not had such an alluring woman under his roof for a hundred years, certainly not one who pulled his interest, made him want things he'd had no right to want anymore.

The letter to his cousin would settle the lass, give her company, and with any luck, keep her out of harm's way. Jeane Macleod would be here by supper tomorrow night, and Maya Harris would no longer be his problem. A good thing. For everyone.

CHAPTER 7

The laird had Maya freed the following morning but under strict orders to remain in the Great Hall and keep herself occupied with either reading or sewing.

Maya had chosen to sew the laird's tunics that needed repairing, taking great pains to ensure the clothing was in a lot worse condition than when it had been handed to her in a wicker basket.

She smiled down at the button she was sewing on the incorrect side of his top. She chuckled at the thought of him trying to fit it through the hole that was also on the same side as the button.

She would pay him back for locking her up like a prisoner. She'd gone for a horse ride with an armed guard. How dangerous could that be?

The sound of a cart and horses pulled her attention away from her sewing. Maya walked to the door, staring out into the bailey as a carriage rolled to a halt. Suppose if one could term the vehicle as a carriage. It wasn't very fine. It looked to have wooden wheels that no doubt felt every stone and rut on the road. No glass windows, only blinds that were tied away at the top.

A woman jumped down with the help of Boyd, who came to greet her. His smile and pleasure at seeing the young woman catching Maya off guard.

She'd not seen him smile before, and to do so left her insides a hot mess.

He kissed the woman's cheek, their words low, and she could not catch what he said to her, but she laughed at whatever it was. They turned toward the door and saw Maya.

The laird's visage physically changed, all pleasure wiped from his features, and Maya felt the loss of his happiness to her very core. Why did he dislike her so much? She would be his friend if he only let her. She did not want anything from him. How hard was that for the man?

He gestured to Maya as they came to stand before her. "Jeane, this is Maya Harris. Her family sent her here for a possible union with me, but unfortunately, I have informed Maya lass that we will not suit."

Maya shut her mouth with a snap, glaring at the neanderthal Scotsman. Did he have to be so honest? So blunt! And so full of shit.

"Do not tease your cousin, Macleod, I'm not here for your hand, no matter what my family may wish," she said, no longer having to keep to Mrs. Fletcher's story of why she had turned up at Druiminn in the first place. Not now that she and Boyd had come to an agreement the first night they met.

As much as she would like to put Boyd at further ease with the truth of her arrival here, she wasn't sure how he would react to knowing that she was from the future. Even with the laird's history with the Fae. From what history stated, he disliked the Fae, and rightfully so. They did steal his wife, after all, but to have a woman claiming to be from the twenty-first century? He would demand she leave when she could not. Not without the tapestry. There was little doubt in Maya's mind that he would think her being here was a trick being played on him by the Fae. He would loathe her presence even more then, and that would equal her to being royally screwed.

"'Tis so nice to meet you, Maya. I was delighted to receive the missive from Boyd to come and keep you company." The woman left Macleod's side and came over to Maya, linking their arms and walking her back indoors to the Great Hall. "I just know that we're going to be great friends."

For all of Macleod's brutish ways, locking her in her room for one, his suggestion to bring his distant cousin to stay had been a good idea. From all accounts, the woman was sweet-natured, a happy, young woman pleased to be of service to her laird cousin.

"I hope so. I'm glad that you're here too. The past week has been less than ideal."

"Oh, really? What has happened?" Jeane pulled her over to the chairs that Maya had been sitting on before her arrival.

"There is no one else here. Other than the female servants, I'm the only woman. And not to be disrespectful to the laird, but his conversation skills are not that forthcoming." Maya tried to be nice, the least offensive she could be about Jeane's cousin, but Macleod had been a quiet, non-talkative host from the day she arrived.

She had months left to be here. She could not endure weeks and weeks on end of no one talking to her.

Jeane reached out, patting her leg. "Well, I'm here now, and you can speak to me as much as you like. From the missive I received from Macleod, you may walk around the grounds outside the bailey so long as he is present. We shall endeavor to do so each day."

Maya threw Jeane a dubious look. "I doubt the laird will want to accompany us every day on a walk. He'll be telling you too soon that you'll have to stay indoors to be limited to the back of the castle that looks out over the ocean."

Jeane raised her brows. "Och, doona worry about that. He will accompany us. He knows better than anyone that to be locked up in a dank, dark castle will drive you mad. He will escort us, or he'll have two women causing him mischief. For all of his strength, his power in this land, Macleod desires peace at home. And so to keep it, he'll walk with us. Doona doubt my word. Now," she said, clapping her hands, pulling a maid from somewhere behind a column in the hall. "We wish for bread and cheese and tea."

The maid ran off to do Jeane's bidding. Maya smiled, relaxing back in her chair, enjoying the woman's company immensely already. Being stuck in sixteenth-century Scotland may not be so bad after all.

Not with Jeane Macleod by your side.

Inviting his cousin to stay had been a colossal mistake. Boyd had done his best over the past month to keep himself occupied enough not to have anything much to do with his cousin or his guest, Maya. But this evening, he was hosting a celebratory bonfire to thank his people for their hard work over the summer before the cold Highlands winter set in.

With the preparations for the night of revelry, he'd been able to keep Jeane and Maya busy with chores, and for the past few weeks, they'd not bothered him with wanting to take long, unwelcome walks about Macleod lands like a pair of frolicking eejits.

Did they not know that he had many things to attend to on any given day? His people did not want him strolling about his lands as if there was nothing more pressing to do than look about like a pompous laird too proud to care about the running of castle life, his people's needs and wants.

Maya must have learned this absurd need for walking when growing up in England. No Scottish Highlander would ever take up such a ridiculous pastime.

He bathed and dressed in a fresh tunic and tan trews, wrapping his leather belt and attaching his dirk. His jerkin lay over a chair, and he slipped it on, finishing off his dressing with a shawl of tartan in the Macleod colors over his shoulder.

Tonight they would drink, listen to music, and enjoy the last two months of summer. By the time he stepped out into the bailey, the music was playing. People were dancing, and the bonfire stood set and ready for lighting.

"Aye, Macleod, will you do us the honors?" one of his clansmen called out, holding up a torch that was already alight.

He walked over and took the torch, turning to face the wooden structure about to go up in flames. "Thank you all for your hard work and loyalty to clan Macleod. Enjoy this night, for there are many days ahead of hard work to make this year's crop one of our best."

Cheers went up, and Boyd threw the torch on the pile of wood, standing there a moment to watch as the flames took hold, licking the timber to a roaring flame.

He stepped back, the heat of the fire prickling his skin. He looked past the bonfire, and through the flickering sparks, he spotted Maya. Her appearance as bright as the moonlit night, her skin white and glowing under the night sky. Tonight she wore a deep-red kirtle, her hair falling about her shoulders, and flowers seemed to have been braided through her dark, long locks.

She was talking to Jeane, laughing and drinking wine, her cheeks flushed from pleasure. She was so beautiful that for a moment, he debated going to the lass, asking her to dance. The idea of making the rest of her body flush in satisfaction, in pleasure, threatened to buckle his knees. He could not look away, nor could he act on the need that grew wilder with every passing day.

He spent half his time avoiding the lass so that he didn't have to want her as much as he did. When she was out of sight, he could push her from his mind.

But tonight, seeing her in a pretty gown made him doubt his resolve.

Why, he could not fathom, he hardly knew the lass, and yet… There was something about her that drew him. Oh, there was little doubt she was comely, a pleasing lass with a body that would make any man salivate, but his attraction was more than that. It went beyond his control. And that was what scared him the most.

He was married. Neither he nor Sorcha were dead. Sorcha may live in another realm, but that did not change the fact he'd promised himself to her until death parted them.

To act on a need, on a desire that went soul-deep, went against everything he was as an honorable man...

Maya looked about the bailey, and her eyes met his through the flames. He did not miss her heated, satisfied inspection of him. Boyd breathed in a deep, calming breath. He would not touch her.

He would not.

"Macleod," his head guardsman said beside him, pulling his attention away from Maya. A welcome reprieve that would settle him and stop him from fantasizing about a Sassenach.

"Douglas," he returned. "Are you enjoying the bonfire?"

"Aye, and I'll enjoy Samhain even more, for all the hard work will be done by then."

Boyd chuckled, nodding in agreement. "Any more news on Clan O'Cain? Have they been spotted on Macleod land again?"

"Nay, not as yet. But I doona think they'll know what's good for them. They'll be back, and when they are, we'll be ready for them."

"Kill them and bury the bodies. I doona want them returning to O'Cain lands. The laird Dougall will figure out soon enough that his clansmen were dealt with."

Douglas frowned, rubbing his jaw. "You will have trouble if we kill them. Mayhap we just injure them enough that they will not be back these ways anytime soon."

Boyd had been fighting with the O'Cain clan for years, and he was fatigued of it. His long life, over 127 years, was too long. He was weary of all the conflict, the petty thieving, and raiding. It was time he took a harsher stand. He would and could not allow his clans peoples' hard work to be thieved without any punishments. Clan O'Cain needed to know that Clan Macleod would not abide their crimes.

"Kill them. That's an order," Boyd repeated.

He walked off, speaking to his clansmen and giving the lasses compliments he knew kept them swooning over him. If he could not touch them, at least he could show appreciation with the spoken word.

"You're flirting with them all. Is the laird allowed to do such a thing?"

Maya lass.

He sighed, steeling himself to look at her. To gaze upon her natural beauty without the urge to pull her into his arms and show her what happens when no words were necessary. He had thought to keep away from her tonight. Hell, he'd been avoiding her since the day she arrived. To have her this close muddied his mind and his resolve.

"There is no harm in a pretty compliment for the ladies fair." She chuckled and squealed a little when Thomas swooped in behind her and stole her before him for a reel. Boyd narrowed his eyes at the lad, not willing to have Maya for himself, but he'd be damned if he'd allow anyone to have her either.

She would return to England a maid, or whoever ruined her would have Boyd to face. He ignored the taunting voice in his mind over what his punishment would be should he be the one to ruin her in his bed.

CHAPTER 8

Maya squealed as strong arms wrapped about her waist and pulled her into a Scottish reel around the bonfire. The night was simply a perfect evening.

Not a cloud in the sky took away the moonlight, the air smelled clean and fresh, the people full of gaiety, laughter, and hope. Maya reveled in being here, of being lucky enough to have time traveled and landed in a location that looked after her, cared and protected her.

She could have been unfortunate to have traveled back to any time and place. The idea didn't bear thinking of.

Thomas, the young man who escorted her on her ride last month, smiled and laughed, showed her how to do the steps when her feet refused to cooperate.

She could not hold back the boisterous laugh that escaped her when Thomas was swooped out of the way, and another clansman came before her, taking her hand and claiming her as his dance partner.

This swapping went on throughout the reel. By the

time the musicians stopped, and she too halted to catch her breath, everyone laughed at the actions of the young men.

All but one.

Maya took a glass of wine from Thomas, her original partner, thanking him before taking a long sip. She looked over the top of her glass and spotted Boyd, standing behind his people, his dark, hungry gaze on her.

A prickling of awareness thrummed through her body at his inspection. He looked displeased. Thunderous even, and she wondered at it.

She was nothing to him, they had agreed to tolerate each other and nothing more, but perhaps she couldn't dance with the clansmen. Had she broken some rule about guests and servants?

Little did Boyd know that in the twenty-first century, she too was a servant, no better or less of a person for being so. No better than any of the people who served him daily.

The rules in these distant times could go to the devil if anyone thought she would stop being who she was just for the sake of propriety.

Maya started for him, determined to find out why he was glowering when everyone else was so happy. His eyes followed her around the fire, before she came to stand beside him.

"Are you not going to dance tonight, Macleod?" she asked, taking in the revelry of his clan that continued and grew more boisterous every hour.

"Nay, I doona feel like dancing." He didn't say anything more for a moment, but then out the corner of her eye, she watched him finish his ale, gesturing to a servant for more. "Did you enjoy you dance with Thomas? If you like the lad so very much, mayhap I can persuade you parents to let you marry a Macleod clansman. He's a fine lad. Will bed you well."

Maya choked on her drink, not quite believing he would say such a thing. She rounded on him, hands on hips. "Bed me well, will he? You asked me once whether I learned manners as a child. I wonder now the same about you."

He shrugged, his broad shoulders distracting her for a moment. "The lad likes you. Why even now he's watching to see if he can steal you from under my nose yet again."

Maya turned and smiled at Thomas. He was a dear lad, but she was twenty-seven, at least ten years older than the boy. As handsome as he was, that was a little too much difference in age, in experience, even for this medieval time. She wasn't a cougar, not yet anyway.

She bit back a chuckle at her own thoughts. "I'm not interested in Thomas, but I will not deny myself the pleasure of a dance when asked."

"He dinna ask you. He forced you into it."

She met Boyd's hard gaze and read interest and confusion both in his eyes. He was such an odd man, this immortal highlander. She couldn't help but wonder if he was bored with it all. Weary of life, after living more than his share. And after what he just said, she couldn't help but wonder if he was a little medieval feminist too.

"Will you walk with me, Macleod? I would like to see the stars from the ocean side if you will escort me." The opposite side of the castle, away from the revelry and bonfire light, would let her see the stars more clearly.

"'Tis a moonlit night, the stars will not be as visible."

Maya hadn't thought about that. But with a determination that would not be denied, she linked her arm with his and pulled him on. "Take me, anyway."

His eyes burned down at her before he covered her arm with his hand and started for the back of the castle. He did not speak, his long strides eating up the distance, and before she knew it, they were there. Standing at the shorter stone wall that lined up with the castle wall that circled the bailey. The wall allowed them to look out over the cliff where Druiminn castle sat, keeping those safe from falling into the ocean below.

"I cannot help but wonder how many bonfires you've seen. How many clansmen you've watched grow old and pass away, while you, all the while, remain the same."

A muscle ticked in his jaw as he stared out over the ocean. "I've seen too many of my clansmen die. My childhood friends turn into old men, frail and weak. I would not wish this curse on anyone."

Maya looked down at her hands, anything but to look upon him and see the pain etched onto his features. The emptiness, the loneliness that shone from his emerald eyes. His curse would not be an easy thing to live with, even if the idea of immortality would appeal to so many.

"To break the curse, you have to find love. Why not try? To keep living this life that you lead, do you not think it's allowing the Fae Queen to win?" To Maya her words sounded ridiculous, but she was also in sixteenth-century Scotland, so who was she to say what was true or not.

"I canna love again, nor marry for I am already married." He turned, staring down at her. "No matter how much desire, satisfaction, or my personal needs tell me to enjoy my manhood, I canna do so."

He was looking at her so intensely, his breathing ragged and as uneven as her heartbeat. Maya licked her parched lips, biting her bottom one as she stared up into his eyes, unable to look away.

"You still desire, but you deny yourself?" she whispered.

"Aye." He nodded once. "I still want." He paused. "Women."

The pit of her stomach thrummed. They were alone here, their voices hushed and just for themselves to hear. Never had she ever felt so flushed, her body yearning for the touch of a man she had no right to be meddling with. A man she hardly knew for crying out loud.

But, oh, Boyd drew her in. Like a moth to a roaring flame, she wanted to throw her body into the fire and let herself burn. Let him use her to sate his long-denied need.

A little part of her knew that to be bedded by the highlander would be a night of wild, possibly rough sex. She'd never had sex in such a way, but she wouldn't say no to this man. Not if he asked nicely.

But as he stood beside her, determination to remain distant all but palpable from him, she knew he wouldn't make a move on her. His honor forbade it, and it would be a tremendous woman or emotion indeed to change his mind. What a shame that was. That he would continue in this vein, be a leader of his clan, a laird, a chief, and yet not live at all.

"I do hope that one day that changes, Macleod," she said, giving him a small smile.

A muscle in his jaw worked and he looked over her head, out to the sea beyond. "It will not."

Maya nodded, knowing that with his steadfast tone, the conversation was over. "Shall we return to the party?" she asked him.

He nodded and strode away, not waiting for her to join him. Maya shook her head. In her time, there was still a clan Macleod, chiefs that came after Boyd, so he must break the curse, or his wife returned and saved him from this endless existence. Or perhaps, the line came from another clan member, Jeane maybe, but she was unmarried, so…

Maya didn't know much of the clan's history, other than the tidbits she'd picked up since working at the castle. But something must happen to change his life. The fate of these people.

But what, she was still to find out. Maybe she never would. That's if she managed to safely return to the twenty-first century and survive her time in the sixteenth.

CHAPTER 9

Maya was determined to change the laird's fate. After she returned to the bonfire, she could not find him again, and for two days, he wasn't anywhere about the castle or grounds.

His cousin Jeane grew concerned when he did not return for supper the next evening. On the second day, they were told the laird had ridden out with a group of men the morning after the bonfire, but as to why they did not know. He returned that evening, strode into the Great Hall with a group of clansmen, dropping deer, rabbits, and other game on the hall's floor.

His housekeeper Mrs. Fletcher was all aflutter at the meaty gifts, seemingly thrilled by the arrival of fresh food. She set the servants to pick up the animals and take them to the kitchens.

Jeane strode up to Boyd, stopped him from moving to the dais, hands-on-hips and a fierce scowl on her forehead. Anyone looking at the Scottish lass would know she was pissed off.

Maya sat at the table, watching the play between the

distant cousins and enjoying herself immensely when the laird appeared troubled by the fear he'd unwittingly caused.

"You could have told us you were going hunting. We've been fraught with fear that something had befallen you. That you had been attacked in some way."

He reached out to pat her shoulder, and she slapped him away. "Doona try and make peace. I'm angry with you, Boyd Macleod. You ought to know better than to disappear for days on end and not tell a soul."

Boyd, having had enough of being scolded like a child, stood tall, crossing his arms and accentuating his broad chest, which still sported the blood from his kills.

"I doona have to answer to you, lass. My men knew where I was. You should have asked them if you were so worried."

Jeane, a little lost for words at his reply, narrowed her eyes. "You tell your family, your guests when you are going to hie off into the Highlands. And we did ask your men, and they were vague in their answers."

Maya's gaze slipped below the base of Boyd's tunic. The laird had very lovely legs in his trews, his muscular thighs tensing as he stood staring down his cousin. As for his arms, they too were toned and sun touched. His hands especially big. Heat kissed her cheeks at the saying over what big hands and feet meant for men. Over the past two days, her dirty dreams had returned of her and Boyd. Of him making love to her with delicious slowness that left her burning and aching for more. In her dream Boyd seemed to be quite the lover and very well versed in how to make a woman satisfied.

She had never dreamed in such a realistic way before. Worse was that the more she dreamed of Boyd Macleod, the more she thought about him during daylight hours. Maya caught herself thinking of his hands and what they were capable of. Like right now, seeing his arms flex as he helped pick up the deer and hand it to clansmen, Jeane still beside him, berating him for his disappearing act, she couldn't help but sigh at how lovely he was.

She chuckled, and right at that moment, he looked across the room and met her eyes. Like a physical caress, she could feel his interest. Did he think about her at all? Did he ever wonder what it may be like to kiss her? Even if that went against his rules of chastity?

Mrs. Fletcher came up to Maya, filling up her wine glass. "Ah, see, my English lass, the laird is curious about you. Did you see him looking for you, wanting to check that you were still here?"

Maya grinned at the meddling housekeeper, even as her stomach flipped at the thought. "Your plan will not work. I'm not here for a husband, and he doesn't want a wife. He's married, which I'm sure I don't have to remind you of."

Mrs. Fletcher waved her concerns away, leaning on the dais and looking back toward where Boyd stood discussing and celebrating their kills. "I canna help but think his leaving the castle these past two days was to get away from you. You tempt him, lass. Now, I doona want you to fear that he'll force himself on you, for he would never do that to a woman, but should you be open to a tryst, well, I think you may find a willing participant, no matter what he says to oppose."

"I'm not the type of woman who readily sleeps with men. I usually like to date them for a while first, Mrs. Fletcher."

The older woman looked at her curiously. "I doona

know what date means, lass. What has a date to do with being courted by a man?"

"Everything." Maya laughed. "To date someone in my time is courting. So what I'm saying is I'd like to be courted a little first before I let him have me." Not that that was entirely true. Not when it came to Boyd Macleod, but no one else, not Mrs. Fletcher or Jeane, needed to know that. There was something about this particular highlander that Maya knew she would give herself to. And probably from the moment he kissed her.

If he ever managed to get past his own rules.

"Well, you just wait and see. I've known the lad since I was a little girl, and over the years other clans, English and Scottish noble houses, have thrown their daughters before him. Never before have I seen him look at the lasses with such a hunger as he looks at you. 'Tis a fact, and one I'll stand by."

Maya shut her mouth and watched as the housekeeper wandered off, pouring wine for others. She wasn't sure what she thought about the possibility of turning her dreams into reality, but would it be so very bad if she was the one to change his fate—the one to save him from himself and his never-ending life of not living?

She may never break the curse. He may never fall in love with her, but at least for the few months she would be here, a little fun could be had. She was a twenty-first-century woman, after all.

She'd be a damn idiot if she didn't try to get in the sack with such a hot guy. A nice one too. Her romance-reading friends would never forgive her if she didn't give it a good go.

And neither would she.

But how to drive him mad, without letting him know

he got to her as well? If Mrs. Fletcher's words were true… Now that was the question.

No matter how many days Boyd avoided Druiminn, there was no getting away from his thoughts. They plagued him, night and day. Even in his sleep, he dreamed of her.

The dark-haired Sassenach haunted him with her disinterest. He'd almost convinced himself that was why he was so captivated with her, but on his ride back to the estate, after a good two days of hunting, he'd realized why she fascinated him so.

A part of him that he had buried the day he lost Sorcha rumbled inside him. Told him not to let this lass leave like all the other women who had tried to catch his heart. Told him to learn to know her. Maya gave him the one thing he'd never thought to have again.

Hope.

Would she be willing? That he could not say, but it did not mean that trying to persuade her to be interested in him could not end in a mutual satisfaction until she did decide to leave.

Suppose she was not the one that was his destiny. The one, the Queen of the Fae foretold would break the curse.

He had lived long enough. It was time to at least try to find his soul mate and let his old, weary self pass on like his ancestors before him.

Which in itself brought forth a thought that had been troubling him. Not since Maya had arrived, but for years before. If he did not find love, how would his clan go on? Without a son, there would be no more Macleods, and something told him that the future would not be so kind to an immortal highlander as the people of this time.

He was often talked about, was forced to lie, and state he was Boyd Macleod's grandson. The falsehood would only keep him alive for so many more years before they would come for him.

Come for his life that even his clansmen would be unable to defend, and when he did not die due to being immortal, he would have to leave. There would be no peace in the Macleod lands once those in power knew of his otherworldly curse.

Boyd strode to the dais, determined to spend some time this night with Maya. Since the night of the bonfire, he'd whispered her name on his lips. Knowing that it sounded as sweet as he thought the first time he'd heard it.

She watched him walk toward her, her gaze taking in his form and leaving him with little doubt she liked what she observed. Such looks were not new to him. Many of the lasses of his clansmen, the female servants, watched his every step. With a flick of his chin, he could have them over a table or up against a wall, skirts lifted and pleasure nothing but his aim.

But he did not want those women. He wanted the English lass. The image of her spread out before him, wet and willing, made his blood boil.

He bit back a growl, seating himself before she noticed his cock standing at attention.

"Maya lass," he said, watching her from his chair.

She threw him an amused glance. No fear. No trepidation or meekness. Did she suspect his troubles? Did she suffer the same as he? The lass was so unlike anyone he'd ever met before.

"Macleod," she returned, putting down her glass of

wine. "I hope you're sorry for the worry you put your cousin through."

He glanced across the hall, spotted Jeane on the lap of Gordon Lennox, a trusted clansman who still sported blood on his tunic like himself after their hunt. He wondered if his cousin had found another to replace the husband she lost in battle.

"Are you not as upset as Jeane, lass? 'Twould be most upsettin' if you are not."

Her dark-blue eyes widened a little in surprise before she chuckled. The sound reeked of disbelief. "No. I didn't think a man like you would be gone for long, and I certainly didn't think you would get yourself killed. I think your cousin has forgotten that you're immortal."

He smirked. "Aye, I think Jeane forgets that fact too, but I do like her. Through the years, she's been a favorite of mine, the closest relative I have now, and I doona like to scare her. I will apologize in earnest on the morn."

He stilled when Maya reached out and touched his arm. "You're a good man, Boyd Macleod. No matter how scary you try to make yourself appear to women who travel here to woo you."

"Woo me? Is that what you are doing?"

She shrugged. "While I do not want to marry you, I would be a liar if I said that I did not find you somewhat attractive. Any woman alive would be blind not to."

Her words sent fire to course through his veins.

"You are a pretty lass too, while we're giving each other compliments." He let his gaze travel over her kirtle, lingering where her breasts rose above the bodice with every breath. Her waist was small, the kirtle accentuating her slim figure.

Their eyes met, held, and he let her think what she

would from the look he gave her. A rose-colored blush kissed her cheeks, and it took all Boyd's restraint not to close the small gap between them and take her lips. Lay claim to her.

He swallowed. He'd not kissed a lass in a hundred years, but by God, he wanted to kiss Maya Harris. Kiss her until she saved his soul.

CHAPTER 10

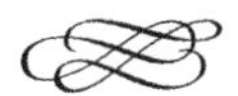

The following day Maya woke early and dressed to meet Jeane downstairs before the clansmen had entered the hall to break their fast. Today they were leaving the castle grounds to go to some secluded pool beside the river that ran before Druiminn Castle. The local women used the pool, sheltered by rocks and trees, to bathe and catch up on local gossip, or so Jeane told her.

So well hidden from those who did not know it was there, it made it the perfect location for such activity.

Maya quickly ate the porridge Mrs. Fletcher laid out before her, too excited to eat much else. It had been four days since she'd been able to bathe, and her hair alone, itchy and too oily for her sanity, needed a good scrub.

What she wouldn't do to have shampoo or a toothbrush right at this moment.

One of the castle maids bustled into the hall, looking about the room before she spotted Maya and came toward her. The woman's determination caught her attention, and Maya stood, going to her before she reached the dais.

"Miss Maya, I have a message from Mistress Jeane.

She'll be unable to attend with you this morning at the pools. She's come down with a megrim and is feeling poorly. She told me to tell you to go along without her. She apologizes for not accompanying you."

Disappointment stabbed at Maya. She could not go without a respectable chaperone, and Mrs. Fletcher was too busy with her castle chores to take time off so that Maya could wash.

"May I bring something to her to make her feel better? I cannot go without her, so please let me know if there is anything that I can do."

"'Tis nothing for you to do, Miss Maya." The maid bobbed a quick curtsy. "Good morning to you."

Maya watched her go. She would go out into the vegetable garden and pick some ginger. Ginger biscuits made people feel better when they were ill. At least it was supposed to help women who were pregnant. If someone had a megrim, whatever that was, some sort of grimace of the body Maya assumed, then a cup of ginger tea or biscuits would surely help.

"I will walk you down to the pool, Maya lass. You shouldn't be going without my escort in any case."

Maya gasped, having not heard Boyd enter the hall. Somehow he was behind her, his deep, gravelly voice making the hairs on the back of her neck stand on end.

She refused to shiver or sigh at his presence. She didn't need him knowing that he affected her. Last night at the dais she had fallen into his beautiful green eyes, and almost kissed him. And not anywhere, but at the main table, before all his clansmen.

Forced back to medieval Scotland or not, she was not here to fall for a guy totally out of her league, but neither could she ignore the attraction she had for him. Other than her two friends, Molly and Heidi, she may not have a lot to go back to in the twenty-first century, but that didn't mean she could do what she liked here. Boyd had been alone for so many years. He needed to find his soul mate, and while she knew that wouldn't be her, she also knew that the attraction she felt for this man was nothing like any she'd had before.

Maya turned and regarded the magnificent man towering over her, reveling in his presence. His tunic that hugged his muscular form, the clan-colored shawl thrown over one shoulder, and trews would make any woman purr with pleasure. His dark eyes and chiseled cheeks with a sprinkling of hair made him look wickedly handsome. A dirk hung from the belt about his waist, and she would lay money that the laird had a sgian dubh in the stocking on his right leg.

"I'm going to bathe, Macleod. Do you think it would be appropriate for you to attend me?"

"Nay, I often escort and keep guard over the women who use the pools. 'Tis no different and will not be inappropriate should I take you too. Go and get your things, and I shall meet you in the bailey."

Maya didn't need any further prodding. She ran up the stone staircase, grabbed her things and met Boyd out the front of the castle. They left via the castle gates and started down a small worn track that led toward the river.

It wasn't long before the tall tree foliage left dappled light on them, the undergrowth much damper and cooler than up at the castle. The sound of trickling water ran somewhere in the distance.

"I used to swim here as a lad. The pool is deep in parts but shallow in others. Perfect for bathing."

"Will it not be cold?" she asked, rubbing her arms as

the air chilled further the deeper they went into the forest and the louder the running water became.

"'Tis a mystery as to why the pool is the way it is, but you will not be cold. I promise you." He threw her a wicked glance, and goosebumps rose on her skin. Maya had the absolute feeling his words had a second meaning to them.

They only walked a little farther, and the forest gave way to a clearing of green grass, a steaming aqua pool, almost perfectly circular within its position. The pool was secluded by a massive rock face that curved around it. Small flowers grew within the grass and upon the rock's lower edges, giving the pool the look of a well-landscaped oasis.

"The water is heated?" she gasped, walking quickly to the water's edge, reaching in to feel it. Delicious warmth engulfed her hand. The thought of being submerged in the pool, bathing, and relaxing for an hour or so was beyond exciting.

"Aye, the water is heated from the underground. 'Tis a natural phenomenon." He looked about, frowning a little. "I'm surprised there is no one else here this morning. I'm sure other women will be along soon."

Maya wasn't bothered to have the pool all to herself. Communal bathing wasn't something she was used to doing, and nor was she used to a hulking, light-haired god of a man keeping watch over her. He better not try to sneak a peek. Or perhaps she wouldn't mind so much if he did.

"I'll be alright on my own." She stared at him, didn't say another word, just waited for him to realize she was waiting for him to leave.

"I'll, ah," he stammered, stepping back the way they

came. "I'll be waiting up the path a little for you. Shout if you need anything, lass."

"Thank you. I will." Maya watched until Boyd was out of sight, and then she quickly stripped, placing her towel, or linens as they called them, close to the pool before stepping into the warm water.

She ducked her head, coming up and laughing at the wonderous feeling of so much warm water about her body. The hip bath she had to use in the castle was tiny and made it hard to bathe properly.

"So you are the lass Macleod has taken an interest in. I wonder what he would do if I sent you home right now."

Maya gasped at the sound of the female voice behind her. She turned and felt the blood drain from her face at the vision of the woman who stood on the grassy bank.

No, she did not stand. She hovered, her silk-slippered feet standing on nothing but air.

Oh, dear God. Was this woman a ghost! Was she seeing dead people now as well as time-traveling?

"You're not real," she said, squeezing her eyes shut. She opened them again, fear churning in her stomach when the woman did not disappear. Simply stared at her with flickering silver eyes, long, white flowing robes, and hair as colorless as Boyd's.

"Who are you?" she asked, wrapping her arms around her chest to cover her breasts.

The ghost smiled, and yet, the gesture did not meet her eyes. They remained cold and aloof. Even surrounded by the warm water, Maya shivered.

"I'm known as the Gyre Carling, Nicnevin, but to my own kind, I'm called Titania."

Her own kind? What did that mean? The floating woman

lowered herself and came to stand on the grass, peering at Maya.

"You're a beautiful woman, as pretty as Sorcha." At the mention of Boyd's first wife's name, the woman's eyes flickered, as if a light illuminated behind her iris. "I can see why he's taken with you."

"Macleod is no more interested in me as I am with him," she lied, knowing full well that some of the looks Boyd had bestowed on her meant Maya could take their *knowing* of each other further. Take it all the way to the bedroom if she wanted.

The woman walked along the bank, staring up at the surrounding forest. "I did not think that Macleod would ever find love again. I'm surprised that you are here. How is it that you came to be in sixteenth-century Scotland?"

Maya frowned, a warning voice in the recesses of her mind telling her not to trust this woman. Not to tell her anything. "I've traveled from England. I'm not from anywhere else. Your questions make no sense."

The woman's laugh echoed through the trees, sending them to rustle as if a strong wind had suddenly risen. When she spoke next, her voice was odd, disjointed, and seemed to pierce her skin like a thousand needles. "Do not mock me, human. I know you're from a time hundreds of years from now. I need to know how you came to be here."

Maya stepped back farther into the pool, distancing herself. "You're the Fae Queen. You forgot to mention that name with your many others."

"I will return."

The woman disappeared just as Boyd ran into the clearing. He held his sword in his hand, and the thunderous scowl on his face sent fear to thrum through her veins.

"Where is she?" His roaring voice made her jump, and Maya feared both Boyd and the queen right at that moment.

Maya pointed to the sky because that's where the woman went—disappeared into thin air.

The Fae Queen. The fairy who cursed Boyd for eternity was now interested in her. Wanted information. But why?

This was destined not to end well. Not well at all.

CHAPTER 11

Boyd put everyone at the castle on watch. He doubled the men keeping watch surrounding the castle lands. He had them positioned on the outer castle wall, his archers ready for anything that came their way. Around the clock, he had guards within reach of Maya's sleeping quarters.

He would not let the Fae Queen get her troubling, mischief, life-ruining talons into another woman under his care.

Even if that woman wasn't the one he loved.

Maya Harris was at Druiminn under her family's wishes. They did not need to lose her to the Fae Queen. Have notice of her disappearance or death.

Boyd did not want that on his conscience. Maya would be safer if he returned her home, but the thought of sending her away, of not seeing her again, shredded his innards.

Even so, it would be for the best. With determined strides, he closed the distance to her room. After what happened at the heated pool, he'd asked Maya to remain in her quarters for the remainder of the day. He needed time to place his men on guard and notify the clan that the Fae were causing trouble once more.

He rapped on her door, listened as the sound of her feet on the wooden floor beyond creaked as she made her way across the room.

She peered out, swinging the door wide when she realized it was him.

He walked in without being invited and shut the door firmly on the two guards who stood watch.

"You need to leave, lass. 'Tis not safe for you here any longer, and while I know your family may be disappointed in you not finding a match with the Chief of Clan Macleod, I shall sleep better knowing you are hundreds of miles away. Back in England where you belong."

The blood drained out of her face, and she stumbled back. Boyd reached out, stopping her from falling. "What is wrong with you, lass? Did the Fae Queen do something to you before I could get to you?"

The idea of Maya being used for the Fae Queen's sick amusement made his blood boil. He would not tolerate any further difficulty from the Fae. Not even if it cost him his life. He'd lived long enough in any case. He would die with honor, knowing he saved at least one innocent from the queen's wicked touch.

"No, the queen didn't do anything to me. But I can't go back, Macleod. I have nothing to go back to."

She shook free of his hold. Walked to a chair beside the fire and flopped into it as if life had beaten her down.

He joined her, leaning on the mantel. The peat and wood fire in the room burned well, and the space was comfortable and warm. Even though they were enjoying warm days, the castle was thick-walled, cold, and damp without the fires running all year round.

"Your family will welcome you back. I shall write them a missive. Explain why we doona suit. But you canna remain here. The queen knows you are here, and her interest is piqued. She will not leave you alone now."

Maya reached out, clasping his hands. Her eyes held his, a beseeching light burning bright, or were those tears he saw forming?

"I cannot go back to England, Macleod." She shook her head, biting her lip. "I'm not from England. At least, not your England."

Boyd frowned, her words making no sense. "What do you mean?" A discernment of foreboding ran down his spine, and he was certain the next words out of her mouth would not be to his liking.

"Please don't be angry with me, or Mrs. Fletcher. She didn't know what to do when I arrived, and neither did I."

"Explain yourself, lass," he stated as evenly as he could. He took a calming breath, smoothed his forehead, where he could feel a scowl forming.

"I'm not from the sixteenth-century England. I'm from the twenty-first century."

For a moment, Boyd could do nothing but stare at the lass. He opened and closed his mouth several times, trying to form words. What was she talking about? Twenty-first century? Had she hit her head at the heated pools today that he had not seen?

"I touched the tapestry that you're now having made. The one that depicts you losing your wife Sorcha to the Fae. I know all about that story. In my time, I touched it, and it sent me back here. I landed in the Great Hall, only to find Mrs. Fletcher staring at me as if I were a ghost. I suppose in a way, I was."

His mind whirled with the lass's words. Was she from the future? He ground his teeth, thinking over her arrival, her oddness. It made sense that the Fae Queen, after a hundred years of silence, would show her face on his lands when something caught her attention. A woman from the twenty-first century would certainly do that. The queen wanted Maya, but for what ends he could not fathom. Not yet at least.

"What did the Fae Queen ask of you, lass? Tell me. It could save your life and that of my clansmen."

Maya bit her lip as she contemplated his question. Even with him as mad as he was with the situation, the action made his blood burn hot in his veins. The lass had intrigued him from the moment he saw her, and now he understood why. She was from the future. Was not used to their ancient way of life. The Scottish culture, or speech. Maya was misplaced in time. That was what made her so different from all the other women paraded before him.

"She asked me how I came to be here. I did not tell her," she quickly added.

Boyd was pleased to hear that she did not, but that did not mean the queen was not lurking about, listening to their conversations.

"Doona talk to her again. She's after you for some reason, needs to know that truth. I will speak to Mrs. Fletcher and tell her not to tell a soul."

"So you won't send me away? If you make me go back to England, I'll be homeless and with no way to return to my time. I need to stay here until the tapestry is finished," she whispered, looking about the room as if she expected the queen to be sitting nearby. "I was hoping that when you hung it up in the castle, that if I touched it again, I would return to the twenty-first century."

The thought was a sound one. As sound as any such thought could be when one was discussing time travel. Magic.

"I will not send you away. I trust that what you say is true. That I have lived for a hundred years cursed by the Fae is proof enough that time travel is not without possibility. We will hope that when the tapestry is complete, you can return to your time."

She smiled a little at him, and Boyd realized he would miss the lass. She was a breath of fresh air in the stale castle walls.

"Thank you so much, Boyd," she said, using his given name. She jumped from her chair, throwing herself at him, wrapping her arms about his neck.

Boyd froze at the feel of her womanly curves against his chest. Her breasts flattened against him, the sweet scent of lilies wafted from her skin and hair.

She smelled divine, clean after her bath at the heated pool. Automatically, his hands wrapped about her waist, holding her against him.

He indulged in the feel of her. How many years had it been since he'd felt a woman in his arms? A woman who wanted to be with him in such a way and not afraid to hold him?

Boyd shut his eyes a moment, reveling in her embrace. He'd missed having a woman. He missed their feminine curves, their sweet kisses.

Worse, he wanted the woman in his hold more than he'd wanted anyone before. And now, soon, she would leave. Return to her time, and there was nothing he would do to stop her. The choice would be hers, and he knew she would make it. Leave him. Leave him in the past where he belonged.

Maya held Boyd tight, refused to let him go, even though she knew she should. She had already hugged him for longer than what the gesture required. He would think her an idiot soon if she did not let go.

His silver-white hair tickled her nose, and it smelled of herbs as if he too had bathed recently. She was uncommonly aware of the corded muscles that made up his abdomen. His large hands that ran up her back and held her against him. Heat pooled at her core. She breathed deep, knowing that no matter how much she may deny her thoughts, she wanted the man in her arms.

It had been almost a year since she'd been with a guy. They had only dated two weeks. After he'd had her in his bed, she'd not heard from him again—the bloody asshole.

Maya pushed the thought aside. Her mind solely focused on what Boyd was doing. His hand started to stroke her back, her impromptu hug having altered somehow in the past few seconds.

Neither of them seemed in any rush to let the other go. Maya pulled back, meeting his gaze. The hungry, determined burn in his eyes made her stomach clench. His chest rose and fell with labored breaths. Was he forcing himself to hold back, not to close the small space between their lips and kiss her? She wanted him to kiss her. She licked her lips in preparation, heat pooling between her legs in an embarrassing flood of need.

The word *finally* fluttered through her mind. She wanted him terribly.

His attention snapped to her mouth, and she felt him stiffen, his every muscle growing taut. He lifted one hand, swiping a lock of hair off her cheek and placing it behind her ear.

"I shouldna kiss you, lass, but I canna help myself," he groaned.

She shivered at his words, trepidation running hot through her veins. "Would it be so very wrong if you did kiss me?"

A shadow flickered in his green orbs before he stepped back, distancing them. "Aye, it would be wrong of me, against my vows. I'm sorry, lass. I canna kiss you."

He set her aside with little effort. Her feet curled into the animal fur beneath them, and she willed herself not to follow him as he strode to the door.

"Goodnight, Maya lass. I shall see you on the morn."

Maya did not reply, not sure she could hide the disappointment from her tone if she did. She knew he was battling a war within himself over his wants and needs and his past. He was married, yes, but he had not seen his wife in a hundred years. Surely, his holding out hope for her return was madness.

One positive thing was at least she no longer had to hide from Boyd who she was. No more pretending she was an English noble lady looking for a husband. He would ensure she had access to the tapestry when it was completed and delivered, and she could go home.

The thought ought to bring relief, and yet it didn't. If anything, a hollowness opened up inside her, and she doubted it would ever close again.

CHAPTER 12

Maya stood out in the bailey, patting one of the few horses stabled in the castle grounds and spoke to Thomas, the young clansman having just arrived after riding out on to the Macleod lands, checking on the harvests and ensuring no Fae or enemy clans were lurking nearby.

"You look very fetching today, Maya lass. Are you enjoying your stay at Druiminn?"

"I am—"

"'Tis inappropriate to talk to my guest in such a forward manner." The curt words grumbled behind her made her start, and she turned to find Boyd storming over to them, his eyes hard and narrowed on Thomas. Boyd's white locks were half up today, tied off his face, the remainder of his hair falling down his back.

Instinctively Maya stepped in front of Thomas to keep him from harm.

"Take the horse back to the stable and give it a thorough wipe-down."

Boyd's words brooked no argument, but thankfully he did not try to harm the poor lad.

"Good day, Thomas," Maya said, turning with a raised brow at Boyd's reaction.

"No matter what you told me last eve, Maya lass, to my clansmen, to everyone other than Mrs. Fletcher, you are still a proper, chaste English noble lady. Doona start flirting with me clansmen, or your guise will be naught but a memory. The Scottish lasses may not take too kindly to you, either, winning young Thomas's heart. Do you understand?"

She narrowed her eyes, studying him. "Are you jealous?"

He choked, or at least it certainly looked like he was choking. Perhaps on his words, if he was going to act like such a caveman.

"I am not envious of the wee lad." He closed the space between them, his chest grazing her bodice. Her heart pumped fast, but she did not dare move. Boyd seemed on edge, and she wasn't sure how far she could push him before he snapped. Surely his reaction to her speaking to Thomas should not be so volatile. Had something else happened to him today that had upset him? Perhaps the Fae Queen visited him this time.

She shrugged, feigning disinterest. "Then do not storm across the yard and tell him off for talking to me as if you were. It's not like he was going to kiss me or anything. We were just talking. He asked me if I liked it here."

He growled. An intelligent woman would walk away, leave him be, but Maya could not. Whether he kept away from her or not, she could not let him think she cared which way their relationship traveled. To do so would give him power, and she could not risk her heart like that. Not when she would leave this place. Leave Boyd to the sixteenth century, where he belonged.

Instead, she patted his chest, grinning up at him. "Cheer up, Macleod. I'll be gone soon, and you'll not have to worry about me chatting up your clansmen." Maya chuckled, stepping around him, but he rounded on her, scooping her up without an ounce of trouble, and threw her over his shoulder.

Maya gasped, clutching at his back to hold on. "Put me down, Macleod. This is totally uncalled for."

The Great Hall passed her view, and then she was in Boyd's solar, deposited before his desk. He slammed the door shut, his breathing ragged, his chiseled chest under his tunic rising and falling with each breath.

And then everything changed.

Maya didn't have time to think about his actions, to remind him that he'd regret kissing her, a notion she hated. But as his lips took hers, ravishing her mouth, his tongue tangling with hers, his hands firmly against the sides of her face, she knew she wouldn't say a word. Not yet.

Right now, she could do nothing but return the kiss. Take all he would give her and revel in the enjoyment of having him this way.

He growled against her mouth, and she bit back a moan. The mere idea that she made him want her left her on edge and needy.

He picked her up, her bottom settling on his wooden desk. He didn't give her time to think about what he was doing before he was between her legs, his large hands clasping her thighs and raising them on his hips.

Her body did not feel like her own. If he kept kissing her as if his life depended on her touch, she might burn up in flame.

He, too, was hot to the touch, his chest heaved against her, his corded muscles on his arms and shoulders hard and flexed.

What was she going to do with this man? If he denied her after their first kiss, declared it a mistake, she wasn't sure she could survive. To be able to pass a pleasurable time with Boyd while she kicked up her heels in sixteenth-century Scotland would make her time here go all the faster.

A knock at the door sounded, and Boyd wrenched back, staring at her as if she'd grown two heads.

"Who is it?" he barked, his voice hard and annoyed.

"'Tis Douglas. There has been another sighting of O'Cain clansmen. Down near the Druiminn township itself."

A muscle worked in Boyd's jaw. Maya wiggled off the desk, putting her dress back to rights, which had ridden up her legs. Boyd watched her, his eyes a piercing green. He appeared torn as if he wasn't sure whether to go with his clansmen or continue what they had started.

He decided on the former, turning and striding from the room. Maya watched in silence as he left and didn't miss Douglas's amused glance before following his chief.

She sighed, missing Boyd's touch already.

The door to the solar slammed shut, and Maya was once more alone.

"Maya lass, what a wicked little minx you are turning out to be. I see you are progressing well with Macleod."

Maya gasped, rushing about the desk to put space between her and the intruder. It was the woman from the heated pools again, but this time she appeared more human, less ethereal. She certainly had less glow about her, that was for sure.

The Fae Queen, it would seem, could change her appearance.

"Kissing a man isn't anything miraculous. Macleod is not the first man I have kissed, and he will not be the last."

The queen smirked, tipping her head to one side, studying her as if she had never viewed a human woman before. As if she were a funny little object one had found and didn't know what it was.

She chuckled, the sound echoing as if they were in a cavernous cave.

"Oh, my dear, I do like you. And perhaps if you believe that Macleod will not be your last embrace, I may have to ensure that is so."

No sooner had she appeared, she was gone again, vanished into thin air. Maya looked about the room, going over to where the woman had sat. She swiped her hand across the empty space, seeing if she was really gone.

She was, and her disappearance was as strange as her words. What did she mean by what she said?

Maya shivered, leaving the room. Whatever she meant, she did not like it or the fact that it would ensure she would see the Fae Queen again.

When was the only question.

CHAPTER 13

Boyd rode hard down to the small village on the outskirts of the castle, just as the O'Cains who dared cross his lands for nefarious reasons were mounting their horses. They were brazen and idiotic, and several of their horses had dead sheep thrown over their backs, the blood of their slit throats running down the horse's girth. It would slow down their departure. Make them easier to catch and punish—stupid fools.

The O'Cain men spotted Boyd and the few clansmen he'd taken with him. They shouted to go, some darting into the forest, others mounting the horses and fleeing without their cache of sheep. They would not get far. Their arrival was just what Boyd needed this day. Bone and flesh to slice, to make pay for the frustrations still coursing through him after kissing Maya.

He'd not meant to kiss her, damn it. He was determined to let her go. Keep her safe until she could return to her home and proper time. Not make her his lover. Not take her for himself. To do so would only make her parting harder.

To have kissed her, to have reveled in her soft lips, her sweet-tasting mouth, the little sighs and purrs she made when he kissed her would drive him to insanity if he did not stop thinking of it. He was chief of his clan. She was a mere woman. He would not allow her to have such power over him, make his mind divert, and ponder the softer emotional sides of life. That was not who he was. Not anymore. Distance is what he needed from the lass. But something told him after their kiss; such duty would be hard kept.

They could not be allowed to kiss again. Each time he thought of the lass or dared kiss her, he broke his vow to his wife even if Sorcha had forgotten him these past hundred years.

The pain stabbed at his chest at Sorcha's loss, of not being able to have Maya. Of the children he'd never seed, the normal life denied him because he'd made the mistake of loving a woman half-Fae.

Still, with all that stood between him and Maya, his past, his curse, the future he could not give her, he wanted her—burned for her as hot as the midday sun in a desert landscape.

He kicked his mount into a gallop, drawing his sword and shouting out a battle cry as they closed the space between them and the O'Cains. They would fight this day, and mayhap a little of his ire would dissipate at the spilling of enemy clansmen's blood.

Boyd wanted a bloody, deadly battle, as short as this one would be. The O'Cain men were no match for him and his men's strength and speed. They came up to the riders, and Boyd's first blow knocked a man from his horse. He tumbled onto the grassy riverbank, a sickening crack announcing he would not rise again. Boyd moved on to the rider ahead of him. His horse was fast, but still, it took too long to close the space between them. Impatience churned his guts. As he came abreast of him, Boyd sheathed his sword against his back and lunged for the O'Cain instead. They toppled to the ground. Pain tore through his back, his shoulder when it connected with a rock.

The man yelped, but Boyd didn't let him go. After they stopped moving, he came over him, punching the bastard several times before taking his head in his hands and breaking his neck.

He stood, staring at the man for several seconds before walking away and dismissing him as the worthless enemy he was. His men battled around him, their swords drawn, stronger, angrier than the O'Cain clan, who stood no chance.

Boyd had warned the enemy clan to keep off his lands, stop stealing, and there would be no more bloodshed.

But not anymore. "Burn the bodies," he yelled out to Douglas, who had done away with his opponent.

"Aye, Chief."

Boyd walked back to his horse, his arm smarting with pain. He rolled his shoulder, hoping he had not done too much damage. Not that he could be injured. Not really. He was immortal, forever breathing no matter what condition his body was left in after battle. It would heal, and all the quicker due to his curse.

"They are becoming bold," Douglas said, coming up to him and looking over the five O'Cain men, lifeless and bloodied on Macleod land.

"I canna understand why they continue to provoke. They're like a disease that doesn't want to wane. I'll no longer send them back, bloodied but alive as a warning. I'll merely kill each one of them. One by one if I have to until there is no O'Cain clan left."

They walked back toward the castle, leading their horses, watching as several of his clansmen dragged the bodies up into a wooded area out of sight of the well-used road they stood on.

"Has there been any reports of the Fae? Between the O'Cains and the queen, I'm losing patience."

"No sign of her yet. But the men are nervous. I've heard them speaking in the barracks. Thinking it best that Maya ought to be sent back to England."

Boyd stopped walking, turning to face Douglas. "They are fearful of Maya? It isn't she who is the problem. The Fae Queen has taken an interest and no more than that. She is not Fae herself if that is what they are thinking."

"I think you need to speak to them, Macleod. Put them at ease. We doona need them revolting on the clan as well as everything else that is troubling us of late."

Douglas's words made sense. It was understandable that his men were nervous. The Fae made even Boyd concerned more than he should allow them to. They had otherworldly power. Could take people at their will, never to be seen again. They had taken his Sorcha, and for a hundred years, he'd not gazed upon her pretty face.

The thought that the Fae now wanted to play with Maya, take another under his care, would not happen. He would die before he'd allow anyone else to fall into the Fae's fickle clutches.

"I will talk to the men. Maya is no threat, but the Fae and enemy clans such as the O'Cains are. I will remind them of this fact and their loyalty to me. Anyone who causes trouble after the fact can go. Leave. I'll not be tolerating scaremongering."

"Aye, 'tis a sound course," Douglas agreed.

They mounted their horses and rode back to Druiminn, only to find the castle yard full of his men, many of the servants outside, staring up at the castle as if it were something to fear.

"What is happening here?" Boyd yelled, dismounting, handing his horse to a stable lad who ran over to them.

"The Fae, Macleod. The queen has returned."

Dread circled his heart. Before the clansman's words were finished, Boyd was already running into the castle. His only thought was Maya. Was she still here? Was she in danger? What if the queen had done something to her? The Fae loved nothing more than tricks and fickleness, to tease and confuse those they taunted.

"Maya," he called, running through the Great Hall to start up the stone stairs leading to the second floor.

The castle was eerily quiet. No servants went about their chores. No sound other than the ocean beating against the stone fortifications of the castle outside.

Like a vision, Maya stepped out of her room, her face pale, but otherwise unharmed. "Are you hurt, lass? What happened?" He clasped her shoulders, shaking her a little as if that would help her tell him quicker.

"What happened?" She frowned up at him. "Nothing has happened to me. I'm fine."

Boyd moved past her and strode into her room, looking about. The room was empty, except for the distinct scent of lilies that always floated about Maya. "The Fae. They were here?" he asked, turning to face her.

Her shoulders slumped, and she nodded, moving over to her bed and sitting. "Oh, that. Yes, the queen was back. She didn't stay long, though. It was really strange."

"What did she say to you?" Boyd kneeled before her, taking her hands, urging her to tell him everything.

Maya frowned in thought. "She spoke as if asking herself a question about us. Said something about me not making you my last conquest."

Boyd stilled at the words. *Conquest?* "Have you had many?" he asked, hating the thought of Maya with anyone, faceless foes whom he'd like to strike a sword through.

Her cheeks flushed a little, but she did not look away. "I've been with other men, yes. I'm twenty-seven, do not forget."

Boyd couldn't form words. She wasn't a maid? He cleared his throat, forcing the words past his clenched teeth. "You've been with other men, do you mean that you have slept with them?"

She crossed her arms, a small frown between her eyes. Her lips thinned. "I have been. What about you? Have you been with many women? How many? What was it like? When did you lose your virginity?"

Boyd stood, striding across the room to lean on the mantel. "My life is not up for discussion."

"Well, why not?" Her words sounded behind him, and he turned to find her staring up at him, still glaring at him like a small banshee.

"Women are meant to be chaste. Maids until they are married. You are not married."

She rolled her eyes. "Times have changed. Women no longer have to do what their fathers or men in general tell them to."

"I doona think I would like your time."

She shrugged. "And yet again, you may. If our roles were reversed, and women in this time held more power, would you like to be told what to do? Who to marry? What alliance you should make for the good of your family?"

Boyd crossed his arms, narrowing his eyes. "Nay, but it isn't like that, so I have no concerns."

"Well, if it were, you would like it no more than I would. My time for all its difficulties, and there are many, at least affords me a life that I can do as I wish. Mine to make, to enjoy, to do what I want."

"You should have told me that you were not a virgin."

"Why?" she asked, her blue eyes pinning him to the spot. "Why should I tell you? It's a personal thing that I need not tell anyone if I do not want to."

"Oh, but I would know when I took you that you were not a virgin. To trick a man in such a way 'tis shameful."

She shook her head, shutting her mouth with a snap. "I'm not trying to trick you into anything, and how would you know? I could fake pain, and you would be none the wiser. You men are so infuriating sometimes. I'm starting to see why you've not found love in all this time you've been immortal. You're a chauvinist."

"What the hell is a chauvinist, lass?" He'd never heard of the word before, and he doona like being called things he did not know the meaning.

"It means you would like a woman to do as you say, know her place, and yield to your whims. That will never happen with me, and not any woman who turns up here to marry you if she has any backbone to speak of. Any pride left running through her core."

"Aye, really?" he said, stepping close and placing them nose to nose. With his temper running high, his mind had one thought and one thought only. How damn beautiful she was when fired up, angry as hell, and willing to defend her beliefs. As odd as they were. She was as free and untamed as the Highlands. "Better a maid than a woman who's been with half of England and Scotland combined. No wife of mine will have been so free with her liberties."

The crack of her hand hitting his cheek echoed through the room. Maya fisted her hand at her side, pulling it away, hating that he'd poked her to the point she lashed out. Damn him. She'd never hit anyone in her life, and she hadn't wanted to hit him either. "I'm sorry," she said, swallowing hard as a red handprint formed on his cheek.

"Hit me again, lass, and I'll have you over my knee with your ass reddened within a breath."

She gasped, stepping back. "You wouldn't dare."

Boyd strode to the door. "Strike me and find out."

CHAPTER 14

O'Cain Stronghold, Duntulm Castle, Skye

Dougall stood in the hall of castle Duntulm and watched as his clansman, bloodied and worn from his flight from Druiminn, strode into the hall. The other men who were sent out to raid Macleod lands nowhere in sight. An ominous view that could only mean one thing, that their mission had failed.

He crossed his arms, pushing down his temper that yet again, his men had failed, that his clan had lost lives. Good, fighting men whom Clan O'Cain could not afford to lose. If his men could not raid and claim their spoils successfully, Dougall would be forced to do the raiding himself. Not that he minded such a feat. It had been some time since he'd had a good, bloody sword battle with a rivaling clan. And he would like nothing more than to lob off the head of Boyd Macleod, to see for himself if he were immortal as everyone in the Highlands thought him to be.

"My laird, we were attacked. Macleod and some of his

men caught us at Druiminn before we could get away. Everyone was killed."

"You survived it would seem," he said, narrowing his eyes on the lad. He'd sent some of his best men, confident they would return with cattle and mayhap a few pretty lasses to warm the men's beds. That they were bested once again by the bastard Macleod would not stand.

"Narrowly. I hid in the forest and made my way back here once darkness fell. The men," he said, wiping his face as if to clear his vision of what he had witnessed. "They were murdered, struck down without the opportunity to defend themselves. Macleod ordered their bodies to be burned."

Dougall fisted his hands at his sides. No matter how he intended to use them, the thought of his men being killed was never something easy to hear. Macleod was growing bold, and it was time the ancient laird died. He'd heard the rumors, of course, that the laird was immortal, but no man survived when his heart was ripped from his chest and his head put on a spike. Macleod would be no different.

"Macleod spoke of losing patience with the O'Cain clans. Do you think he'll incite war?"

Dougall laughed, hoping it would be so, and if not, then he would encourage one himself. He wanted the rich, fertile lands Macleod held. He wanted to grow his clan and be the greatest landholder in Scotland. His people would be well-fed, happy to follow his lead. The Macleod's time at Druiminn was limited.

"That is my hope," he said, staring at the battered clansman and feeling nothing but annoyance at his failure. "And if he does not, then I shall have to do the honors. He will not know what has hit him after I have finished," Dougall said more to himself than to his clansmen.

Macleod would die when they met in battle, and nothing, not even the Fae, would change Macleod's fate. Not this time.

Macleod stood at the stone wall at Druiminn Castle, looking out over the ocean that continuously rocked against the castle walls below. At night, the sea sounded angry and annoyed. He was livid over what was happening on his lands. The danger the O'Cain clan posed for his people. The raiding, stealing of his assets that kept them all fed. They did not just steal his cattle and sheep, but they destroyed crops in their raids. It had to stop.

The O'Cains were growing bold, leading up to something, but what he did not know, but he could guess.

They wanted a war. And war they would get if Dougall O'Cain needed one so badly. The young laird had only inherited last year. Boyd supposed the green lad needed to show how big his balls were. He would ensure they were shoved down his throat when he killed him, if only for his own amusement. They need only to come at him and his people one more time, and he would be forced to strike back, hard and deadly.

"Boyd?"

He inwardly groaned, steeling himself to look upon Maya. Another distraction he did not need. Along with his growing infatuation with the lass that left him distracted when he needed to be on edge, watchful, and ready to strike at a moment's notice. His name on her lips left an ache to thrum deep inside his chest, and he wanted, damn it, to hear it again and again.

He had left her earlier this night, knowing he needed to

clear his head from the day's troubles. That she had hit him and his words afterward were dishonorable. He'd never hit a woman in his life, even on their ass and he would not start now.

"Maya lass, what are you doing out so late? I thought you went to bed hours ago."

She leaned on the stone wall, looking down at the waves below. He instinctively took a step toward her, the thought of her tumbling to her death spiking fear in his soul.

"I couldn't sleep. I kept thinking about what I did to you. I'm sorry I hit you," she said, looking at him quickly.

He grinned, trying to dispel the despair he read in her eyes. "Doona worry, lass. My skin is as hard as leather. You dinna hurt me, but I should apologize as well. I would never hit you, lass. I hope you know that."

She watched him a moment before looking back over the inky-black ocean. "I may not have known you long, but I know that is true." She sighed, the sound lost. "I keep thinking about home, and if the tapestry shouldn't work, doesn't send me back, then what? What shall I do?"

"You will stay here with me." He would not send her away, even if he was never to have her warm his bed. He could not do that to a woman without a family or clan to protect her.

"You would let me live here with you. Forever?" She watched him a moment, grinning a little. "You have a kind heart, Macleod. Are you sure you want me to know that about you?"

He shifted on his feet, not sure he liked the term. Kind of heart did not sound strong or warrior-like at all. It sounded English, weak, and feeble. "Doona confuse who I am, lass. I doona have a heart. Not anymore." Not since the Fae had stolen his wife from him a hundred years before.

"You lie, but I shall keep your secret." She smiled a little at him. "Thank you for letting me stay here. Even if I shall grow old while you remain young, and I'll forever be jealous of your good looks while mine leave me."

Boyd hadn't thought of that. Good God, should Maya be stuck here for the rest of her life, she would grow old and, in time, die. The idea of the sweet English rose aging while he did not made his stomach churn. Of course, he'd lost friends in such a way before. At 127 years of age, that happened, but something about seeing Maya age and pass on disturbed him more than it ever had before.

What did that mean?

"We shall figure out a way to get you home, lass. Doona concern yourself."

"And what about you? Have you thought more about finding a sweet Scottish lass that you can love to break the curse? Don't you think it's time?"

He narrowed his eyes on her, mulling over her words and not in the mood to have such a conversation. "What do you know of Clan Macleod in your time? Tell me."

She leaned her petite bottom against the stone wall and crossed her arms. Her straight, white teeth bit her bottom lip, and his cock twitched in his trews. He sat atop the wall and focused on the stone castle before them, a tower of strength of solid stone, a reminder of his power and ability to deny himself the lass beside him.

"There are ancestors, a Laird Macleod in my time, so you must have children at some point. I wish I could tell you who it was that breaks the curse for you, but I do not know. But it is rumored that your family has gifts." She looked up at the stars, their flickering lights reflecting in her orbs. She was a pretty lass. Sweet and kind. He could see himself courting such a woman.

"What kind of gifts?" he asked, knowing that other than his immortality, there were no gifts for the Macleods. Only curses. Seeing everyone around you grow old, year after year, was no reward.

"I hadn't been working at the castle long, so I do not know exactly."

"You worked at the castle. What was your use?"

She chuckled a little, meeting his gaze. "I was a cleaner —a maid. I only started working there a couple of weeks before... Before," she waved her arms toward the castle, "all this happened."

"Such a beautiful, intelligent woman as yourself should not be waiting on the laird. You should be sitting beside him. Married to him."

She barked out a laugh, and he frowned. "I doona mean for my words to be amusing, lass."

She chuckled still. "I'm sorry, but no. I'm no better than anyone else, and I like working as a cleaner for the estate. I meet so many people from around the world, visiting and taking in the Scottish Highlands. While it would be lovely to be married to the current Laird Macleod, he's already taken. I'll just have to perv on him from afar, I'm afraid."

Perv? "You speak in a foreign tongue, lass."

"I just mean," she went on, "that he's handsome, and while I do enjoy seeing him when we're lucky enough to catch a glimpse of him, I'm not going to try and steal him from his wife. I love my job, and I would like to return to it if I should ever be lucky enough to return home."

Boyd studied her. The time she spoke of seemed strange and unreal. He could not think of the castle having anyone other than himself living within its walls. "What is

Scotland like? Have we claimed our independence yet, lass?"

She threw him a dubious look, unsure how to answer such a question, especially when she knew he would not like what she told him. "There was a vote a few years ago, but unfortunately, Scotland decided to stay part of the United Kingdom."

"Gods blood, what?" Boyd stood, the scowl on his face deep set. "We had a chance of independence. To pull free from the English reign of terror, and we dinna go?"

Maya stood, coming over to him and laying a hand atop his arm. His face had blanched, and she'd never seen anyone look quite so ill so quickly before. "The country does have its own parliament, so it isn't all bad."

He didn't look convinced, and she supposed, nor would he. To hear such a thing, knowing that his clansmen, all the Scottish people alive today, would love to be free from England. To hear that his homeland voted to stay would be a knife through his heart. Hers went out to him. "I'm sure one day Scotland will be free. But times are so different from how they are now. There is no clan warfare, hasn't been for hundreds of years. Scotland is peaceful, one of the most beautiful and most visited places on the planet. England is not looking for war any longer. I think should you see it, you would like the Scotland of my time. What your Scotland has turned out to be."

As beautiful, rugged, and magical as the man who stood before her. What wasn't there to love about that?

CHAPTER 15

Maya came downstairs into the Great Hall the following morning late after her nighttime chitchat with the laird. A conversation she would forever remember and cherish when she thought about it. That he was interested in her time and thought she should be married to the current Laird Macleod was a compliment that few women would not think sweet.

She spied him sitting at the dais, leaning back on his chair, one foot lazily sitting atop the table.

His breakfast seemed consumed, but he continued to look out over his clansmen and women who sat eating, breaking their fast. Maya started toward him, pushing down and ignoring the fluttering that always rose within her when she saw him. Of late, and especially after their kiss, her attraction to him had grown. Her hope that she could help him find love and break the curse seemed an unachievable dream, so she would have to settle for biding her time, enjoying his company as friends and hope that he bestowed one or two more of his delicious kisses.

His gaze slipped from the hall and landed on her, his dark, hooded eyes watching her every step.

Maya took a deep, calming breath. Never had she ever reacted to a man as she responded to this laird. His eyes, dark and hungry, held promises of nights of pleasure. She had little doubt that the women who lived under his care here at Druiminn thought him hot. She found him hot as hell. His chiseled jaw and cheekbones were enough to make a woman want to touch them. He always sported a little stubble growth over his jawline, giving him a rugged, dangerous appearance. Her fingers twitched at her sides, and she fisted her hands to still them.

She swallowed, not quite believing that the powerful laird kissed her. *Her.* A normal English woman of no particular expertise or standing in the world. Just a normal person like so many others, but Boyd Macleod had wrenched her into his arms and kissed her.

It was quite marvelous really.

Maya bit back a grin at her wayward thoughts as she stepped up on the dais. He turned in his chair, facing her. "Good morning, lass. You look handsome today."

Maya looked down at her yellow kirtle and didn't think the color helped her pale skin, but she smiled in any case, liking that he liked her gown. "Thanks. And you look very relaxed this morning."

"I have several tenants coming to see me today, requesting an audience about matters around my lands. I thought that maybe you would like to sit with me and watch."

"Really?" she asked, breaking some bread a maid placed before her before dipping it into a bowl of porridge that she'd come to like more than she thought she would.

Especially when it looked like white glue with chunks in it, nothing like the porridge she ate in her time.

"'Twould give you a chance to see what I do for my people, try to stop any disagreements from the outlying farmers who seed and tend my land."

Maya couldn't stop the smile from bursting forth. "I would love to sit by and listen. Being stuck in this time with you, and your people, I do want you to know that I'm enjoying it much more than I thought I would."

He threw her a crooked smile. She sighed, knowing how easy it would be to fall into lust with the man who, with one look, could make women shuffle up their skirts.

"You dinna think you would enjoy living here at Druiminn? What worried you so much?"

She chuckled, chewing her bread. "Besides the fact that there are no toilets, no showers, no toilet paper? Those are just a few things to start. Not to mention there is no deodorant."

He slipped his legs off the table and turned fully to face her. "While I doona pretend to know what any of those things are, deodorant has me intrigued."

His brogue made the word almost unrecognizable, and Maya chuckled, leaning toward him. "You spray it under your arms, so you don't stink."

He frowned, sniffing his underarm. "I doona stink, I hope."

"Oh no, you smell lovely." Maya froze as the words slipped past her lips before she could wrench them back. Heat burned her cheeks, and she knew there was no stopping the blush covering her face.

"Really?" His tone was cajoling and charmed. "I smell nice, do I, lass? Well..." he said, his head too close to hers. His breath tickled her ear, and she gasped when his lips brushed the whorl of her ear. "You smell as fresh as the rain on a cold Highlands morn, as sweet as a rose newly bloomed." He breathed deep beside her and didn't rush to back away.

Maya could not move, nor did she want to. If she were honest with herself, she'd wanted to hear such things from his lips, to have him kiss her again. She craved it nearly as much as she craved coffee.

Her hand reached out, settling on his muscular, long leg and the soft leather trews he wore. Her attention snapped to the clan, eating their breakfast before them, and was relieved to note none knew what was happening at the dais. It was Boyd's turn to still, his breath hot and heavy.

"What are you doing, lass?"

She faced him, placing them nose to nose. "Touching you."

His nostrils flared, a muscle in his jaw worked, before he wrenched his chair back, standing. "Eric, let us prepare for the tenant farmers," he yelled out to the young man who often accompanied Boyd. His secretary or squire, she supposed.

Maya huffed out a disappointed breath, missing already the feel of his body under her hand. She listened to him talk to his clansmen, watched as his men organized chairs and the hall to accommodate those who would attend today. As the hall was divided into seating rows, facing the dais, she supposed Boyd would sit here when he discussed their grievances or ideas, whatever it was they did during these events.

"Maya lass, good morning to you." Jeane sat beside her, her cheeks rosy. Maya frowned, reaching up into Jeane's hair and pulling out a long piece of straw. She held it up before Jeane, grinning. "Late night?" she asked, smiling when Jeane's cheeks turned an even darker shade of red.

"Shhh, lass. Boyd will find out, and there will be hell to pay. He thinks I'll never marry again, but that isn't the case, not when the devilishly handsome Douglas Albany kisses me as he does."

"Really?" Maya said, happy for her only friend. She cast a glance out into the hall and spotted the very man himself watching his Scottish lass with nothing but devotion in his eyes.

"He looks nice, Jeane." Maya squeezed Jeane's hands in support. "I'm happy for you."

"Thank you. I'm happy too, for the first time in what seems like years."

Maya poured them both a cup of honey wine, handing a cup to Jeane. "Do you think you'll marry him?"

"He's asked me, and I've said yes. I merely have to tell Boyd. I hope he approves."

"I cannot see him disapproving. They're friends, are they not?"

"Aye, they are, but Boyd will not expect it of me, and he'll worry that I shall be hurt again should anything happen to Douglas. Considering that Douglas is Boyd's head guardsman."

"Let us hope nothing happens ever to Douglas or yourself, and Boyd approves." Maya finished her breakfast, and they spoke of going back down to the bathing pools should Boyd agree. For all of Boyd saying she smelled like a rose, Maya did not think that was the case. They spoke of the farmers who would attend today and how long that would take. By the time they finished, Boyd was ready to sit back beside her and start his day.

Jeane excused herself, and Maya watched as discreetly

as possible beside the hall door as Douglas and Jeane made their farewells for the day.

She cast a glance at Boyd to see where he was looking, but he was staring at her. Maya started, having not expected him to be watching her. Or the spark of desire that flamed to life whenever he was near made her want to do things with him, no matter who was around.

"I know of their dealings, Maya lass. Doona trouble yourself in trying to lie for my cousin."

Relief ran through her like a balm. "Oh, thank God for that," she said, sighing. "I didn't want to lie to you since you've been so good to me, but I'm glad you know."

"Like I told you, lass, there is nothing that happens in this castle or on my land that I doona know about."

The doors to the hall opened, and in walked all the farmers, young and old, who had business with the laird. They were dressed in worn tunics, stained trews from their work on the land. Their wives, who followed them, were a little less disheveled. Even so, their status of being the lowest class in the clan was obvious.

Maya's heart went out to them, and so very thankful that in her time, at least, people were able to gain help when living on the poverty line. Perhaps she could speak to Boyd and try to get him to change his people's living conditions. Help them have a better quality of life.

The farmers lined up behind each other, their gazes flicking between Boyd and herself, and she could see that her seated beside the laird was of interest to them.

"Gregory, what can I do you for?" Boyd asked the first gentleman. The older man, possibly in his late sixties, stepped forward and pointed a gnarled finger at Maya.

"You can start by ridding Macleod land of that witch. Her being here has brought bad luck on us all."

Maya felt her mouth drop open. Boyd stilled, and no sound whispered in the Great Hall. Boyd leaned forward, and even from where Maya sat, she could feel his anger, that he was holding his fury in check. She didn't dare move or speak. Nor could she stop looking at him in all his glory, a Highland laird, straight out of the history books, powerful, strong, and in charge of all he commanded.

He was captivating and scary as hell.

"What did you say, Gregory? Perhaps you would like to repeat your question before I give you my reply."

CHAPTER 16

The clans people gathered, yelled in Gaelic, others in English, but none of what they said boded well for Maya. That she knew for certain. Farmers raised their arms, flailing at the clansmen who stood to the sides, everyone ill at ease over what was said, some against, others for the charge she was a witch and bringing bad luck to the clan.

Fear spiked through her when Gregory, the farmer who had accused her, stepped forward, daring to lean on the table and shout at her to her face.

In a flash, a blade, long and true, was at the farmer's throat, a nick of blood spilling from its point. The room went silent at the sight of Boyd holding the man within an inch of death.

"There will be calm here," he bellowed in both Gaelic and English.

The farmer's eyes were wide, his mouth turned down in a defiant frown, and Maya wondered if he would be foolish enough to continue with his claim.

"My chickens have disappeared, Macleod. How do you explain such a thing?" one woman shouted.

"My crops are trampled, ripped up overnight, and with not a sign that it was men or their horses. 'Tis like they came from the sky," another declared.

Their faces were pale, and Maya could see they believed something otherworldly impacted their lives. After what had happened to her, her own trip through time, nothing seemed out of the box anymore.

Boyd drew his dirk back from the farmer's throat, pushing him away. The older man stumbled into the gathered crowd, holding his hand up to stem the flow of blood oozing from the wound.

"I am willing to hear you, but doona think I shall tolerate disrespect to my guest or my authority. We are not a rabble like our enemy clans, fighting within ourselves. We doona act that way. We shall remember who we are and what our clan stands for."

Maya didn't dare say a word. Everyone seemed so upset that she was here, and it only reaffirmed that she could not stay. Even if she was a little infatuated and in lust with the laird, this time wasn't for her. If they thought her a witch, what would they think if they knew she'd arrived from a future time none of them could comprehend?

It was odd that they seemed to not fear their laird, a man who neither aged nor could die. She could only put it down to the fact that perhaps the people under Boyd's care could only take so much magic in their lives. The Fae meddling in their Scottish lives was one thing, time travel another altogether.

"Maya is not the problem," Boyd stated, his voice calm but with an edge of steel that even she could discern. "If your animals have been dying or disappearing overnight, if your crops are trampled and ripped out, 'tis because the O'Cain clan are determined to start a war. We have caught their clansmen twice on our lands, the last time not far from the castle itself. If they are bold enough to try to steal from under my nose, they will have no issue with stealing from the farms on outlying Macleod lands."

The farmers and some clansmen who also showed concern over her presence took in Boyd's words, their eyes narrowing in thought. The room quietened, calmed somewhat. Still, Maya kept her eyes lowered, trying to show the people she did not mean them harm, that it was not her being here that caused the strife.

"What I have failed to tell my people is that the Fae Queen has returned. After a hundred years, she is seeking to cause discord. Between the Fae and the O'Cains, I have little doubt as to who is behind your misfortune."

Audible gasps sounded, the women's eyes widened in fear. Maya wished she could go to them, comfort them in their concern, but she dare not. Right now, Boyd and she were outnumbered, and should they not like or agree with the laird's words, she wasn't sure where that would leave them.

Probably dead. At least she would be. Boyd couldn't be killed.

"Maya lass is no witch, but she is being mocked by the Fae, for reasons I doona know. But I will discern. As for your farms, I shall have men sent out to our farming lands to watch over you and keep you safe and free from theft and strife. Your concerns are heard, and I will not let any further harm come to you. Doona worry, I shall not fail you again."

Boyd's speech seemed to soothe the clansmen, farmers, and soldiers all. Maya wiped the sweat from her palms on her gown, taking a deep breath to dispel the nerves eating at her insides.

"All will be well, lass. Doona fret," Boyd said, catching her eye before turning back to the crowd gathered before them. "Now, is there anything else that is needin' to be discussed? If so, come forward and speak with me."

The clan dispersed a little after Boyd's announcement. Yet, some farmers remained and came up to the laird and told him of their issues. They ranged from asking for two families being joined together in marriage, grievances between farmers that had nothing to do with Maya, thankfully, of cottages that needed repairs, new thatch before the winter snow storms settled on the Highlands. Of sick children in need of care.

As he listened, Maya watched how Boyd ordered his men to carry out the repairs or send for the apothecary. Every trouble or request was met to the farmers' satisfaction. Maya did not think it was always so that lairds of great lands such as the Macleods would look after their people so well, but she was glad Boyd seemed willing to be a fair and kind leader for his people. Even after the trouble when first they spoke.

It made him all the more inspiring.

The discussions took several hours, and it was just past luncheon when the last farmer left the hall. Boyd stood, stretched; and ordered wine in his solar. "I shall see you at dinner, lass. There is a pile of correspondence that I need to attend to."

She nodded, watching him go just as Jeane came into the hall. "Maya lass. Come, I have a surprise for you."

Maya stood, her bones aching, her bottom almost numb after the many hours of sitting, only too glad to go with Jeane to see her surprise. With any luck, it would be an hour-long massage. How she'd love to have one of those right about now. One day, she promised herself. When she returned to her own time in the world. A spa day sounded perfect.

Boyd read through his correspondence from several allied clans, all of whom voiced their troubles with the O'Cains and the clan's increasing raids and thievery.

It could not go on. Boyd had been lucky that to date, no one had been killed other than the O'Cains on his land, but he knew that luck would not hold for long. Eventually, he would lose men, women, and children, perhaps to the bastard clan, and that he could not allow to happen. The O'Cains would be brought to heel.

Douglas strode into his solar, and Boyd stood, noting the man's ashen face. "What is it?" Boyd asked, knowing something was wrong.

"'Tis Jeane and Maya. They have disappeared. We canna find them anywhere."

Boyd picked up his sword and plaid, throwing the woolen tartan over his shoulders, and strode from the room. Thoughts of O'Cain men having Maya and his cousin made the blood in his veins run cold. They would rape and kill them, use them for their misdeeds, and not care how much they tortured them before ridding them of their mortal shell.

He walked through the hall, straight out into the keep, calling for his men to saddle horses, ride out in search of the women.

If the O'Cains didn't kill them both, then he surely would when he got his hands on them. They knew not to go anywhere without his escort. How dare they go against his orders for a second time?

"Look down near the heated pools, at Druiminn, and along the river. Mayhap they have gone to bathe or visit some of the crofters on the land. Bring them back to the castle. I shall deal with them here."

Boyd mounted his horse, kicking it into a gallop out of the gates, and started down by the river. There was no sound other than the horse's hooves breaking the ground beneath him, of its heavy breathing the farther he traveled.

What felt like hours passed, the afternoon darkened, and he knew soon they would be out of light. That if Maya and Jeane were out somewhere in the Highlands, they would not be able to search for them until the breaking dawn.

He returned to the castle to the news they had not returned. He jumped from his horse, panic rising in his gut.

Where the damndest were the blasted women!

"We rode out toward O'Cain land, but there isna any sign they have been on our lands. Some outlying farmers returning after today's hearing have not seen either lady," Thomas said, a frown between his brow.

Boyd ran a hand through his hair, unsure of what to do. What else could he do? He was powerless in situations like this. If the lasses had left and stumbled into trouble, they could be anywhere by now if they were not already dead.

"They were not down by the heated pools." Douglas looked as ill as Boyd felt. Damn the idiot women. Would Jeane never learn to do as told? As for Maya, she was as tenacious and obstinate as his cousin.

He would redden both their hides when he saw them again.

If you see them again.

He pushed the taunting voice away in his head. Not willing to contemplate such a thought.

Laughter and women's chatter caught his attention, and he turned to see Maya and Jeane climb the stairs that led down to the seafront the castle overlooked.

Everyone present in the yard, servants and clansmen alike, stared at the women, the two completely oblivious to the clan's concern as they continued to walk and chatter away like old tavern wenches.

Boyd crossed his arms, staring at them until they saw him. Both women caught his eye, their smiles slipping as they took in the clan watching them. No one present pleased with how they had spent the afternoon—looking for two senseless lasses.

"Is something the matter, Boyd?" Jeane asked, wrapping her arm around Maya's as if to protect her from him.

"Go to your rooms, both of you. I shall speak to you both before we break our fast this night."

Maya's large, blue eyes met his, and he could see she was as confused as his cousin. None of that mattered right now. Anger thrummed through him at the thought they had disobeyed him for a second time. That they had placed themselves in danger still made his emotions high. How could he keep them safe when they both continued to go rogue on him and his rules?

Not that they had done anything wrong from the appearance of it all. They were both perfectly fine down by the sea on that part of the castle grounds. His anger arose from the fact he'd not known where they were. That he may have lost Maya before he'd come to know her as much as he hankered to.

His attraction to the lass was impossible to deny. There were days where he'd thought of nothing but Maya. Of her long, dark locks so unlike his own. Her lithe form her kirtle accentuated most pleasantly. Even the guilt that arose within him with his lustful thoughts had not materialized of late. Did it mean he was ready to move forward? Maybe never love again, but at least find comfort within the arms of a woman after so many years of being alone.

Sorcha had been a passionate, beautiful, and caring wife. For years he'd soothed his screaming soul that she would be faithful to him, that she would not have married a being of her kind. Even now, the thought of such a thing made his stomach churn, and yet, he knew she would have. A hundred years was a long time to remain chaste, to go on without passion and love.

Boyd wasn't so certain he could do so any longer.

CHAPTER 17

Maya was chilled after walking about the rocky shore that castle Druiminn overlooked. They had searched the small ponds left filled with water at low tide, looking for crabs and small fish, shells and driftwood, anything really that caught their eye.

The afternoon had been pleasant, full of laughter and fun. However, her feet were as frozen as a block of ice, and if she placed them any closer to the fire, they might catch alight. Even so, they remained cold to the point her toes ached.

The dancing flames reminded her of Boyd and his fiery temper. Whatever was wrong with the man? They had not been out of the castle grounds. The whole afternoon they had been in sight of a guard who stood watch over them.

His anger at seeing them walk up the stone stairs to enter the bailey made no sense at all.

Footsteps sounded on the wooden passage before a light knock sounded.

"Come in," she called, knowing by the steps it was

Boyd. He entered, shutting the door behind him. His dark-green eyes took in her room before settling on her.

"Are you cold, lass?" he asked, closing the space between them. He kneeled beside her, picking up her feet. "They're freezing."

She gasped when he placed them on his legs and rubbed her skin briskly. His large, coarse hands sent heat to spiral through her, and not just her toes. Maya couldn't hold back the small grin of pleasure his touch wrought through her.

"We were walking around in the shallows while the tide was out. I was searching for fish and crabs. When the sun dipped behind the clouds and then the mountains, needless to say, it grew too cold to stay out. They'll warm up soon, I'm sure."

"You'll catch your death."

She watched him avoid her eyes, and she couldn't help but wonder why. Although she had a good idea. Not that she had ever been overly aware of men or how to read them, but Boyd wasn't like most men. He was a highlander, wore his protection of others like a badge of honor, and his concern for her was true. But not to look at her, well, Maya couldn't help but hope it was because to look at her would mean she could look into the green depths of his eyes and read him like a book. And his growing feelings for her.

His touch on her feet changed, grew languorous. His fingers dug into the undersides of her feet, massaging the cold flesh back to life. "If you tickle me, I may kick you in the nose. Don't press too hard." She grinned at him, and finally, he glanced up. It was all she needed to understand. To know he was hiding behind his shield of himself.

He didn't say a word, and he didn't need to. Maya slipped her legs out of his hold, placing herself closer to him. He did not move, nor did he reach for her, but she knew what she was about, what she wanted.

Boyd.

"I want to kiss you again," she admitted, watching those very lips that fascinated her, that were as soft as silk and deadly as sin, open a little with an intake of breath. Maya shuffled closer still. He smelled of leather, of man and spice. She licked her lips, wanting to taste him. To lose herself in his arms. If only he would allow himself to find some small piece of pleasure in his long life.

He pulled back, denying her, but Maya wouldn't let him go so fast. They had been playing this cat-and-mouse game for days. She reached up, clasping his stubbled jaw. Pain flicked in his eyes, and she knew he was fighting a war within himself, a pledge to remain chaste, without love, without a woman who was not his wife.

He may not love her. Hell, she certainly didn't think what she was feeling right now came anywhere near love, but she did like Boyd. She certainly lusted over him, and she was a twenty-first-century woman. If she wanted a man, nothing was stopping her from going for him so long as he was willing.

Every time she caught sight of Boyd around the castle, her breath caught, her mind running wild with the idea of having him lose control with her in his arms. He'd come to her room to chastise her, she was certain, but as of yet, he hadn't said a word.

"Don't deny me again," she whispered, her lips all but touching his. She could feel his breath shiver over her lips. His need was palpable. Expectation ran through her like liquid fire. Every muscle in his body tensed, and still, he did not reach for her. He fought to the very last not to have her. To make her his.

. . .

Boyd wrenched out of Maya's hold and stormed from the room. Her door slammed against the stone wall on his way out. The sconces lit his way as he blindly fled to his rooms like an Englishman being chased by a Scotsman. How ironic that it was an English lass, a Sassenach who pursued him now.

To his very core, he knew he could not deny her. For it was his wish as well as hers. He closed his eyes, slamming his door closed, slumping against it as if to keep his needs on the other side. At bay, even for one more night.

It didn't help. He craved her. He wanted to lay claim to her. By God, he wanted to tup her until he lost himself within her warmth, until she cried out his name into the Highland night. To kiss her breasts, to kiss the sweet liquid heat between her legs.

He groaned, wrenched off his tunic, and stumbled to the basin of water in his room, splashing his face with water—anything to rid himself of the flames that crawled over his skin.

"Boyd?"

He clasped the wooden table, closing his eyes, willing himself not to move. "What are you doing in here, lass? Leave now, before it is too late."

Her hand, featherlight, ran up his back, following a scar he'd gained as a child during one of his first skirmishes with the O'Cains.

"It is already too late," she whispered, the feel of her lips skimming along his spine his undoing.

He turned, wrenching her into his hold, slamming his mouth down against her lips with punishing need. Her mouth, soft and willing, moved, opened like a flower, and took him to a place he'd never thought to be in again.

Another woman's arms.

Boyd swept her off her feet, covering the distance to his bed in only a few strides. He didn't break the kiss, needing to know she was his for this night at least. What happened after was as unknown as the future, but now, right this moment, he never wished to let her go.

He lay her on the bed, standing back to untie the leather belt holding his trews in place. They dropped to the floor with a clang.

Maya's eyes went wide, gliding over him, her cheeks warming to a rosy hue. Pleasure spread across her features, and it pleased him that she liked what she saw. That she did not shy away from his size.

She kneeled on the bed, licking her lips, and he groaned. For the first time in a hundred years, Boyd bared himself to a woman. Body and soul.

Maya reached out, ran her finger along Boyd's impressive cock.

Wow. She blinked. Twice.

She had an inkling that he would be large, but this was seriously more than anything she'd ever seen before. What a marvelous gift time traveling was turning out to be. For it could have been so much worse. She could have ended up anywhere, really, been murdered on her first day back in time.

Her insides fluttered, clenched with expectation for what was about to happen. A part of her mind couldn't quite believe she was about to have hot, dirty sex with a Scottish highlander. And not just any Scottish man, but a medieval laird.

A fantasy come true for any woman with such a specimen to do with as she pleased. His cock jerked, and a small bead of pearly white seed appeared on its tip. She licked her lips, the urge to lean down, taste him, take him in her mouth, overwhelming. She'd never been one to like doing such a thing to her lovers in the past, but there was something about Boyd that made her want to. The very thought of it made her squirm with need.

She wrapped her hand around him fully, noting her fingers didn't quite reach the pad of her palm, and pulled him toward her.

He growled. "Do you like what you see, lass?" He hissed when she stroked him a second time.

Maya met his dark eyes promising retribution for her play. "I like it a lot."

As quick as a flash, he pulled her from the bed, turning her. A wall of solid muscle met her back, his hands sliding down her stomach, her hips, before fisting her kirtle in his fingers, edging up her dress.

His ragged breaths whispered against her neck, sending delicious shivers to run down her spine. This was too much, and they had barely begun. His mere presence, his removal of her dress, slow and teasing, his hands playing over her arse, her stomach, to tease the undersides of her breasts already had her on the brink of release.

It would not take much to send her over the edge.

Dampness pooled between her legs, more than she'd had with anyone else in her life. And he knew what he was doing to her. He played her like a musical instrument, made her purr to his wicked ability.

Her gown slipped free, and his fingers moved quickly to untie her cotton shift before that too was removed and thrown somewhere behind them.

His lips skimmed her neck. "Do you know how much I want you, lass? Do you have any notion of all the things I want to do to you?"

His firm cock gave her a good idea. He reached around, clasping her breasts, his fingers kneading her nipples to aching peaks. His cock slipped between her arse, grinding there, teasing her in a way she never thought would be an erogenous spot for her. But, with Boyd, well, everything was.

"I'm going to make you come so hard, lass, that you will never want another."

Her breath hitched when he nipped at her neck, his body engulfing her, owning her—holding her at his mercy. Maya pushed back against him, urging him on. "I can hardly wait."

CHAPTER 18

Boyd didn't think he'd ever feel so out of control as he did right now. The lass had his head spinning, her willingness to be with him, to chase him down and demand what she wanted was a light to his flame.

He kissed her neck, breathing deep her sweet flowery scent, licking along the contour of her neck to see if she tasted as sweet as she smelled.

She did. Better, in fact.

"I doona think I can wait, lass."

She reached behind, holding his hips and grinding herself against him. His cock ached, his balls tight as a fist. She'd unman him before he'd even sank himself into her soft, welcoming heat at this rate.

"What are you waiting for?" she gasped when he set his hand over the thatch of curls between her legs. Boyd frowned, feeling her, and his curiosity got the better of him.

He turned her about and kneeled. He felt his eyes widen at the sight of her sex. *Where the hell was her thatch of curls?*

"You are almost bald, lass. Whatever have you done to yourself?"

She chuckled, running her fingers through his hair. He glanced up, saw the need, the lust that burned in her dark-blue eyes. His mouth watered with wanting her, and he knew that while he was on his knees, it was only right that he give homage to her cunny.

"I've been waxed." She smiled, tipping up his jaw to look at her. "It'll grow back, especially now that I'm in the sixteenth century. There are no beauty salons here that I can book into."

Boyd didn't understand all that she said, but he could grasp her meaning. "Women do this to themselves in your time? Why? Do men not like a woman in her original, beautiful form?" He ran his hands up the insides of her legs. He could smell her desire, earthy and potent, and his cock twitched.

Soon, he promised himself. Soon he could have her for himself.

"Some do. Not all." She gasped as his thumbs swiped across her partly bald mons. Oh yes, she was wet, ready, and in need of him.

"Lie on the bed, Maya. I want to see you."

She did as he asked without fear. He wondered for a moment if more women in her time were so eager, willing to spread out before a man and let him have his way. A liberating time that were he able to time jump, may prove interesting to visit.

He wrenched her to the side of the bed. She let out a squeak of surprise at his manhandling before laying her legs over his shoulders. She squirmed, clasping the animal fur bedding as his thumb glided over her sensitive nubbin.

"You like that?"

She purred, staring at him, her eyes blazing with lust. "Yes," she whispered. "But I would like your mouth more."

So would he.

Boyd need no further prompting. From almost the first moment he'd seen the lass, he knew they would end like this. Together. Taking pleasure from each other. He licked along the inside of her leg. Maya chuckled, wiggled, as the action tickled.

"You taste divine," he said, before kissing her sex. She opened for him like a flower as he took her into his mouth. She was wet, hot, a heady scent of desire and need. All the things that made him hard, made him want to wrench himself up and impale her until they were both sated.

He licked and kissed her, fucked her with his tongue. She moaned, her fingers digging into his hair, pulling him against her as she raised her ass, grinding herself upon his mouth. Taking as much as he was giving.

Her breaths hitched, mumbled words spilled from her mouth as he laved her excited flesh.

Boyd, his favorite chant of all.

The word filled a place inside of him long empty, gave him hope, made him want and need things like all honorable men in the world.

She was close, he could sense it, taste it on her weeping bud, but he couldn't allow her to come. Not yet. He wanted to be with her when she shattered. Be one and the same.

Boyd pulled back, ignored her whimpering, her clutching at his shoulders, and came over her, rubbed his cock against her wet, swollen cunny.

"Oh fuck yes," she gasped, wrapping her legs about his hips and trying to drag him close.

"I'm going to tup you now, lass. Make you mine. Tell me that you want me."

"I want you," she gasped. Her hands came up and grasped her breasts, rubbing her pinkened nipples to hard little beaded peaks. Boyd almost came watching her play with herself.

He took a calming breath, needing to satisfy her before he took his pleasure. Determined, even after a hundred years, to be a good lover.

"Mmmm," she panted as he pushed the tip of his cock inside.

Boyd closed his eyes, forcing himself to calm. His arms shook, his hand guiding himself into her.

"You feel so…" Boyd couldn't find the words or hold himself back. She was too hot. Too wet and tight. He thrust into her, impaling her to the very hilt of his cock.

Pleasure ran down his spine, into his balls, and through his body. Gods blood she felt good. Too good.

She pulled him down to kiss her. Their mouths melded, the kiss wild and demanding. He thrust into her, again and again, deep and long.

She kissed him back, her tongue tangling with his, her fingers clasping his hair, punishing and forceful.

"Boyd," she panted, kissing the side of his mouth, his jaw, his neck. He closed his eyes, reveling in her pleasure. Both of their pleasures. He wanted to stay like this forever, in her arms, emotions rioting inside him.

Completeness, fulfillment, hope.

She ground against him, lifted her arse, and his balls tightened, demanded release. He deepened his thrusts, took her to the point of savagery, but nothing could stop him now from taking his pleasure, of spilling his seed into her womb.

Maya kissed his shoulder, throwing her head back as her cunny tightened about him, convulsed and contracted with the first tremors of her release. Boyd tupped her until she broke. Her scream rent the air, sure to be heard throughout the castle.

He cared not. His moans mingled with hers as heat licked his spine. The first vestiges of his orgasm ripped through him, made his breath hitch, his heart stop. He took her without heed, pumped every last ounce of his seed into her, let her tight, convulsing sex drain him of every drop. Exhausted, he slumped down beside her on the furs, pulling her into the crook of his arm.

Their breathing ragged, their bodies damp with sweat, he stared at the ceiling, not remembering sex with a woman ever being so intense, not even when he was married.

He frowned at that truth, as painful as it was to admit. But it gave him hope. Mayhap Maya had been right, and it was time to break the curse. He did not know if it was the lass in his arms who would be the honorable one to free him, but after today, he was starting to think that mayhap she could be.

No one ever in his long life had stirred him as much, made him need like the Scottish highlander he once was.

"I didn't hurt you, did I?" she asked, her chuckle vibrating against him as her hand slid up his stomach to play with the fine hairs on his chest. "I'd hate to have broken my new toy so soon."

He laughed, the sound carefree and true. Another new and strange fact of how he had changed since her arrival. "Nay, lass. You dinna hurt me at all. Just give me a minute, and I'll show you that I'm in perfect working condition."

She grinned up at him. Her long, brown locks splayed

over his arm and pillow. Her long, lean body curled against his, her perfect creamy flesh pale and pure against his dark sun-kissed skin. He met her gaze, and something shifted inside him, cracked open, and burst free.

"Good, because there are so many things I want to do with you, and we only have a couple of months before I leave. There is much fun to be had before I go."

He pulled her close, the idea of her leaving sending a spike of panic through his gut. "Aye," was all he could reply. Discourse failing him for a moment. The idea of his future, as bleak and mundane as it was before she landed on his hall floor, winding him of breath.

"Best we continue then," she said, rolling to sit atop him.

He was instantly hard. "Do your worst," he taunted.

Her eyes took on a wicked glint before she did, in fact, do her worst and left Boyd gripping for purchase when she was finished with him. Hours later.

CHAPTER 19

Maya woke the next morning, stretched out on the cool linen sheets, the furs that covered her, luxuriating in the memory of what she and Boyd had done the night before.

Multiple times.

She rolled over, expecting to see him asleep beside her, and was met with an indentation of his large, muscular body imprinted on the bed, but no man.

Where was he? She sat up, looking about the room but found it empty, no sign of him anywhere.

She slumped back down, staring up at the ceiling, and screamed.

Sitting upon one of the rafters was the Fae Queen, her face contorted into a semblance of disdain.

Maya blinked and squealed a second time when the immortal now stood at the base of her bed. "Ah, so you have woken. Our own sleeping precious after your night of revelry with the laird."

A chill ran over her, and she glanced down, ripping up the blankets over her bared chest. "What do you want?"

The Fae wiggled her finger at her, clicking her tongue. "I heard that you had consummated your relationship with Macleod. I did not think he would crumble under your spell so soon, but alas, I was wrong. He proves himself to be as weak as any human male."

Maya wanted to voice that Boyd was anything but weak, but bit her tongue, kept her mouth closed less the queen thought to punish her for her retaliation.

"I don't understand why you keep haunting me. What do you want?"

The queen shrugged, strolled about the room with a graceful air, and yet menace oozed from her every pore. "Macleod displeased the Fae a hundred years ago. Dared to love one of our own. I shall punish him for as long as it pleases me."

Maya shook her head. "Why? Has he not paid enough for living all these years without the woman he loved? He's been alone all that time, has he not disbursed his penance to you?"

"His *wife*," she said, disdain masking the title, "is trouble in the Seelie Court. Has been since the day she arrived there. The silly fool thought it wrong the treatment of the Macleod and wants me removed as queen. Ha!" She laughed, the sound echoing about the room as if they were in a great canyon. "She is as foolish as Macleod thinking that the Fae's wrath is done with him."

"Are not fairy's supposed to be kind? You are part of the Seelie Court, you say. I thought it was only the Unseelie who made strife," Maya stated, sick and tired of being taunted, threatened by this being. Immortal, magic or not, she was not going to be bullied. She jumped from the bed, as naked as the day she was born, and stood nose to nose with the Fae Queen. "I may not know much about

Scottish lore or tales of the Fae folk, but I do know that much about you."

If she thought to make Maya cower, she would not. Even if her stance against this female, this evil little fairy got her killed. The room's tone changed, the air crackled with anger, and the queen seemed to start to glow, but not white. Instead a deathly pale gray.

"You would be foolish to believe that the Fae are either kind or cruel. A mistake that your laird pays for to this day, but alas, I see you could be his savior, and I'm not so certain I have finished playing with him yet. He is quite amusing to watch, year after mortal year, a lonely, mundane, pathetic man."

"If Sorcha is causing trouble for you, I hope she is successful in bringing you down. God knows you seem like a trouble maker."

The queen laughed, but her eyes flashed silver, hard and cold. "Do not fall in love, my little human. I should hate to have to take you away from the laird as well, but," she shrugged, floating and gaining height away from Maya, "now that the wheels of pleasure, of emotions, have started, even I cannot stop that, but it doesn't mean that I will allow it to continue. Be warned, mortal."

The queen disappeared without a trace, the only sign that she had been there an odd scent that reminded her of mildew.

Boyd strolled into the room at that exact moment, a maid behind him holding a tray of food squealing in surprise. His eyes widened, his mouth falling lax.

Maya glanced down at herself and gasped, running to the bed and pulling off an animal fur to cover herself, having forgotten her nakedness.

"I'll take the tray," she heard Boyd say to the maid,

kicking the door closed when he came into the room. He threw her a lopsided grin, his eyes filled with mischievous light.

"Do you often walk about your bedchamber naked, lass?"

Heat bloomed on her cheeks, and she shook her head. "No, of course not. Not often," she ventured.

He placed the tray down on a small cabinet, walking toward her and reminding her of a wild lion she'd once seen seeking to mate during breeding time at the zoo.

Even after her less-than-pleasant interaction with the Fae Queen, her body reacted as it always did when she saw Boyd. It sizzled to life, her wants and needs demanding attention. The queen warned her not to fall in love with Boyd, but somehow Maya thought it was already too late. She was falling for the rugged Scot, and there was nothing that could change that fact, not even a threat that she didn't know would materialize or not.

He reached out, lifting each of her fingers that pegged the animal fur closed at her chest. The fur slipped from her hold and pooled at her feet, leaving her exposed, naked to his gaze.

His eyes ran the length of her, a slow, torturous inspection that left her breathless. Moisture wantonly pooled between her legs.

"I have affairs to attend to in the keep, but you, lass, well, you make me want to pull you into my arms and make sweet love all morning."

Was he going to leave her? Oh no, no, no, she couldn't allow that. Not with the heat that licked at her skin from his mere inspection. "You cannot look at me like that, Boyd, and not attend to affairs here first," she stated, determined to get her way.

. . .

Boyd could not believe what his lass had uttered, but her determination to get her way was as true as her nakedness. She wanted him. Wanted him as much as he burned for her. He'd awoken at dawn, determined not to let the lass from the future complicate his life, change the structure of his days.

But she had, and with very little effort on her part.

His mind alone could not stop thinking of her abed upstairs, asleep and utterly tupped to within an inch of her life. He had forced himself to remain in the solar, read reports from allied clans, talk to Douglas about today's training. Of what his clansmen were saying after their travels to the boundaries of his land.

All the while, his mind had stolen to their hours of lovemaking. To Maya's willingness to let him have his way, to kiss and pet her wherever he wanted, to lathe kisses on her in her most private of places, to touch and savor her body like the goddess she was. Even now, he burned for her, longed for when they could be alone.

His men were assembled in the courtyard, ready for a day's training. They had to prepare for the O'Cains, for another melee would soon follow. Being distracted as he was for the past weeks with Maya here at Druiminn, he felt his ability required study within himself.

"I doona look at you in any other way than I normally do," he answered, knowing full well he looked at her like a man starved of a woman a hundred years.

She shook her head, closing the space between them, her delicate hands sliding up his arms to lock at his nape. "You are looking at me as if you want an encore to last night's events. Do not say that you do not."

Oh hell yes, he wanted an encore. He wanted more than that. "I doona have the time, lass. I must go."

She pouted up at him, and he groaned. Damn the woman and his growing inability to say no to her. "Well then, if you must go and leave me hanging, I suppose I'll have no choice but to do it myself."

The very thought of Maya touching herself made him rock hard. She sauntered over to the bed, crawling onto it before lying on her back. Boyd felt every muscle in his body grow taut. For a moment, it was hard to breathe. He clasped the bed in support. This woman would bring him to his knees if she followed through on her threat.

"You wouldn't," he hedged, a small part of him hoping she would.

She raised her brow in defiance. "Wouldn't I?"

Her hand slipped over her stomach, one finger outlining her belly button before moving farther to the manicured curls that had held him in fascination last evening. His attention shifted to her face, and he found her eyes focused on him. Her breathing increased, her breasts rose and fell in a motion of enticement. With wickedness he never thought to see in a woman, her hand slipped between her legs, clasping her sex. She arched her back, a soft sigh of satisfaction passing her lips.

It was all it took. Boyd was on her in a heartbeat. His men, his training, missives, and safeguarding his home forgotten, at least until he'd sated their needs. Possibly more than once.

CHAPTER 20

Maya knew she was playing with fire the moment she touched herself. The fire that burned in Boyd's eyes was enough to singe her, even with him at the end of the bed, watching her with an intensity that left her reeling.

When she followed through on her teasing, touching herself, she hadn't thought Boyd would break so quickly. How wrong she was.

He came over her within a breath, taking her hands and pinning them above her head. With his free hand, he ripped at his trews, opening them only enough to release his delightfully large cock.

He thrust into her without waiting for her to catch her breath. Took her in hard, maddening, deep strokes that sent her mind reeling.

His green orbs, so like the color of the Highlands, sizzled with fire, need and something else, she thought. Dominance perhaps, but definitely possessiveness.

Maya wasn't certain how that made her feel, but what she did know was right now wasn't the time to delve into those new and mysterious emotions crackling between them.

With only her legs to hold him, she wrapped them about his hips, lifted herself up to meet his claiming.

It didn't take Maya long to feel the tightening of her body, her breathlessness as release was upon her. She came, hard and quick, convulsing about him as he spilled into her. His muffled panting of her name warm against her ear.

Boyd slumped beside her, and Maya stared up at the ceiling for the second time this morning, remembering what she needed to tell Boyd about the Fae Queen.

He lay an arm over his eyes, his chisled chest, tight stomach rising quickly with each breath. She grinned, noting he was practically fully dressed except for where his cock, still half-hard, lay against his trews.

"You are a distraction, my lass. One that keeps me from my responsibilities."

Maya didn't want to be a distraction, not if it meant his home and clansmen were put at risk, but she also knew that she wanted to see him. Often and alone preferably.

"I won't seduce you again," she teased. "At least not when I know you're needed elsewhere. Would that suit better?"

He turned his head, watching her. "Aye, that would suit better, but it is yet to be seen if it can be done. I doona think I can keep my need of you at bay. Not even for a day."

Pleasure thrummed through her, and she curled into his side, throwing her leg over his waist. She clasped his jaw, making him meet her eye. "Is it so bad that we enjoy each other's company?"

"Nay, 'tis not bad, but we shall try better. The clan are

already suspect of you, we doona need them thinking that you have possessed my soul."

Maya laughed. If only she could be so lucky as to possess such a man, make him hers. But she could not. This time here in old Scotland was just a passing dream. A mistake in the make-up of time itself. It would right its wrong, throw her back home and then she would be left heartbroken that the man she'd come to like more than any before him, had long left the world.

The Fae Queen was right. She needed to guard her heart. Before she lost it in sixteenth-century Scotland, never to be returned to her again.

Dougall O'Cain sat in a crofters cottage, only several miles from Druiminn Castle, the stronghold of his enemy and the laird he would rid the world of himself if there was any justice in the world.

He sat across from the newly married couple, both of them roped to chairs, the woman's mouth at least shut with a tied bit of cloth.

"Tell me about your laird's guest? She's English, and quite beautiful I'm told. Does he hold her in high regard?" Dougall asked, narrowing his eyes as the young Scot clenched his jaw shut. The English wench may be a way in which Macleod would fight. If he could get his hands on the outlander.

Dougall flicked his head at the lad's continual silence, and a knife appeared at the throat of the young woman's neck. Her tears marked her cheeks as they steadily fell, her whimpering growing on Dougall's last nerve.

"She's English. Some say she has our laird besotted for the first time since his wife disappeared. He is defensive of her, stood up to his clansmen and women when they questioned her staying at Druiminn. Some of the clan thought her bad luck, that she was causing the strife on some of the outlying farms."

Dougall laughed to himself, knowing it was no wench from England who was causing the issues the Macleod clan were having. That, in fact, it was his men raiding, stealing, enjoying the spoils of the fertile land.

"What do you think of the lass? Do you think she's a witch?" Dougall was no fool, and he didn't want to set out to seize Macleod land if he were up against more than a mortal man and his rabble of people.

"Nay, I do not. Macleod would never jeopardize his people by allowing anyone with dark magic to remain at Druiminn. Not even if that person were a woman."

Dougall rubbed his jaw, not so certain that was true. The Macleod laird was immortal from all reports, cursed by the Fae for going against the rules. Not that he believed such a tale. No man lived forever. The young laird was simply a doppelganger of his forefathers, not a continuation of the same man. And yet, to dismiss the rumors as he had of late, left him uneasy.

Had the Fae played a part in cursing the laird, he did not wish to anger them whether he believed it to be true or not. The Fae could curse his people, his land never to bear a good harvest again. Make his cattle and sheep barren, never to breed.

"I want you to travel to Druiminn after we leave. I want you to let Macleod know that I was on his land and that under my sword, he will fall. Immortality means nothing to the O'Cains. Tell your laird that we're coming for him, and he will lose, both his lands and for the second time, his wench."

Dougall wrenched from the chair, striding to the door. "Rape the woman, and make the husband watch. I need Macleod to know I'll not spare his people."

He walked from the cottage to the muffled screams of the woman, the shouts of the man. He smirked, gaining his seat on his horse. "We'll return to O'Cain stronghold. I have achieved all I want for now." But soon he'd return with an army of men, outnumbering the Macleod, and the rivers on his land would run red with blood. The land would soon be his, and he'd allow nothing to get in the way of that.

No English wench. Not witchcraft or the Fae. Nothing.

CHAPTER 21

Chapter Twenty One

The following afternoon Maya found Jeane out near the stables, speaking to Douglas. They stood, close, heads bent, watching several clansmen rub down horses, the mounts sweating and breathing heavily after their run. The bailey was busier than normal. Men walked about, fully armed, looking as if they were on their way to battle or just returned from it.

"Och, Maya lass, 'tis good to see you. I feel like I have been neglecting you the last few days. I hope you doona think that I am," Jeane said, stepping away from Douglas as if her interest in him was forbidden.

"Never," Maya said, nodding hello to Douglas. "Have you seen Boyd today? He left early this morning, and I've not seen him about the castle. He's not in his solar."

A shadow crossed Jeane's eyes before she blinked, and it was gone. Did Boyd have something to do with the horses that had come back labored and tired? The men who walked about armed? The pit of her stomach twisted, and she couldn't help but wonder if something was afoot.

"You've just missed him, lass. He's headed down to the heated pools to bathe. There was a small skirmish a few miles from here."

Fear spiked through her. A cold sweat chilling her skin. She pulled Jeane aside, needing to know more. "Is everyone okay? What happened?"

Jeane walked her through the bailey toward the back of the castle that overlooked the sea. "More O'Cain men are causing strife. Late last night or I should say this morning, a farmer sought solace and help after the O'Cains attacked his farm. Dougall O'Cain himself sent a warning message to Boyd."

A warning message? What did that mean? Was the clan going to go to war? Maya hated the idea of such a thing, so much death and destruction, and for what? Nothing really, not when all was said and done. "What was the message?" she asked, not quite certain she truly wished to know.

"That Boyd would die by his sword and before the year was out. Boyd and several men rode out this morning to seek retribution. To see if they could intercept Dougall O'Cain before he crossed back into his lands, but could not. They did, however, come across others thieving livestock and dealt with them appropriately."

Maya wasn't foolish enough not to know what dealt with appropriately meant. She sighed, unable to pull forth an ounce of pity for the enemy clan, not if they were hell bent on causing so much strife. It was amazing that anyone survived these hard times in history to continue their families far into the future. She supposed Boyd's family was one of the few who did not get lost in history. They still had the title and a laird in the twenty-first century, but this O'Cain laird sounded like trouble to Maya. Oh, how she would love to tell O'Cain that his fight against Boyd was in vain. That he would not win. History had already proven that point.

"I shall go to him."

"No," Jeane said, clasping her arm in a punishing grip. "You cannot go without a chaperone, and most of the men have just returned from battle. They will not want to escort you."

"Jeane, I'll be fine. It's five minutes from here, and Boyd is there."

Jeane bit her lip, a frown between her brow as she thought over Maya's words. "He'll skin me alive if you should meet him there alone."

"I will tell him I went without telling anyone." Thankfully Jeane let her go, and Maya strode quickly out of the bailey and down into the trees, being sure to follow the well-worn track to the heated pools.

The closer she came, the more she could hear the water falling into the pool, the intermittent splashing as Boyd bathed in the water.

She stood in the trees before the clearing, enjoying the sight of Boyd as he washed his arms, his stomach flexing and showing off his impressive midriff. All the troubles of just before floated away at the sight of him. So strong and able. Tall and muscular, a god of the Isle of Skye and hers, for the time being in any case.

With no one else present, Maya made herself comfortable leaning against a tree, smiling to herself as he dipped his head, attempting to wash his tangled hair.

"Do you need help with that?" she asked, chuckling

when he started at her voice, his eyes finding her quickly enough in the undergrowth.

He frowned, searching the trees for others. "Are you alone, Maya?"

His voice was calm, but she could hear the censure in his tone. She sighed, walking toward the pool, kicking off her leather boots, and dipping her toes in the heated water. "I am, but before you go all highlander on everyone back at the castle, no one knows that I came here. I heard someone say that you were bathing, and I wanted to join you."

One of his eyebrows rose in disbelief, if eyebrows could rise in such a way. "You are not allowed to leave the castle grounds without me. 'Tis not safe for you, lass." He stood, several yards into the water. Her attention dipped to his chest, his stomach that she only now realized was bleeding. She gasped, going to him and forgetting she was still fully clothed. "You've been cut," she stated, touching the wound. She pushed it together, a sizeable slice just above his belly-button. Thankfully it wasn't too deep, but still, his gasp pulled her away from inspecting it.

"Aye, I wasn't quick enough to get out of the way of that strike. Doona flash yourself, lass. It'll heal in a day or two."

Her touching of the wound aggravated it, and it started to drip blood. She cringed. "I've made it bleed, sorry."

His amused chuckle brought her attention back to his face, and she looked up to find him smiling at her.

"What are you laughing at? It's not funny. Look," she said, pointing at the wound. "It's bleeding worse now." She frowned in thought. "You need to return to the castle and have it bandaged."

He reached down and splashed some water on it. "It'll be well. 'Tis only a small cut."

Maya regarded him a moment, hoping he wasn't injured anywhere else. "You fought today. Was it bad?"

He shook his head, pulling her against him and holding her tight. He didn't seem to want to do anything else, content just as they were. Maya wrapped her arms around him, holding him hard in return.

"The O'Cains attacked an outlying farm. Raped the wife and beat her. Her husband traveled all night to tell us after she passed away. I could not allow the O'Cains to get away with such treatment." He placed a small kiss on her shoulder. "If it is a war that they want, then they shall have it."

Maya's stomach churned at the idea of the farmer's wife's pain at being beaten and raped. This time was so hard, cruel, and dangerous.

"I don't want anything to happen to you," she admitted. The idea of Boyd being injured or killed spiked fear into her more than the fact she may never be able to return home. She didn't know much about clan battles, the history regarding the Isle of Skye. The clan wars, and who won them throughout the ages. All she knew was that the Macleod clan was still around in her time, but that did not mean they were a direct line to Boyd. The laird today could be a distant relative, Jeane's bloodline even. He may have died, been killed, even with the immortality curse shadowing his every step.

"I don't want to even think about you going to war. I'm sorry for the farmer and his wife though. He must be devastated."

"He is. To lose a wife is never easy, but to lose one at

the hands of someone else while you're made to watch is a punishment meant for no one."

Maya thought over his words, wondering if, in part, he spoke of his loss that he'd been made to stand by, to watch as Sorcha was taken from him. At the same time, powerless to stop it.

"You will seek retribution. When do you think you'll do that?" she asked, knowing that immortal as Boyd was, she wasn't so certain how far that immortality cloaked him. What if he was so severely injured, cut into pieces like the historical fabled William Wallace, what then? What would happen to him if such a fate befell him?

"We need to prepare. A month or two, if I know the O'Cains at all. They will wait for their clan to pull together, train and plot. But doona flash yourself, lass. It'll not be me who'll die. I can assure you of that," he stated, stepping back and continuing to clean his body, reaching between his legs and lathing his private bits. For a moment, she couldn't do anything but stare and admire the virile, hot Scot.

"I should leave you to your bath. I'll sit on the bank and wait for you." She turned to go, and he clasped her about the stomach, pulling her up against him.

"Nay, lass," he breathed against her ear, sending goose-bumps to prickle over her skin. "I doona want you to leave me."

Maya closed her eyes, having not thought that her coming down to the pool would end in such a pleasurable way, but now that Boyd suggested it, having him, here in this clear, warm water, was all she wanted.

"Perhaps you ought to help me out of my gown, then?" she suggested, looking over her shoulder and meeting his eye.

Heat flickered in his green orbs, a wicked grin on his lips. "'Twould be my pleasure, lass." He reached down into the water, lifting the half-sodden dress up and over her head, throwing it onto the grassy bank.

He ran a finger down her spine before his lips followed his finger's progress. "Your skin is so soft and smooth. I doona think I've ever seen anything so lovely."

Maya closed her eyes, reveling in his touch. His hands moved over her, teasing and caressing her body. He clasped her breasts, kneaded them. Teased her nipples to hard little points, before sliding his hand down between her legs.

"You make me want you, all of you, forever," he groaned against her shoulder, kissing her neck, her ear, working his way around to her nape. He ground himself against her, his hard cock sliding against her bottom.

Maya moaned, reaching up behind her to hold his face as he kissed her neck. Heat pooled between her legs. She wanted him too. So much. More than she ever thought to want anyone in her life, but right now, right at this moment, if he did not take her, she would surely die.

CHAPTER 22

Chapter Twenty Two

Need roared through Boyd. His rock-hard cock wept to take her. She was simply the most perfect woman he'd ever known. She made him laugh, forget his troubles, was kind and sweet. And gods blood, she made him burn.

He kept her pinned to his front, bent down a little, and took her from behind. Her sigh of pleasure mingled with his. So tight and wet, unbelievably ready for him. Her need as great as his.

He rocked into her, holding her stomach, his other hand playing with her puckered nipple. Tonight he'd kiss her sweet peaks, but right now… Now he required release, to forget, even for a moment, the threat against the woman in his arms, his clan, and home.

She moaned his name, and it almost unmanned him. He tupped her harder, giving her what she wanted, what they both did, and then he felt it. The first tremors of her release, convulsing on his cock and milking him of his. He came hard and quick, her name on his lips like a sacred plea. She moved against him, taking from him what she wanted, her pleasure, before slumping back against his shoulder. A tup as quick as that was enough to make one dizzy.

Their breathing ragged, he pulled out, turning her to face him. "What am I going to do with you, lass?"

She wrapped her hands around his neck, leaning up to place a light kiss on his lips. "More of the same, I hope."

A little delirious, for a moment he couldn't remember what he'd asked her, and then he did. "Aye, of course," he agreed, but that was not what he meant at all by his statement. How could he let her go when the time came? When the tapestry was ready, how could he stand by and allow her to touch it, possibly catapulting her back through time to her old life?

He pushed her long, dark locks from her face, needing to see her sweet mouth, her little nose, and large, luminescent eyes that he'd come quite enamored of. "I will miss you, Maya lass."

She tipped her head to the side, her eyes dimming a little with sadness. "I'll miss you too."

"Tell me why you cannot stay?" he asked, already knowing the answer to his question. This time was not her own. She was born centuries into the future, had a life there, friends and family who would want to know where she was. This time was hard, ancient to her way of living, and dangerous. Already there were clans aware of her presence and willing to hurt her to get to Boyd. He couldn't allow that. Even though he wished he were selfish enough to have her linger, live with him here, forever.

"As much as I'd like to, you know that I cannot. There must be rules to time travel. Certainly, I'm misplaced, and my being here would have to have a changing effect on the future. I do not want to risk that, no matter how alluring you are for me to remain."

Of course, he understood. Still, it did not make it easy to hear. Would she stay if he fell in love with her? Told her that she was his savior? If she fell in love with him? An unattainable dream, it would seem.

Boyd swooped her up into his arms and lowered her into the water, bathing her after their lovemaking.

He swept his hand over her body, paying homage to the sweet delicacy between her long legs, her breasts that required wiping multiple times. She chuckled, moaned in his arms as he brought her to a second orgasm. Boyd stared down at her, marveling at her beauty, her trust in him after only a few short weeks.

And the years loomed ahead, lonely and devoid of life, only honor and duty, and he wasn't so sure when Maya left, there would be anything left to live for. Not in this time, at least.

The Fae Queen hovered in the tress, masked by magic, and watched Boyd Macleod savor and cherish his Maya lass from the future with an affection she'd not seen before.

Not even with his wife, Sorcha.

Her eyes narrowed, anger thrumming through her and threatening to break the hold on her invisibility spell. This was getting out of her control, and she would have to do something about it.

Her curse against the laird she had thought unbreakable, certainly his love for Sorcha had led her to believe so. How wrong she was after watching the two lovers frolic in the water. Two carefree lovers who looked as if there were no troubles in the world.

No longer would she tolerate such a farce. She would have to move on Maya, ensure she returned to her time or some other such place that no one would think to look. No human went against the Fae and merely walked away unharmed. He deserved to pay for breaking the rules, and a hundred years was not nearly long enough. A blink in time for the Fae. No, he deserved to live alone and lonely in his grand castle.

Titania smirked, thinking of the laird when he found his new lover gone. Oh yes, this would be fun indeed, now she just needed to decide when to take his lady. The sooner, the better, by the looks of it, before they fell in love and broke her hold on the laird forever.

Maya linked her arm around Boyd's a little while later as they walked back to the castle. Sated and somewhat tired after their pleasurable afternoon, they spoke little as they walked along the worn track, lost in their thoughts. Boyd didn't elaborate on what else the Laird O'Cain had said to the farmer who had sought refuge at Druiminn castle, but nor did he need to for her to know it wasn't good.

That the farmer's wife had died was serious enough, heartbreaking for the man and women in general who were susceptible to such violence, now and even in the future.

Men could be such assholes sometimes, no matter the centuries.

The clan was on edge. Maya could see it in their haunted eyes, the way they stood, looked about. They appeared permanently on guard. O'Cain had issued a warning threat, and everyone knew that the enemy laird would follow through.

One day and soon.

Walking through the bailey, Maya spotted Jeane sitting at a table with a group of women, each employed with cutting up and peeling vegetables. "I'm going to go help Jeane. Do you mind?" she asked Boyd, who had stopped to watch several men train with swords.

"Nay, lass, do as you will. I shall remain here."

Maya threw him a small smile before joining Jeane, seating herself and picking up a knife to slice the vegetables. For a moment, the clanswoman didn't speak before Jeane put paid to their silence.

"Doona stop talking on Maya's behalf. She's just like us, a woman. You may speak freely."

Maya didn't expect the women to be overly friendly with her. Not after the gathering where she was accused of being a witch. Although Boyd had explained her presence, the people remained distant and afraid.

"Is it true that you are here to win our laird's hand in marriage? 'Tis an impossible feat, doona you know? He'll never marry again. Our laird had one love and one love only, and she's gone now."

Maya glanced up from cutting a carrot to find a young woman with long, red hair pulled off her face by two long braids, staring at her with a knowing smirk.

Was the lass jealous? Did she want Boyd for herself? The thought sent anger to simmer in her blood. "What do you know of Macleod's wife? He hasn't spoken much of her." Or at all, not to Maya, at least. She dearly would love to know about the woman who held his heart in her hand. From what she could remember of the tapestry she was beautiful, but other than that, a historical figure, forgotten in time.

"My great-grandmother remembered her. She's passed on now, but my mother knows all that my great-grandmother did during her life. My family lives just outside the castle grounds near the river. We've been loyal to the Macleod clan for centuries."

"That is amazing," Maya said, noting the pride that blossomed on the young woman's face. Better than disdain. "May I ask what was said about Sorcha?"

"Some say she was a changeling, thrown into the mortal world when just a babe. Brought up by human parents and not knowing the power, the truth of her life."

It was all so odd listening to them speak of the Fae, of other worlds and realms. Of immortality, but then, she had time traveled, had seen for herself the Fae Queen, and could not disprove the women's tales. To do so would be equal to imagining herself as crazy as they were, and she was not crazy. All of this was real, was happening, and valid. There was little doubt about that.

"Sorcha grew up on a large estate near Loch Carron, was brought here with her parents as a possible match for the Macleod's son. They fell in love during that summer and were handfasted before the first snowfall the following year. The one and only time the laird has been happy."

"Until now." Maya heard Jeane's whispered words and ignored them.

"And then she was taken," Maya pressed, needing to know as much as she could. To make sense of the past at Castle Druiminn.

"Aye, a year after they were married, just over there

near the bridge that crosses the river, it happened. The Fae found their missing child, now a woman, and demanded her return. Of course, they coudna just take Sorcha. They had to make Macleod pay for daring to love a Fae."

Maya looked out across the bailey and spotted Boyd standing with Douglas, a tightness about Boyd's mouth telling Maya that their conversation was not pleasant. More bad news, she supposed.

"Do you think Sorcha will ever return?"

Another young woman nodded enthusiastically. "Oh aye, she will. She loved our laird, and as soon as she can, she will return. Their love was as grand as any mountain range, as deep and endearing as the ocean floor. Sorcha will be back, she's a Scot at heart, and her heart was left here at Druiminn."

Maya swallowed the panic that seized her at the thought of Sorcha returning. What would Boyd do if she did? What would happen to her? He'd probably have the tapestry finished earlier than planned and shove her hand against the silk image quicker than she could say his name.

Jeane threw her a consoling look. "Whereas I doona believe Sorcha will be back. A hundred years have passed. Nay, the Fae lass has moved on, has another life, just as our laird needs to do. Find someone else."

Everyone at the table turned to look at Maya, and she fought not to fidget. Wishing she were that someone Boyd needed while also praying she was not. How could she choose between two times, two lives? Sorcha had no choice. A little voice inside Maya wished that she didn't either, for she wasn't sure how she would choose when it came time to make that decision.

CHAPTER 23

Chapter Twenty Three

Before long, Maya had been at Castle Druiminn a month, which left her only three months until Samhain and when Boyd was expecting the delivery of the tapestry.

She had thrown herself into castle life, helping Mrs. Fletcher with running the house as best she could. She had not been brought up to run such a grand home, an old and historic castle such as Druiminn.

Still, she helped with chores in the garden, walked daily with Jeane, sometimes to the seashore at low tide, or even to the heated pool, since Boyd seemed affable enough to let them go down there with only three armed guards now instead of himself and an army of men.

Today Jeane needed Maya to help her look in on a small cottage that was being built not far from the castle and was to be a home for the apothecary the estate had procured.

"You are not to leave the path or Jeane's side. Look in on the building work, but dinna venture farther. 'Tis not safe," Boyd said to her, clasping her face in his hands, a warning light in his eyes. "Your usual guards will accompany you."

Maya wrapped her arms lazily about his neck, grinning up at the overprotective laird. He was truly adorable when he got the little worry frown between his brows that she'd come to treasure.

"I'll be fine, Boyd. The cottage is visible from the top of the castle battlements, and the three guards you have following us about will surely protect us. We're just going to discuss the layout of the house inside. I think Jeane has suggested a cellar must be built into the structure."

"Aye, I know all about my cousin's plans. Mayhap it's time that she returned to her home."

"No," Maya declared. "You wouldn't take her away from Douglas so soon, would you? You know he asked her to marry him, don't you?"

"Nay, I dinna know that. When?"

"A few weeks ago," she said, stepping out of his hold and picking up the woolen shawl over the chair before the fire. Over the last few weeks, they had not parted from each other's side, not at night at least, and it was perfectly lovely that they did not.

Maya had started to dread October. As the crops grew higher in the fields, so too did her time become shorter with Boyd. All the while, Boyd grew more and more distracted through the day over the impending threat that the O'Cain clan had issued. That the Fae Queen had been absent this past month, too, did not help. Maya had not seen her since she appeared floating in the rafters, and a sense of expectation hung over the castle. As if at any moment everything could change, and not for the better.

"I shall give them my blessing to marry," Boyd said, pulling her from her thoughts.

"They will love that. And you should. I know Jeane would prefer to have your approval." She grinned at him from over by the bedroom door. "You know that the more time they spend together, the less time she needs to keep me company, and I can be all yours."

"Hmm, well then." His brogue turned deep and cajoling as he stalked across the room. "Mayhap I'll seek her out now and tell her I approve so she may run off to Douglas and allow you to stay with me."

Maya laughed, leaning up to kiss Boyd before pushing him away jokingly when he went to grab her. "No, today we're doing something important for the clan. And I will tell you this, Boyd Macleod. The little building we're going to discuss being built still stands in my time, so it needs to go up. You'll not distract me from my purpose."

"Fine, lass. Do as you will, but know when you're free, I'll be in the solar." He winked, and she laughed as she closed the door, starting down the hall and knowing all the while she had a goofy, lopsided smile on her lips.

Maya met Jeane out in the keep where she took a basket from Mrs. Fletcher. "Food for the workmen, lass," the housekeeper said, pride in her voice. "We doona need them hungry when they're working."

"Good morning, Mrs. Fletcher. A lovely day," Maya said, smiling at them both, the smell of fresh-baked bread wafting up from the basket.

"Och, aye it is, Maya lass, but alas will not be for long. Soon we'll have our first frost, and then the winter snows will be upon us," Mrs. Fletcher said, looking up to the sky as if the weather was already turning.

"I hope you like the cold," Jeane said, smiling. "Scottish winter is sure to be different to an English one."

"I think I shall be okay." Maya met Mrs. Fletcher's eyes and knew the older woman was thinking of her return to her own time while Scotland would brace for winter.

They thanked the housekeeper again before starting out of the castle. It only took several minutes to make the small cottage. Several men were digging a hole within a wooden boundary that outlined the cottage walls. Others were unloading a cart of rectangular stone, similar in color to the castle that she could just see through the tops of the trees.

The day was warmer than the last this past week, and Maya went and sat under a tall pine watching as Jeane discussed the cottage with a man who looked to be in charge of everyone else working there.

She started when two men in light-colored trews and matching tunics sat beside her, pinning her between them. "Hello, Maya. How lovely to meet you at last. I've heard so much about you."

Maya looked between the men, a sense of power emanating from them in waves. She went to stand, and they both clasped the tops of her arms, holding her still. "Do not move or make a scene, human. With a flick of my fingers, all who stand before you could be dead. Would you like that on your conscience?"

The man's eyes flickered a chilling silver, and she stilled, knowing these were no men at her sides but the Fae. She swallowed her panic, bracing herself for their reasons for being there. "What do you want?"

The other *tsked tsked* her question, tipping his head to

the side as if he'd never seen a woman before, or at least a human one. "It is not what we want, but our queen. Your presence is required at court."

"What court?" Maya took a calming breath, unable to breathe or think clearly.

"The Seelie Court that she rules over." The other Fae slid his hand down her arm, taking her hand, squeezing it, warning her not to make a scene. It only heightened her fears, and she felt her eyes prickle with tears at being at their mercy. She neither liked nor trusted the Fae, and it would not start now, even if the men seated beside her were more beautiful than anyone she'd ever observed in her life, Boyd included.

"I have done nothing to your queen, and her interest in me is unnecessary. Let go of my hands," she said, trying to pull free of their grasp.

"I'm afraid your wishes are not heeded. Let us go, and we shall see what our queen commands."

Maya screamed out for Jeane, and the last thing she saw was her friend's ashen face as the Scottish landscape she'd been admiring only a moment before melted away and a world she could not even imagine formed before her.

The Seelie Court.

Boyd sat at his desk, looking at the maps that showed where his army was stationed and where they would march when they took on O'Cain. Just north of here, Glendale stood, a clearing, a flat gully suitable for conflict. The port nearby would also serve in helping him bring in allied clans to help with the fight.

If they stood any chance of beating the O'Cains, once and for all, the war needed to take place away from

Druiminn. Preferably in a location that would benefit his clansmen more than the O'Cains.

A commotion erupted out in the hall, and multiple footsteps sounded outside, heading toward his solar door. Boyd reached beside him, drawing his sword, and stood, waiting for whoever dared to storm his home.

But when the door slammed open, and a crying Jeane ran into the room, a gray, ashen-faced Douglas by her side, he knew something had happened to Maya.

"What?" he bellowed. "Where is Maya?"

"She's gone, cousin. Two men from the Fae world have taken her. She was sitting under a tree, just watching, and then the next I remember, she screamed out my name and disappeared into thin air." Jeane clicked her finger, signaling just how quick Maya's disappearance had been.

"Where were her guards?" he demanded from Douglas, who dipped his head before he answered. "They were not far. But no one would have been quick enough to stop the Fae. I saw with my own eyes it was instant. One moment she was there, and the next, she was not."

Gone? Boyd clasped his chest, certain the pain ricocheting there would kill him, immortality or not.

The queen would not dare take another from him, and if she had, the Gyre-Carling would pay for it with her life.

CHAPTER 24

Chapter Twenty Four

Maya opened her eyes and blinked. She felt her mouth gape at the sight she beheld. The Fae Queen moved ahead of her, walking casually through the group of people, or Fae people, if Maya understood where the queen had taken her.

This could not be happening. How was such a thing even possible? Maya clasped her hands before her, sweat prickling her palms as the Fae stared with interest, not all of the looks welcoming. One would have thought the Fae were sweet beings, kind to all, but from the disdain, the judgment on their perfect features, that was not the case.

Maya needed to remember that she was an interloper here, an outlander in their court, and Boyd's life as well.

The court seemed to be within a garden amongst a thriving forest. Flowers, vines, and moss littered everywhere she looked, the trees, the gurgling river that ran through the court like background music. It was one of the most beautiful scenes one could imagine, and yet, she knew they did not want her here.

What was the queen doing? Why continue to harass her and Boyd, for that matter, in such a way? Was the queen jealous? Had she coveted Boyd for over a century, only to lose to another of her kind? Or, Maya thought, more realistically, she was just awful. A troublemaker who was never happy unless she was causing strife.

"My people, pay no heed to my human. I shall not keep her here long, but I wanted you to see who it is that has captured the Laird Macleod's heart after all these years. Who our esteemed Sorcha has been replaced by."

Maya caught the eye of one Fae, her long, curly blonde hair framing a face that was so angelic and perfect it made her sigh. Flowers and diamonds threaded about her long locks, giving her a regal appearance. She was tall and slender and utterly flawless. But where others looked at her with aversion and annoyance, this woman looked upon her with pity, her eyes warm where others were cold. She stepped forward, two large, scantily clad men guarding her sides.

"What is the meaning of this, Titania? The court warned you not to interfere in Macleod's life and the journey he is on. How dare you break that oath and bring a human here."

The queen chuckled, her eyes blazing silver. "I brought you here, did I not? Another human."

"She is Fae and free of her human chain. Do not disrespect her," one of the men said to the queen, his voice low and hard.

Realizations struck Maya, and she knew who the Fae

woman willing to stand up against the queen was. Who she had to be without a flicker of doubt in Maya's mind.

Sorcha.

Boyd's first wife. His only love. The woman he remained immortal for if only to find her again one day. Or because he had not found another to join the place in his heart where he loved.

Maya swallowed her disappointment, knowing she could never live up to such standards. She wasn't special, certainly not magical, and as for looking like Sorcha, Maya couldn't help but wonder what it was that Boyd found so interesting in her.

Sorcha glanced at her, a small smile playing about her lips. "Do not doubt your allure, Maya lass. There is much to love."

Could Sorcha read minds? The question materialized in her mind, *Can you read my mind?* Sorcha gave the smallest nod before turning back to the queen.

Oh dear Lord, that could be embarrassing.

"You must return Maya to her world. Already too much time has passed, and you threaten Macleod's future. You created the curse, but you are not to interfere in how or when it is broken."

"I am the queen here, Sorcha. Be obedient and quiet before I have reason to punish you along with your husband."

A mumbling went through the room, the Fae uncomfortable and alarmed at the two women crossing swords. The queen's threat against one of their own.

Maya watched the queen and did not miss her quick reading of the Fae within hearing, noting their displeasure at her words and thinking better of being more divisive.

The queen smiled. "Very well, I shall let her return to

Macleod, but I thought you should meet the woman who looks to succeed you in Boyd's heart. Is she not a disappointment? Do you not think, Sorcha that your replacement would have been something grander than this?" The queen gestured toward Maya, and self-consciously Maya's gaze dipped to her woolen gown and plain leather boots. Somewhere in her journey from the real world to this faery realm, she had lost her plaid shawl. Maya wrapped her arms around herself, conscious of how cold she felt and how dowdy she looked compared to everyone else here.

The Fae were the most judgemental and awful beings Maya had ever met in her life, and she decided if she never saw one again after returning home to her time, it would be too soon.

She blinked and stumbled back when Sorcha appeared before her, her face one of curiosity, her silver eyes so like the queen's, and yet somehow Sorcha's were warm where the queen's were cold.

She spoke several words that Maya couldn't understand before tipping up her chin, peering at her. "I think you are most perfect, Maya lass."

That Sorcha used the same endearment that Boyd did, sent warmth cascading through her. Did the woman already know of her? The queen brought her here to annoy her kind, but something told Maya that Sorcha had known of her for longer than anyone knew.

"You will do well for Macleod, and know that I am happy that he has found you."

For a moment, Maya could do little else but stare at the woman, beyond beautiful, and it stripped her of her voice. Boyd had loved this woman. Had loved her with his body, married her even. Her skin was so perfect, luminescent, her eyes large, her lips a soft, perfect pink.

However was she to compete with such beauty?

"Do you miss him?" she couldn't help but ask. A small part of her was fearful that Sorcha did and that one day, she would return him. Rebel against the Fae's rules and return to her one true love.

A man that Maya was herself starting to adore, cherish more than she ever thought possible. What she felt for Boyd was new, strange, and yet, right. So right that she ached to get back to him.

Sorcha smiled, a wistful look on her face. "I shall always miss Macleod, but we were not to be. I learned long ago our union could only be fleeting. A gift in time that I was bestowed and allowed to revel in for a moment. It has taken Boyd longer to understand this fact, but he is changing. A slow process with one so proud and honor-bound as Macleod is, but give him time, Maya lass. Be patient, and you will have your reward."

The queen appeared beside them, her face hard. "Do not overstep your bounds, Sorcha. You do not hold court here."

"And you would be wise to know that your hold on the Fae court is waning," Sorcha whispered, only loud enough for Maya and the queen to hear. "I came without trouble to your court. Followed your decree, but overstep your bounds with Macleod, and I shall ensure you lose your position as queen. I shall have you cast out and never to be allowed to return."

Maya blinked, sensing Sorcha had more power here than perhaps even the queen understood. There was certainly more going on between the two Fae women than everyone knew. Their dislike was palpable, left a sour taste on everyone's tongues when present to their sparring.

"Are you threatening me?" the queen asked.

Maya looked between the two women, not quite believing she was listening to them argue. There was a lot of bad blood between them. Everyone present could see that, but she couldn't say who would be the ultimate victor in this fight.

She looked about the room, the court as interested in the conversation between the two faeries as Maya. Would these magical beings turn against their queen or remain faithful to her rule?

Maya couldn't help but hope they would turn, that everyone would side with Sorcha and allow kindness to be part of their life once again. Living under the rule of the queen would not be pleasant, and Maya certainly wanted to leave. Never to see her again.

"Send her back, Titania. Maya does not belong here, and you lose authority when you make us all abide by our rules, but flaunt them in turn to tease and create strife for a human not worth your attention."

The queen seemed to think on the words before she stepped away, smiling again as if nothing was amiss. "Very well. Back with you, Maya." She flicked her hand, and Maya landed with a thump on wooden floorboards, one knee landing on an exposed nail and scraping her skin. She cursed, sitting on her bottom and rubbing her leg. "Damn bitch," she muttered.

"Maya?"

She glanced up, sighing in relief when Boyd loomed over her, larger than life, his face one of wonderment. Maya looked about, realizing she had been dumped in the room she shared with Boyd at Druiminn Castle.

"Boyd," she whispered, standing. "Oh, thank heavens I'm back."

He wrenched her into his arms, holding her so tight

she could hardly breathe. He mumbled sweet words against her neck, kissing and clasping her as if checking that she was really there. Maya allowed him his strange homecoming. She would enjoy any such lavish attention if it were coming from Boyd. "Och, lass. I thought I wouldna see you again."

She chuckled, rubbing a soothing hand over his back. "Don't be silly. I was only gone a couple of hours."

Boyd held her away, frowning at her. She took in his lovely face, features that had become precious to her, even more so after the queen took her, and she didn't think she'd see him again.

"Maya lass, how long do you think you were gone?"

For the first time, she noticed the stubble on his jaw was longer than normal, a spattering of gray through his dark beard. He'd had hardly any facial hair at all when she'd seen him this morning. His hair, too, was longer, more disheveled, but also a little less white. Was that possible? His hair had always been so luminescent that at times she thought it was liquid silver.

"A few hours. I saw you this morning," she said, the pit of her stomach churning at the disbelief in his eyes.

"Nay, lass." He shook his head, his eyes pained. "You've not been gone merely hours. You've been gone three months."

She gasped.

What the actual fuck.

CHAPTER 25

Chapter Twenty Five

Boyd wrenched Maya against him for a second time. He breathed in deep her sweet scent. Welcoming the feel of her darling self against him after so long denied her presence. It soothed his tortured soul and angered him in turn. The queen would pay for her role in stealing his Maya away.

The first few days of her disappearance, he had thought the Fae Queen was merely taunting him. Making him pay for his growing feelings toward Maya and thwarting her curse, but as the weeks turned into a month, then two and three, all hope fled. Left him with the devastating realization that the queen had, in fact, stolen another he cared for and would not be returning her to him anytime soon.

He had lost her, and he was powerless to change his fate.

Boyd closed his eyes, holding her close and determined never to let her go again. By gods, he'd gone to a dark place with her absence. All he'd thought about these past weeks had been Maya, how he'd never see her gentle face or hear her tinkling laugh. That he would have to live another five hundred years before he could trace her down in her time and be with her again.

Something he was willing to do and had accepted after a month of her absence.

"Three months. No, you tease me. I've only been gone a few hours," she muffled against his shoulder, unable to pull back due to his hold.

If only it had been hours, not months. Too much of their time, stolen from them both. Samhain was upon them. But that was not the worst of what had happened when she had been missing.

"Maya lass," he said, pulling back only the slightest bit so he could look into the dark depths of her blue eyes and revel in their beauty. A beauty he'd thought lost. "You were gone three months. I swear to you, on the life of my people. We haven't seen you for twelve weeks."

She stared up at him, and he could see she was counting time, working out what that meant for them.

"When is Samhain?" she asked, the fear in her eyes crushing his soul.

"A sennight."

Her mouth opened and closed several times. "But we had months left. How could I have been gone only hours for me, but months for you? It makes no sense."

"Nay, lass, it makes perfect sense. Where did the Fae Queen take you?"

"The Seelie Court. She was confronted for bringing me

there. Not all of the Fae seemed pleased with her actions or her interfering in your life."

The thought that the mongrel queen was questioned soothed a little of Boyd's roaring temper. Had he managed to get his hands around that faery's throat, he would have squeezed until she was no longer trouble for anyone.

"Time works differently for the Fae. Quicker than us mortals. A moment in time there can be hundreds of years for us. I will not let her take you again," he promised, laying his forehead against hers, her presence soothing his soul.

"Boyd, we're running out of time. The tapestry will be here soon."

He closed his eyes, pushing away the thought of such a thing. He didn't want to know what the tapestry being in the castle meant for them both.

"Nay, lass. Doona think of it." He picked her up, wrapping her legs about his waist. He strode a couple of steps and hoisted Maya up against the wall. His need for her, his obsession to know that she was flesh and blood, back in his arms for certain, not just some figment of his imagination, too much to ignore. Her nimble fingers tore at his trews, pushing them down just enough to release him. His cock sprang into her hand, and she gripped him, stroking him. His breath hitched, and he moaned when her fingers tightened around his flesh.

He ripped her gown out of the way and took her, fast and hard, pinning her with his weight as he fucked her against the wall. So tight, so wet. His mind spun, celebrated that she was back with him, home, safe and sound.

Her fingers dug into his shoulders as he drove into her. She rocked against him, taking as well as giving pleasure. It was too much and yet, not enough. Would never be enough.

How would he ever let her go?

Boyd increased his pace, taking her with a primal need that he'd never felt before. She whimpered in his arms, her head laying back against the wall, her gasps pushing him to give her more. To take as much as he could give her for as long as they lasted.

If only this would last forever.

Maya held on to Boyd as much as she could as he fucked her. *Hard.* This was not sweet seduction, a home welcoming at all, but a taking—a resounding statement of what was his.

Her.

She gasped as he took her, his large cock filling her to completeness, too much and yet, never enough. The wall, cold and hard against her back, grazed her flesh as he laid claim to her body. But she didn't care. All she wanted was Boyd. With each stroke, each maddening thrust, a promise, a declaration was made.

She was his and no one else's.

Maya was perfectly happy about such an avowal. Boyd had come to mean so much to her. When she'd been in the Seelie Court, her only thought was getting back to him. Not to her own time, her friends, her work, but Boyd. Her sixteenth-century highlander.

She moaned, could feel her orgasm building, thrumming just on the edge of release. And then she tumbled. She gasped, whimpered his name, kissing him deep and long as he too followed her to release.

His cock seemed to swell, filling her, giving her what

she wanted. Her body drained him of his seed, taking and giving as they both rocked to a slower tempo as their orgasms ebbed away.

She wrapped her arms around his neck, placing her face a scant distance from his. "It has never been like this for me. Not with anyone."

He kissed her, long and slow, their tongues tangling, his lips teasing and beckoning her to fall. But Maya knew the truth. She had already fallen. Weeks ago, perhaps. Possibly even from the very first moment she laid eyes on the Laird Macleod.

How could one not love such a man? A man of honor, strength, and loyalty. He trusted her, welcomed her into his home when she had nowhere else to go. A kind man, no matter what anyone said. What was there not to love?

He didn't say anything. Merely walked them to the bed and lay her down. He joined her, stripping them both of their clothes, before making slow, heartbreaking love to her for the remainder of the night.

If a pang of fear had spiked through her at his absence of words, his inability to say what he felt, his actions told Maya differently.

For if love had a physical movement, his cherishing of her told her all she needed to know.

That Boyd loved her as well. As much as she did him.

Dougall O'Cain strode through his army of men, men who had for the last several weeks trained, learned, and fought each other to make their skills precise and deadly.

He had sent out several clansmen to bring in all the young O'Cain men on his land to learn to fight, to join him in making the clan stronger, more prosperous. To defeat Macleod and his ancient clan once and for all.

"The men are ready, Dougall. I doona think that Macleod will stand a chance against us." Dougall nodded, watching the men spar out on the flatlands at the base of their stronghold.

Tents littered the grounds. Fire pits burned, the smell of meat cooking rent the air. His army was strong and healthy. All things that Macleod would not expect.

That his enemy had been distracted the last few months had enabled him to prepare, to plan, to spy.

Macleod no longer held a chance against him and his army. Excitement thrummed in his veins at the thought of his victory. Of taking Druiminn Castle for himself, and all the wealth that came with it.

He would savor the downfall of Boyd Macleod, make the man watch as he took the woman reported to be his love, his savior after all these years.

He would see for himself if Macleod was immortal. When a knife cut you through or removed one's head, he doubted immortality would save anyone then.

"When will we march for Macleod land?"

Dougall rubbed his jaw in thought. "We will aim for after Samhain. Let his men be groggy from their night of revelry and tired from their track to Glendale. Let them face us in battle with a hazy mind and slow hands and bellies full of feasting. It'll be like slaughtering sheep."

He chuckled to himself at the thought of their victory. That within a sennight there would be no more clan Macleod. That all of Scotland and England too would know the O'Cains ruled Skye and that there was no room for anyone else.

Not ever again.

CHAPTER 26

Chapter Twenty Six

Boyd was up to something, and Maya wasn't sure what. Over the days since her return, he had a nervous edge about him. She caught him often looking at her as if something troubled him. He hovered like a man terrified he would lose what he was guarding. She knew that her absence had scared him, possibly even made him realize what she meant to him, and even though he had not said the words, she knew he loved her as much as she loved him.

If only he would declare himself.

With only a few days until Samhain, the clan was busy preparing for the feast to celebrate the end of the harvest season. Already meats were being prepared to cook over the many bonfires. Women were busy preparing cakes to be left for the dead, following the pagan beliefs of the time. Maya had said nothing about this, and nor would she.

After being thrown back to the sixteenth century and having the Fae Queen steal her away for months on end, if the dead rose on Samhain, Maya doubted she'd bat an eyelid.

She walked from her room, shutting her door and finding two maids chatting secretly near a door that led up to the top of the turret. When they saw her, one of the young girls hurried away while the other pretended to wipe a sconce on the wall clean of dust.

The servants had been acting odd as well when she came to think of it. Always someone near that one particular sconce. It would have to be the cleanest item in the castle, without a doubt.

Maya walked toward the stairs, bringing her closer to the maid, and noticed the woman wouldn't make eye contact with her. That she appeared nervous, too, if her wide eyes and jittery stance was any indication.

Maya stopped beside her. "Good morning," she said, hoping the young woman would speak. She did, but it was more like a squeak.

"My lady," she said, dipping into a curtsy before rubbing the sconce yet again with renewed vigor.

Maya reached out, halting her hand. "You've been here a lot lately. Is there a reason you've been loitering about in the hall these past days?"

"Nay, my lady. Not at all." The maid did look at her then, her eyes wide with fear. What on earth was going on? Why would she be scared to answer such an easy question?

"I think the sconce is clean. In fact, I think this whole passageway is the cleanest in Scotland. You do not need to stay here, lass. You can go back downstairs if you like."

The woman shook her head, her mouth pinched. "I

canna, my lady. I'm to stay here and work. Those are my orders."

"Who gave you those orders?" Maya asked, curious. Was it Boyd or the housekeeper, she wondered.

"The laird, my lady." The woman bit her lip, her eyes flicking over Maya's shoulder.

Hmm. Maya turned about and spied the door that led up to the top of the turret. She hadn't been up there—never one for heights—to look out over the lands from the top of a tower had never interested her. Even the thought of it now made her palms sweat.

But why always linger in this part of the hall? "Have you been told to guard the door behind me?" she asked, not missing the young woman's eyes widening at her question.

So she had been charged with such a mission. What was Boyd up to? What was he hiding?

"Nay, my lady. I'm merely cleaning, as is my employment."

"You may go downstairs. The hall is clean enough," Maya commanded, knowing the maid would accept her stern tone. The woman hastened off, all but running down the stairs as if the devil himself were after her.

Maya turned toward the door, wondering if Boyd had it locked as well. Surprisingly, when she pushed on the metal handle, it opened, swinging wide. Stairs leading upward met her gaze, and Maya entered, shutting the door behind her to stop anyone from finding her and halting her progress. She needed to find out what the hell was going on.

The staircase circled twice before opening out into a circular room with coarse wooden floorboards. There were no windows, only narrow slits used during battle for archers. Not so scary and certainly not up on the roof where she would feel woozy.

Maya stepped off the last step onto the floor and turned, taking in the entire space and stilled.

Boyd had been keeping something from her.

"Holy shit," she breathed, taking a small step toward the large silk tapestry, complete and shining bright its many colors that hung before her—staring back at her like a taunting bully ready to pounce.

Her favorite picture was just the same, except where the tapestry in the twenty-first century had dulled with time, now it was bright, new, and utterly beautiful, just as the people it represented were within its weaves.

Maya walked up to it, careful not to get too close lest she forget and reach out and touch the tapestry and send herself catapulting back to the future.

She wasn't ready for that choice just yet. She needed more time here with Boyd. If more time with him would ever be enough. Maya already knew it would not be.

Hastened footsteps sounded on the staircase. Maya didn't need to turn to know Boyd was striding up to her. She closed her eyes, reveling in his presence, knowing that no matter what story the tapestry told, Boyd's had changed since that day.

He was with her now. Loved her, she was sure.

"Maya lass. I can explain."

She shook her head, turning to face him. "Were you afraid that I would run up to the tapestry and touch it as soon as I saw it?"

He cringed at her question, and she could almost laugh that perhaps this was a true fear of his.

"Aye, I thought you would want to say your goodbyes

to everyone and wish us well sooner than I was ready to part with you."

Her heart ached at his words. Maya reached out, clasping his tunic and pulling him close. "I would never do that. You should know by now that I'm not ready to go yet either."

"Lass..." His eyes held hers, so green and pure like the land. "With everything that has happened to you here, I dinna think you'd want to stay."

"I do not want to go." That she knew without a flicker of doubt. How could she return to her time, go on with her days at this very castle, and not pine for the man she loved who'd lived in it hundreds of years before?

He pulled her away from the tapestry, leading her back to the stairs. They made their way to the solar, Boyd making certain the door was closed and bolted.

"You need to know that the queen will be back. She does not listen to anyone, and with the O'Cain clan breathing down our necks, wanting a war, you are in danger here. I will protect you until the day I die, but I doona want to put you in a position where I have to make that choice."

"The queen has been warned away, Boyd. The woman..." Maya shut her mouth, scared to tell him who the woman was who stood up to the queen. What would Boyd do if he knew she had met Sorcha? Would he ask after his wife? Seek answers that Maya did not have to give him? She didn't want to see him pine for a woman who had been gone for a century.

"Whoever the woman was, she isna as powerful as the queen. All Fae bend to Titania's will."

Maya wasn't so sure. Sorcha certainly seemed willing to

test that theory. She shook her head, dismissing Boyd's words. "Not this faery."

He walked around the back of the desk, crossing his arms and facing her. "Nay, lass. They're all the same. They say and do what they're told, always have, and always will. The queen would say anything to keep her people oblivious to her actions. She dislikes me, is not satisfied the hundred years that I have lived without Sorcha is long enough. Now that you are here, and the queen knows how much you mean to me, she'll stop at nothing to make your life hell. To the point that you'll storm upstairs and touch the tapestry without cajoling."

Maya remembered the words from Sorcha. That she was worthy and good for Boyd. No, no one would make her do anything if she did not want to, not even the Fae Queen in charge of another realm.

Boyd would not believe her unless she told him the truth of her time away from him. He would trust Sorcha's word, even if he were angry over the fact she never returned. "The queen will stay away, and the reason I know this is because Sorcha told me. Ordered the queen to back off in a manner of words. My only threat here is the tapestry and the O'Cains, and you will take care of them." Maya sat on the chair across from Boyd. He'd gone pale as if he'd seen a ghost, and his eyes had taken on a haunted hue. "When I am ready, and not a day before, I shall choose my fate. I will touch the tapestry and return home, and nothing else will force me before then."

CHAPTER 27

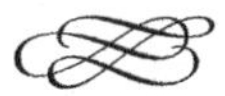

Chapter Twenty Seven

Boyd fought not to react to Maya's statement. How it made his head swim, his stomach tie into knots.

Maya had met Sorcha?

He should have known that with the Fae Queen harassing them as she was, that it was only inevitable that another would step forward and chastise their leader. That it would be Sorcha, he did not expect. He'd not expected Sorcha to be so involved in the Seelie Court. Of course, he'd been wrong before when it came to his wife, what he thought she would do when able, so he really ought not to be so startled.

"You met Sorcha?" After a hundred years of not seeing the only woman he'd ever loved, he had imagined her a figment of the past that he one day hoped would be part of his future.

He wasn't so certain of that anymore.

If Sorcha were to return, what would their marriage be like now? Before the queen had taken her to the Seelie Court, their union had been a happy one. Of laughter and love. She was a fierce warrior, could hold her own in a battle if the need arose, but she was also kind and loving. A gentlewoman. A proper wife.

But a hundred years in the Seelie Court would have to change anyone who ventured there. Boyd could not help but wonder if she, too, had accepted the way of the Fae, embraced her magic and her heritage. As much as he fought not to, he knew that since Maya had walked into his life, he was not the same man he was upon seeing her for the first time.

Over the time she had been here, he had begun to laugh again, to want to go forward, not look back, throw off his curse, and live again, as a man ought. To have a wife, to have children.

The thought of Maya, round and heavy with his child, filled him with a need that overrode all his anger, the resentment he held over what the Fae had done. Over the fact that Sorcha never returned, not even to say goodbye.

He was changing. His hair was evidence of that, slowly with each day it grew darker, more like the reddish brown it once was. No longer as white as the Fae curse had made it.

He couldn't help but hope it was a sign that the curse, too, was waning.

Maya nodded, clasping her hands in her lap. "I did. She was the reason why I was sent back. Had she not reprimanded the queen, I do believe she would have kept me for longer in that realm."

He didn't want to ask about his wife, but he also

required closure. To move forward with Maya, he needed to know that Sorcha was content, happy with the choice forced upon her. "Is Sorcha happy?"

The light in Maya's eyes dimmed, and he cursed himself asking the question. He didn't want to hurt Maya. He needed to tell her that he may want to know about Sorcha but that it meant nothing. Not anymore.

Not since Maya had come to be in his life.

"I do believe so," she replied, her voice strained. "I know that's probably not something you want to hear..."

Boyd went to dissuade her of that fact, but she held up her hand, halting his words. "I understand that what we've been doing these last few weeks, before and after my little sojourn to the Seelie Court, was never going to go anywhere. I am destined to return to my time, and you're destined to remain here. I do hope with all my heart that you find someone to break the curse and that you'll be happy. And maybe in a little way, my being here with you has shown you that it's okay to move forward in your life. That you're not breaking any oaths to Sorcha by doing so."

"Maya," he said but stopped when she stood and all but bolted from the room. He stared at the door for several moments before fear curdled his guts. Had Maya gone upstairs? Was she now going to the tapestry to send herself home?

Boyd wrenched himself out of the chair and all but ran to the staircase. His fear over her leaving dissipating somewhat when he caught sight of her gown slipping into the room they shared.

He joined her there, closing the door and snipping the lock. "Maya lass," he said, closing the space between them, not missing that his lady had tears in her pretty blue eyes. "Och, lass, there will be none of that." He kissed her cheek, her nose, her eyes when she closed them, her tears slipped down her face. Boyd wiped them away with his thumbs, kissing her lips. "Maya, do you not understand yet?"

She looked up at him, wiping her nose with the back of her hand. His heart ached, and he knew, to the very core of his soul, that she was the woman who was breaking his curse. She was the one who made him rise each morning, seek to keep his people and his home safe. She was the reason he no longer pined for a wife a hundred years gone.

"Understand what?" she asked, sniffing.

"I doona ask you about Sorcha to upset you, lass. I need to know that Sorcha is well because to move forward, knowing this truth makes my heart free. My heart free to love another."

Maya's eyes widened, and she looked up at him so quickly that her crown almost knocked into his nose.

"What are you saying?"

He grinned, kissing her slowly, showing her precisely what he meant. "I'm saying, lass, that I love you. That to imagine my life without you is a misery worse than death. I will not ask you to stay but know that I want you by my side forever. I doona ever want to lose you."

Maya didn't know what to say. *Boyd loved her.* She felt nervous and excited at the same time. Along with that also came fear. What would she do? Would she stay, or would she return home? How could she leave him when she knew, beyond any doubt, that she loved him just as much?

"Are you certain? What if Sorcha returns?" she asked,

hating the doubt that plagued her even with his heartfelt declaration. "You won't regret your choice?"

He shook his head, throwing her a *really?* look. "Nay, lass. I will not change my mind, even if Sorcha returned. A hundred years is a long time, and although I haven't been the promptest to realize that what we had, as wonderful as it was, is in the past, I want you," he stated, squeezing her a little. "Only you."

She stared at him, unable to believe that what he was saying was true. Boyd loved her and only her. It was too wonderful for words.

"You doona feel the same?" he stated, his voice hollow when she remained silent.

Oh no, she couldn't have him thinking that. Not when he was so utterly wrong. Maya took a calming breath before she said words that she'd never uttered to anyone else in her life. "I'm in love with you too, Boyd Macleod."

Boyd frowned down at her, wrenching back as if her words pained him. His breathing increased, and he cringed.

Maya watched in awe as the last of his silver-white hair faded and in its place were thick, dark, wavy red locks past his shoulders. So that was what the Boyd Macleod of the fifteenth century once looked like before the curse.

Her heart thumped hard in her chest that the virile, sweet, and gorgeous highlander was hers. It was too much. How lucky was she?

"Boyd, are you okay?"

"Aye, lass. 'Tis fine, I just…" He took two deep breaths, rubbing a hand over his jaw. "A pain 'tis all. No, a weight. I feel as if a weight has lifted."

Maya bit her lip, hope blooming inside her. "The curse.

It has to be that." She reached for him, taking his hands. "I think it may have lifted."

That was what it had to have been. There was no other reason for him to morph back into the laird he'd been one hundred years before. He was mortal, and his love was true.

He loved her without a shadow of a doubt.

His eyes met hers, and she could see he was thinking the same. That what she said was accurate and that him being immortal was no longer part of his life.

"I'm free of it, lass," he said, smiling. Her breath hitched at the look on his face, so much happiness, so much anticipation. "You believe me now that I love you so?"

She chuckled, shaking her head at his teasing. "I think I do, yes."

He bent down and scooped her up into his arms, walking slowly toward the bed. "While I doona know what the future holds for us, I do know that right now, lass, I need you. I need to love the woman I adore."

A lump wedged in her throat, and she clasped his face in her hands and brought his lips down for a kiss.

The embrace, filled with love, and everything that sat between them, joined them like a string that crossed centuries.

A promise of forever.

If only Maya could choose him over everything she'd ever known.

CHAPTER 28

Chapter Twenty Eight

Emotions bubbled up inside Maya as Boyd carried her to the bed, laying her down softly on the furs and blankets. Her stomach twisted in delicious knots. Her mind whirring with the thought that he loved her and no one else. That he wanted her in his life, his future, when for so long he'd been stagnant in the past.

Never before had she ever felt about a man the way she felt about Boyd. She loved him so very much. The idea he was hers was all-encompassing and a little surreal.

Maya wiggled and slipped off her dress, throwing it aside, and watched with satisfaction as Boyd worked quickly with the strings at the front of his pants before ridding himself of his trews.

Her core clenched at the vision he made. Maya bit her lip as he pushed the pants down his long, muscular thighs.

Still, his manhood remained hidden. Blocked from view due to his tunic hanging low on his hips.

She smiled and knew it appeared mischievous. "You know, in my time, what you're doing is called stripping."

He wrenched his tunic over his head, his stomach muscles a beautiful, rippled highway to his jutting cock. So hard and the most perfect penis she'd ever seen.

He reached for his shaft, stroking himself harder still, and heat pooled at her core. "Men strip for women in your time?" He shook his head, clearly confused. "I doona understand."

Maya kneeled, walking on her knees over to the side of the bed and reaching for him. She ran her hand along his stomach, paying homage to the perfect V that directed her gaze to his cock. "Women do as well, but yes, men strip for the enjoyment of women. But we're not allowed to touch."

He frowned, the muscle in his jaw working. "You have been to see men strip?"

She chuckled at his annoyed tone, loving that this highlander could be jealous over her actions, of things she'd done before she even knew him. "I have. I went with friends when I was in college in England. The men were as toned as you, maybe not as tall or muscular, but certainly very nice to admire." Maya leaned forward, kissing his chest, laving her tongue over his puckered nipple.

He growled. "You will never look at another man in that way, Maya."

She smiled against his skin, hearing the warning, the demand in his tone. Her twenty-first sensibilities, her feminism growled in return to his highhandedness, but she let it go. The man she loved was unlike anyone from her time. Things were different here, and although she would never allow anyone to walk all over her, she knew that she would choose Boyd over anyone else.

He was hers. Her soul mate. Her love. She would allow him this one demand.

"I don't want to look at anyone else," she whispered, running her hands over his shoulders and marveling at their size. He was so toned, broad, and devastatingly tall. Just being beside him made her feel delicate and ladylike.

Two things Maya never thought of herself most of the time.

"Now," she said, twining her hands into his hair. "Make love to me before I die from waiting."

A wicked light entered his eyes before he pushed her back onto the bed, rending a little squeal of shock from her. He came over her, covering her body with his.

Maya wrapped herself around him, slipped her legs up about his hips. She couldn't get enough of this man. Knew that she never would. He entered her quickly, a deep, hard thrust that made them both moan.

"Put your hands above your head," Boyd demanded, pinning them with his when she did. He watched her, his gaze overflowing with adoration, with so much heat that her heart ached.

They stayed like that, a slow progression toward climax. He teased, filled, and inflamed her. Maya closed her eyes, unable to keep seeing the emotions play over his face. Of how much she would miss him if she chose to leave this time.

"Look at me, lass," he beseeched.

After a moment, Maya did as he asked. Her body felt aflame, taut, and aching for release. He fit her so well, pushed her along at a steady pace. She was so close, already sat on a precipice, ready to fall.

"You are everything to me," he whispered, leaning down to kiss her. Boyd released her hands, and she wrapped them about him as the kiss melded into so much more than anything she'd ever known. It was a promise, a declaration of endearment, honor, and love.

So much love.

"I love you too," she gasped as, with one final deep stroke, he thrust into her, launching her over the edge. Maya soared, high and long. Her orgasm ripped through her, running out to every point in her body. She moaned his name, dug her nails into his back as still he refused to increase his pace, rode out her climax with maddening, slow strokes that had brought her to release in the first place.

Boyd gasped against her mouth, her name a chant as he followed her, spilling himself into her with abandon.

For a moment, neither of them moved, simply content to lay entwined and joined as they both caught their breath.

Boyd rolled to the side, bringing her into the crook of his arm. "You need to make a choice, Maya lass."

She bit her lip, hating that she had to. Stay or leave. Remain part of the sixteenth century or return to the twenty-first. Her hand idly ran over the light coating of hair on his stomach while she thought. What would happen to him should she leave? Would he revert to being immortal again? His heart broken for a second time? Or would he grow old, remain mortal as he was, eliminating her chance of ever seeing him again in the twenty-first century?

Maya looked up at him and found him watching her. She shook her head, knowing that when it came to Boyd, there was no choice. Never had been if she were honest with herself. Not since the day she fell in love with the highlander.

"I don't want to return to my time, Boyd. Whether there are rules to time travel or not, I cannot leave. My heart is here. How could I live without my heart if it remained in the sixteenth century?"

"Och, lass." He pulled her up onto his chest, kissing her hard and long. "This time is not easy. We're to go to war any day now. Are you sure you wish to stay?"

She would be a liar if she stated that such a future did not scare her. The idea of clan wars was something one only read in history books. To be living in a time where this was a constant threat… Not to mention the Fae and their dislike of Boyd, or at least the Seelie queen's dislike also added a fraction of concern.

With all of this, still, her heart and mind remained steadfast. Her future was in the past, here with Boyd. They would love each other, have a family, be as happy as they could until their time was up.

"I do." She had never been more certain of a decision in her life. "But on one condition," she said, folding her arms on his chest and watching him.

"Aye, anything, lass."

Maya smiled. "I will stay, Boyd Macleod, laird and chief of Clan Macleod if you will do me the honor of marrying me." The shock that rippled over his features was comical, and she chuckled. "What say you? Will you marry me?"

He flipped her onto her back before she could blink. "I'm supposed to be the one who asks, lass."

She shrugged. "Well, you are marrying a twenty-first-century woman if you say yes, and we tend to ask for what we want and go after it when it runs away."

He growled, a rumble deep in his chest that did odd things to her insides. "Aye, lass. I'll marry you so long as you promise me one thing as well."

"Anything," she said.

He slipped to the side, his hand sliding down her front, over her chest, before settling on her stomach. "Be the mother of my children. I dinna think I wanted a family, but after a hundred years of living a lonely existence, a life not at all, the idea of you swelling with my babe, well, 'tis a dream I now crave, more than life itself."

Maya swallowed past the lump in her throat, nodding. "I would love to be the mother of your children if we're fortunate enough to have them." She reached up, pushing his hair out of his face, wanting to see his sweet features. "When can we start?" she teased, pulling him close.

He grinned, a devilish light entering his eyes. "Now 'tis as good a time as any."

Boyd took her lips in a searing kiss, thrusting her into a world of passion for the second time in as many minutes. Hours of lovemaking, cherishing, and desire, and perhaps even starting their family this night. Creating a future—the Macleod clan's destiny that still lived on today, in Maya's time.

Maybe...

CHAPTER 29

Chapter Twenty Nine

Maya stood before the mirror in her room, looking at the dress that Jeane had tweaked and altered for her to wear on her wedding day.

That today was when she would be handfasted with Boyd was something Maya was still getting her head around. How was it possible that in only the short number of weeks she'd been at Druiminn Castle, excluding the time the Fae Queen had stolen her away, that she'd come to love a man so much?

The thought of leaving Boyd was an impossibility she could not face. The idea of touching the tapestry made her stomach clench with fear. No, this was the time she should have been born. A time that the man she loved lived, and not five hundred years from now.

Jeane kneeled and pinned the gown up a little while also adding a pretty edging of lace over the blue-dyed wool twill kirtle. As much as Maya had always thought her wedding gown would be champagne satin, a large wide skirt, and a corset-like princess cut top, the dress she wore today was just as pretty. They lived on the Isle of Skye, hundreds of miles away from any dressmaking shops. No, her gown would do very well. It suited her. So long as she was marrying the man she loved, the day would be perfect.

"Och, lass, Boyd will not know what to do with himself when he sees you. You're as pretty as a Forget-Me-Not."

Jeane had amended the gown to make the bodice slip a little lower on her breasts, and with the white lace running around the hem, she couldn't help but agree that perhaps Jeane was correct.

"I cannot thank you enough for fixing the dress for me. I know it's short notice."

Jeane waved her concerns away, a needle in hand, as she sewed along her dress hem. "'Tis a pleasure to welcome you into the family. It is time that Boyd married and loved again." Jeane smiled up at her, her eyes bright with approval and hope. "His wife, no matter where she is, has gone on with her life. It is time that Boyd also did. I'm happy for you both. You shall make a good wife for him."

Maya hoped that was true. She was certainly going to try. "It doesn't concern you that Sorcha is still alive. I suppose our marriage won't be legally binding because of that fact, but..."

Jeane stood, pulling the gown at her waist and checking the length. "What, lass? But what?"

Maya shrugged, her stomach in knots over marrying a man who still had a wife. Surely some law came into effect when one was abandoned for so long. Not to mention Boyd was over a hundred years old. Some in England and Scotland probably didn't even think he was alive but merely an ancestor of the first Boyd Macleod.

"Does that make me a bad person that I will marry Boyd even if he's still married?" she asked her friend. She wasn't a bad person, had never been the sort to be unkind or do things that were against the law. Marrying Boyd when he still had a wife was morally wrong and not binding by law, but after so many years, did that still stand? She doubted it, and even if it did, she knew Sorcha welcomed her being here with Boyd. She had her approval of sorts. That was enough for her.

"Nay, you love Boyd. How can there be anything wrong with such a thing?" Jeane stepped back, smiling at her in the mirror. "There, lass, the dress is done, and with only hours to spare. Your handfasting to happen tonight when the sun is setting and the moon is rising will be one to remember."

Maya nodded, unable to stop smiling at the idea of being a wife. Boyd's wife. "Will you help me bathe? With several guards, I'm sure it'll be fine to travel down to the heated pools if you like."

Jeane cleaned up her sewing, hurrying about the room. "Now, that would be a welcome idea. 'Tis been several days since I bathed, and I know no one at the ceremony tonight wants to be smelling my armpits."

Maya laughed, untying her gown before stepping out of it. "I'll get dressed, and we'll find some guards to take us down there. I want to be smelling like a flower for my new husband," she said, chuckling at herself. Today was her wedding day! Maya pinched herself to be sure she was awake, and this wasn't merely a dream.

It was not.

. . .

The wedding took place overlooking the ocean at Druiminn Castle, a magnificent and ancient building rising behind them in the twilight. Candles and sconces burned, lighting the area, and some of the village children had sprinkled wildflowers over the ground, covering the soil as best they could. Tonight there was a full moon, only the slightest sea breeze, the air smelling sweet and salty.

Maya walked toward Boyd, who stood watching her beside the castle priest. His dark, hooded gaze shone with love and Maya swallowed hard the lump in her throat. She would not cry. Today was a happy day, one to remember forever. Boyd was all that she'd ever wanted and more, and she couldn't help but wonder how it was that he loved her.

A normal English woman who had no power brought nothing to the marriage, certainly not an allied family to back Macleods in clan wars. No dowry, nothing but herself.

Boyd took her hands as she came to stand beside him, winking at her before turning to the priest. The clan surrounded them. Jeane joined them, tying a thin piece of plaid around their hands, knotting it tightly.

The priest went through the words binding them, asking them to repeat the vows when necessary. Maya couldn't understand a lot of it, but she reiterated as best she could, promising herself to Boyd, the Laird Macleod, until death do they part.

She gasped when the ceremony finished, and Boyd wrenched her into his arms, kissing her soundly. She laughed through the embrace, the catcalls, the laughter and shouts from the clan deafening.

Thankfully after Boyd had spoken to them about her living there with them all, they had come to trust her, know that she wasn't there to hurt or cause trouble. Merely to live, to help like they all did every day until she could return to her time.

That no longer was an issue. From this day forward, she would be a highlander like her husband, a Scotswoman, and wife above anything else. Maya wrapped her arms around Boyd's neck, pulling him close to kiss him with all that she had. The clan laughed harder, but Maya didn't care. She would kiss this man until her very last breath.

Just as she was certain, he would as well.

Titania stood at the Macleod clan's back, watching the laird's people congratulate the bride and groom on their handfasting. She glanced down at her gown of plain yellow wool, missing her silks and satins while in disguise here.

The clan pulled the happy couple into the castle, and she followed, a minstrel starting to play a lively tune that soon pulled revelers onto the floor in the Great Hall to dance.

She watched as Boyd took Maya up to the dais, pulling out her chair and ensuring her comfort with a pillow to sit on and a glass of mead before joining her. He was a fool to have fallen for the woman. It was not because she thought love was a foolish emotion, but merely because Boyd felt so for the woman, gave her power over him. A way to make him do what she willed if it meant that harm would come to those he loved.

She shook her head, taking a glass of wine from a servant who was unaware of who she was. Stupid, simple-minded people these ancient clansmen and women were.

To live each day as a means of survival. To not have the freedom to enjoy the pleasures of life, of what the world held, well, they did not know what they were missing.

Nor would they ever, born a faery. She had traveled to the future and well into the past. To live such as these people would make her immortal soul wither and die.

How pitiful these people were.

She drank down the wine, knowing that in only a few days, Samhain would be upon this clan and others across Scotland. The celebrations would continue, the drinking and feasting. If only they knew that the O'Cains would arrive at the end of harvest.

Titania smiled. The Macleod clan was not strong enough to win a war against the O'Cains. There were more of them, and they were bloodthirsty for Macleod blood.

The laird's in particular.

She raised her glass, toasting the newly married couple. "Enjoy your time, my mortal dears, for it will be as fleeting as your life."

CHAPTER 30

The festivities for his marriage to Maya continued over the next few days, with Samhain tomorrow. Numerous bonfires, stacked high with wood, lay about the castle, both within the keep and the estate's land.

His people came in from his lands to Druiminn. His soldiers happy to revisit old friends they hadn't seen in several months. Some of his men slipped away into the forest or cottages when wanting to be alone with their ladies.

Boyd woke early this morning, wanting to train with his men. As hard as it had been to drag himself away from Maya, her warmth and the comfort she gave him, he needed to return to normal life. He was laird, the chieftain to his people. He could not remain secluded in their room forever.

His spies on Macleod land's border had stated that the O'Cains looked to be building an army of men and preparing to march.

They would be here any day, but Boyd was prepared. He'd expected the move from his enemy. Dougall O'Cain was never satisfied with what he had. He was always looking to gain more. To take what was not his.

Well, he may march toward Druiminn, but he would lose even if Boyd died fighting to save those he cared about, his land, his wife, his people.

Douglas strode up to him, a grin on his lips. "Ach, so the laird has joined us at last. We dinna ever think to see you again."

Boyd chuckled, wishing he had stayed wrapped in Maya's arms or kissing his way down her soft stomach to the patch of dark curls at the apex of her thighs. He smirked with the knowledge they had grown back since the first time he had seen them.

A woman's legs, wrapped about one's head, was the sweetest satisfaction one could have. As much as he enjoyed sparring, verbally and physically, with his men, he knew where he'd prefer to have been this early in the morn.

"You know I have to ensure that you all know how to fight. What with the O'Cains' eagerness for war, I thought it best that I help you train."

Douglas barked out a laugh, but his eyes clouded with concern. "We received a report just this morning talking of our foe. I'm glad to see you so soon. The numbers are not good, Boyd. We're outnumbered from the last count. By several hundred."

Boyd adjusted his stance, unease running down his spine. That was not the news he was hoping for. The O'Cains were more astute than he thought them to be. Normally the rabble clan could not organize a gathering, nevertheless a war.

"Most of the clan will remain here until after Samhain. They will expect to enjoy the revelry, but mayhap we'll need to speak to the soldiers, keep them from imbibing too much good food and wine. If the O'Cains are preparing to march, 'twould only mean they will come to us when they think we're least expecting it. Least prepared."

"And still drunk on mulled wine and beer," Douglas stated, frowning as they watched several clansmen cross swords with each other. The clang of metal on metal music to Boyd's ears.

"What of the women? The castle isn't fortified enough to keep them from harm should the worst befall us on the field."

Boyd turned to Douglas. The idea of Maya or anyone under his care harmed at the O'Cain's hand brought forth in him a wave of anger so great it threatened to consume him. But Douglas was right. Druiminn was a single tower castle. With no impregnable outer castle wall to keep those inside safe, any who stayed within her walls was vulnerable.

Should they survive the forthcoming battle, he would ensure that the castle had modifications, be built upon, and made harder to seize, a second tower perhaps, hidden passageways that would enable those who lived within its walls a way of escape when under attack.

"We'll have boats prepared to evacuate the women and children should the worst happen. They can travel by sea to Duart Castle, stay with the Macleans. They will be secure there and cared for."

Boyd thought over Douglas's idea, unsure it would work. The women could not stay here, not if they were under siege, but that option may not be open to them. "That may be impossible. O'Cains have been ravaging the lands down near Loch Bracadale and Minginish. They have ships, some of which could be near the isles. They'll not think to assume we're watching those ports. No," Boyd said, dismissing the idea of the women and children escaping by boat. "We shall station men at Druiminn and hide them in the forest if need be. Have the men today prepare several sites suitable to enable that."

Douglas nodded, but Boyd could see the worry in his eyes, the same that he held. That the O'Cains may have the advantage at this moment, and there wasn't a damn thing he could do about it. "Send our fastest rider, find out where Donald Mor's men are. We'll be needing them if we're to win."

"From the last report, they are at least ten days away, Boyd. Mayhap if we travel to Glendale, the land is flatter there, and there is a source of fresh water, good for the men. Make Clan O'Cain come to us. With Mor's men set to land at Loch Pooltiel, if we can hold the O'Cains off long enough for them to arrive, we may stand a chance of winning this battle."

Boyd thought over Douglas's words that were wise indeed. "We ride to Glendale the day after Samhain." Boyd looked back at the castle, thinking of Maya. Leaving her here, with only a skeleton army to protect her and the womenfolk left him uneasy. But, there was little he could do about it. He certainly couldn't take her with him, as much as he would like to keep her within view at all times. It was too dangerous, too hard, and he would be distracted, knowing she was back at the base, alone and without protection.

What if the O'Cains worked their way around their forces, got their filthy hands on her? Boyd fisted his hands at his sides before walking over to where the weapons lay ready for use. He clasped a training sword in his hand, adjusting his grip as he got used to its weight, the feel of the weapon in his hold.

One of his soldiers came before him, circling him with his weapon, ready for a fight. The poor lad should not have picked this day to spar, for Boyd was in the mood to draw blood, even with a wooden sword and from one of his own men.

Maya watched Boyd from the steps of the castle, Jeane next to her. His cousin clicked her tongue in censure as Boyd sparred with several men, all of them bleeding, either from their noses or small slices from Boyd's sword. How that was even possible since he was using wood, she could not figure. She cringed when his sword connected with one of the men's forearms, making the soldier grimace in pain.

Maya studied him, wondering why he was so angry. What point he was trying to make.

Boyd didn't hold back, his swings strong and sure, his body sweating, dusty, and utterly delicious to watch, no matter how bloodthirsty. Still, to be out there fighting against Boyd wasn't even something Maya would consider. He looked a little crazed and unstable.

"The O'Cains are close, aren't' they?" Maya said to Jeane, more a statement than a question. This had to be the reason for Boyd's unease. He was worried for his clan, for her.

Jeane pursed her lips, staring out at the battling clansmen. "Aye. I heard Douglas mention that they've been causing strife on Skye and that their end goal is Druiminn. The main O'Cain army may already be on their way."

"To here?" Maya gasped, fear curling around her heart at the thought of those men coming to pick a fight. Not just any fight, but one that ended in one loser and one conqueror.

Oh, if only she had read up on her history of the Macleods more, she would know who won this battle. With Jeane here, a distant blood relative of Boyd's, she didn't know if the current clan Macleod hailed from her bloodline or Boyd's.

What if Boyd was killed? She clutched her stomach, nausea wrenching up, as uncontrollable as the forthcoming war. Maya ran down the steps, rushing to a nearby bush, and vomited. Boyd was no longer immortal. He was mortal now.

How had she not thought of that before?

Which meant he could be killed. That when he fought the O'Cains, he could die, and it would be her fault. His love for her had put him in danger.

She retched again, wiping her mouth with the back of her hand as comforting arms pulled her away. Boyd wrapped himself about her, soothing her with Gaelic words she couldn't understand but wished she did.

"What troubles you, lass?" he asked at length, his hand making round, soothing strokes on her back.

Tears pricked her eyes, and she clutched at him like a terrified child. The idea that within weeks, possibly days, Boyd could be in danger made her stomach churn with renewed vigor.

"When were you going to tell me that the O'Cains are marching toward Druiminn?"

He sighed, setting his chin on the top of her head. "I dinna want to worry you, Maya. 'Tis in hand, and we'll battle miles from here. I'll ensure you and Jeane are safe."

She shook her head, leaning back to look up at him.

She needed to see his face, to see if he was serious and true. "I don't want to be parted from you."

A look of determination settled on his features, immovable and solid like his castle foundations. "I'm afraid that is not an option. You will stay here, or I'll lock you in until I return."

"You wouldn't dare," she gasped, never having heard him speak to her in such a way before.

He stepped back, crossing his arms over his chest. "Doona test me on this, lass, for you will find my word is as true as the sun and moon in the sky."

CHAPTER 31

Chapter Thirty One

"Come now," Jeane said, stepping between them when they both remained at crosses over Boyd's words. "No more disagreements. The Scots have enough of those already."

He wouldn't attempt to lock her in the castle. What if they did need to escape? Leaving them locked away for the O'Cains to come in and do whatever they wanted wasn't safe at all.

Foolhardy more like.

"I will not leave you." Maya was determined to get her way. To stay here without Boyd would be far more dangerous, in her opinion anyway. A small voice whispered that she was being unreasonable, that she should not go to war or be anywhere near one, but she also needed to keep watch on Boyd. Make sure nothing happened to him, that he survived.

The thought of him dying was an unbearable thought to begin with, but the idea of being miles away from him should something like that occur was worse.

"This is not up for discussion. The women and children stay at Druiminn where you will be safe." He looked up at his castle. His lips thinned into a displeased line. "Well, as safe as one can be in such a castle, but I'll ensure you have other options should the Macleods fall to the O'Cains."

Jeane made the sign of the cross, mumbling a prayer. "Doona say such things, Boyd Macleod. You'll curse us all."

Boyd sighed, throwing them a placating look, trying to appeal to their reasonable side. Maya didn't have a reasonable side. Not when it came to living without the man she loved. "I will not be able to focus should I know you're nearby, in danger by being so close to the battle. You must stay here. There is no choice."

"Of course," Jeane said, clasping Maya's arm and trying to drag her away.

Maya didn't move. "What if something happens to you? I won't be there."

"Nothing will happen to me, Maya lass. The O'Cains are no match for us."

Jeane growled, glaring at Boyd. "There you go again, tempting fate, lad."

The whole situation wasn't fair or needed, not in Maya's opinion at least. Why couldn't the stupid O'Cains fuck the hell off and leave Boyd and his clan alone? What was wrong with people in this time that they needed to fight with everyone all the time?

It was absurd, and she was damn well sick of it.

Maya shook off Jeane's hold and pushed past Boyd, starting for the castle. She needed to be alone. To think and plan. What would she do if Boyd did lose and the

O'Cains returned to Druiminn to take their spoils? Whatever would happen to them?

She couldn't stay in medieval Scotland then. As much as she loved the Macleod people, Jeane and Boyd, this wasn't her time. Without the man she loved, living and breathing in it, she could not stay here then.

If she were being made to stay at the castle for the battle duration, she would stay in the tower, within hand's reach of the tapestry. Within reach of returning home, safe from the O'Cains' wrath and destruction. If only she could take everyone with her too. Boyd especially.

Samhain came, and the bonfires lit up the surrounding land. The castle, too, was alight with every candle and sconce burning. The air outside was surprisingly warm, fresh, and clean, and the heavens would soon be out, twinkling over them as if wanting to be part of the celebrations.

Boyd stood to the side of the main bonfire, now well alight within the bailey. Maya stood away from him on the opposite side, a scowl on her brow and displeasure in every word she spoke to him since their argument this afternoon.

It was not how he wanted to spend the last evening with his lass, but then, he also needed her to understand that she would follow his command. That there was no discussion on the matter.

"You look to be getting the silent treatment. 'Tis a shame for a soldier to go off to war with bad blood between him and his wife."

Boyd ground his teeth at Douglas's words. He could not allow her displeasure of him to continue. The lass had to understand his reasons for her to remain, and if she did not, well then, he would make her.

Mayhap make her...

"Aye, I shall secure her understanding. When we ride at first light tomorrow, there will be no hostility between us."

"I wanted to ask before we departed for Glendale if you would give your blessing to me marrying Jeane."

Boyd turned to stare at Douglas, frowning. "You asked her weeks ago, why seek my approval tonight?"

"Because I want your approval and to marry her tonight with your blessing. I dinna seek it before, and I should have. 'Twas wrong of me."

Boyd smiled, clapping him on his back several times. "Thank you for asking, and aye, of course, you have my blessing and best wishes for your marriage tonight. But," Boyd said, pointing toward where the clan priest stood with several men and women, a large tankard of ale in his hands, his eyes glassy and unfocused already, "I would suggest you get married sooner rather than leave it until later. The father looks to be well in his cups."

Douglas looked over to where the priest stood and started off without hesitation. Boyd smiled, watching his closest friend and clan guardsman seek the priest's assistance to marry Jeane. He supposed that meant that Douglas would be family soon. He would have to ensure they had a larger home allocated to them on the land when they returned from battle.

It pleased him that his clan was happy. This night at least they were. Boyd left them to their celebrations, wanting to go over the plans for the next several days. He strode to his solar, wanting to look over the maps, the men, and the abilities one last time before they set off in only a few hours.

A maid brought in a pitcher of beer, bread, and stew. Boyd sat and ate, thinking of all the ways the O'Cains could attack them at Glendale and what to do should that happen. A multitude of battle plays that he saw in his mind's eye and combatted in return. Down several hundred men, they needed to act smart and quick if they were to stand any chance of winning.

The door to his solar creaked, and he looked up to find Maya standing at the threshold. She looked tired and worried. Little gray circles sat beneath her eyes, and he knew she hadn't slept well the night before. Hell, he hadn't slept well either. It had been the first night that they had not come together, made love, and given each other pleasure.

He had not tried to seek her approval or her acquiescence. She needed to think over his stance and agree to it in her own time. Or at least, get used to the idea that he would not be moved and what he said was law.

She didn't say anything, just stared at him, but he understood the silence that fell between them. Tomorrow morn when he parted, it could be the last time they ever saw each other. How could one fill such a space with meaningless words when words would never be enough? Not to encompass what he felt for her and she him.

"Come here, lass," he whispered, needing her more than air. She all but bolted across the room and flung herself into his arms. Holding him with an immovable embrace.

Boyd sent up a silent prayer that his clan, his men, the women and children left behind at Druiminn would be safe. Would survive the next several weeks and be rid of the O'Cains when all of this was over.

He wanted to start a family with his wife. He wanted a

future with her, so much that he knew tomorrow when he rode from Druiminn, his body and soul would not be complete until he was back here again.

He tipped up her face, kissing her hard, showing her without words all that she meant to him. She was his sole reason for living, his future that he wanted with a desperation that scared him.

An emotion he did not need the night before riding into battle.

He could feel the dampness of her cheeks, the tears that fell unheeded. His heart crumbled in his chest, knowing that tonight could be their last together.

"Maya," he said, pulling back. He reveled in her beautiful dark-blue eyes, wanting to remember them forever. "If something were to happen to me, you must not stay. You need to return to your time. I canna die if I know that you would stay. Place yourself in harm's way, when for you at least, there is a way out."

Her lip wobbled, and it near broke him in two, but she nodded, just the smallest bit, and relief poured through him like a balm. No matter the outcome, his lass, his love would be safe.

Would live on somewhere in time, even if he did not.

CHAPTER 32

Chapter Thirty Two

They arrived at Glendale two days later and set up camp across the river Hamra. Boyd walked through the clan's camp. Each of his men was busy with preparations for the forthcoming battle. They sharpened swords, checked armor, viewed the lay of the land, and planned.

It was a week before the O'Cains arrived, late as usual. They set up across the river from each other, both armies within view and ready for what was to come.

"Donald Mor and his men will be here by tomorrow. You have my word." Boyd nodded at Douglas's words, digesting how many men the O'Cains had. He didn't want to unnerve his men, but there were more than he'd thought there would be. He stupidly hoped the estimates had been wrong. Even with Mor and his men's help, when they battled against such numbers, the outcome would not be one he wanted to imagine.

"I have underestimated Dougall O'Cain. What are your approximates of how many he has at his side?"

"At least five hundred we have approximated. Three hundred more than us, including Mor's men."

Damn it all to hell. Boyd rolled his shoulders, the weight of his men's lives like a ring of iron about his body, pushing him down, uncomfortable, painful even. He had led them here, and now many of them could be dead in a day or so.

"We will fight, and we will win," Douglas stated, his words sure, but what did it matter? His oldest friend's eyes held a doubt neither one of them wanted to voice. The battle would be brutal, hard, unforgiving, and they were three hundred men short.

They were doomed.

"Aye," he replied, crossing his arms, watching the O'Cains light fires, preparing for the night. "We shall."

Boyd did not sleep that night, and as notified the day before, on the sunrise, Donald Mor and his men, who would make up the last of his army, anchored boats at the head of Loch Poolteil. The men had fought previously together at other clan battles, both on Skye and the Scottish mainland. Their alliance went back hundreds of years, each clan willing to fight for the other, no matter the cost.

Boyd pulled Donald Mor aside, needing him to know the truth of what was to come. "We are three hundred men short, Donald. 'Tis to be a bloody day on the morrow." He rubbed a hand over his jaw, hating that the night would end all too soon, and come morning, he sent his men to certain death.

Himself included unless a miracle occurred.

Mor scoffed, drinking down his goblet of beer. "Nay,

doona think that way, lad. We've fought harder battles than this, and won, need I remind you. The O'Cains may be an army of many men, but we're an army of skill and stamina. They doona hold power over me or my men, and you shall not allow their numbers to sullen your mind."

Mor was right. The thought of battle, or dying and leaving Maya alone and defenseless, was making him weak. He loved the lass more than anything in the world, and he didn't want to leave her. The idea of them, of a future, was all he wanted now. The damn O'Cain could burn in hell for eternity for wanting to fight. He'd had enough of warfare. After living for so long, partaking in hundreds of battles, his old bones were weary, tired, and he was ready to settle down, rest, and enjoy his life with his new bride.

"You are right. We shall win. To think otherwise is tempting fate." Boyd clapped him on the back, leading him back to his tent. "Shall we finish our drinks, toast our women and our menfolk? Our wives who keep the home fires burning for us?"

An amused light entered Mor's eyes at Boyd's words. "Aye, lad, I heard you married a fine English lass. Is she as bonny as they say?"

"You have heard of Maya?" Boyd asked, surprised that news of his nuptials reached mainland Scotland. They had been married days only. Such news would be impossible.

Mor chuckled. "Nay, lad, I was told upon arrival here this morn, but I did hear you were smitten with the outlander." He drank down his beer, holding it up to a servant to fill it again. "Some said the Laird Macleod would never marry again. You have heard the rumors of your immortality, have you not?"

"Aye, I've heard the rumors." And they had been true, right up to the night he told Maya he loved her. His fate had changed after that declaration, and for the better, he would add.

"While I doona believe all that hogwash that you were cursed, I will admit to being a little curious as to how your hair is so vera reddish brown now. In all the years that I've known you, your hair has always been as white as the clouds. Nor have you aged a day, but," he shrugged, gulping his beer yet again, "as I said, I doona believe in that magic stuff, but it does make interesting debate when there are no wenches around to distract us men."

Boyd laughed, reaching down to his leg and pulling out his sgian dubh, running it atop his finger until it bled. "I am blood and bone just like the rest of you, and on the morrow, should a sword find its mark, I too shall fall. There is no magic here," he stated, never truer words said.

He finished his beer, staring into the fire as they fell into companionable silence. Not even to see Maya again would he wish to be immortal once more. To have seen her face light up, come alive at his words, no pleasure was as great. To be mortal meant to be complete, whole once more after a hundred years. He would not wish that empty, meaningless life on anyone, not even himself.

Not ever again.

The morning mist had not yet lifted from the grass, but still the sound of his men marching into battle echoed like a drum in the valley.

Boyd stood at the front of his men, ready to die for their cause, to protect the ones they loved, their land and livelihood.

The fog lifted and thinned, and in the mist, he recognized the O'Cain clan, and yet their laird, Dougall, was nowhere to be seen. Was the bastard standing at the back, letting others battle first, to die in his place, so that he could try to take what did not belong to him?

The bastard would die today. No other outcome was acceptable.

A drum started to thump somewhere behind Boyd, and he knew it was time. Time to fight. Time to die. Time to do what he must.

His battle cry rent out loud and strong in the air. His men joined him, pulling their swords free, the sound of metal scraping metal music to Boyd's battle-hardened ears.

And then they were running, swords at the ready, as they crashed into the O'Cain clan, their men too running toward war, not away from it. Bodies hit bodies, men dropped around him, both his own and O'Cain. Boyd swung out, slicing, cutting down men as they came for him, all the while he kept watch, looking for the O'Cain laird and his chance to take the bastard to his grave.

Several O'Cain men fought well and long. He blocked several attempts for his head to be dislodged before stabbing one through the throat. The other his stomach, turning to battle his next foe as the man's guts spilled onto Scottish soil.

Sweat ran down his face, stinging his eyes. His mouth tasted of blood, not his own, but others that he had spilled. The scent of death swamped his nostrils. He looked about, searching, always hunting for O'Cain, still, he could not see him. The sight of his men falling, being maimed, slaughtered by the O'Cains at an alarming rate spiked fear up his spine.

Nay, they could not lose.

He roared, fighting with renewed vigor, slicing blindly toward anyone who came within a yard of him. Everyone fell at his hand, and then he spied Dougall O'Cain, surrounded by his men and watching Boyd with malice.

Boyd strode toward him, taking down two more men who ran at him, never once taking his eye off the man who killed so many of his clan.

O'Cain's own private army parted, allowed Boyd to face their laird. "So many men have fought and died today under your command. Yet, it should have been a battle between us. But I know why you dinna choose such a fight." A muscle worked in O'Cain's jaw, not relishing being called the scared leader of a rabble pack.

"A war between our clans or a swordfight between us will end the same way, Macleod. With you dead and your home, your lands finally under O'Cain control." Dougall strode around Boyd, and he turned, watching, waiting for the bastard to strike. "I hope you made your goodbyes worthy of eternity. For you shall not see your precious Sassenach again." O'Cain laughed, and several of his men joined in. "Mayhap I shall take her to be my wife. Tell me, Macleod, are her lips as tight about your cock as her cunny?"

A red haze descended over Boyd's eyes, and he lunged, swinging his sword at O'Cain's head. He would not stop until he saw it severed from his evil corpse.

O'Cain blocked his hit, stumbled back, but righted himself soon enough. Boyd wouldn't kill him unless he was standing. He never killed a man who wasn't wielding a weapon and in control of his destiny. No one would ever accuse a Macleod of being anything but noble in battle.

Their combat went on, both wielding their swords and delivering blows intended to be life-ending. Boyd would not lose this fight. To do so would mean all that he ever loved would be lost. He could not have that.

Boyd noticed some of his men were fighting the guards around O'Cain and himself, gaining the upper hand. He moved fast, swinging his sword, trying to learn his foe's moves and counteract them. It didn't take Boyd long to know O'Cain wasn't the best when it came to fighting, but he was a strong man, his every thrust jarring Boyd's arm with its power.

The thought of Maya kept him going, pushed him forward, toward life, not death.

O'Cain stumbled back, both their breathing labored. Sweat poured down Boyd's face. His hand ached with the weight of the sword. He just needed an opening, an opportunity to shove his sword into the man's gullet, and all of this would be over.

The sound of men fighting around him was deafening, drove him, and then he saw her. The Fae Queen walked up to them as if there wasn't a war going on about them. As if she were merely taking in the Scottish land and enjoying what she saw.

Boyd stilled as both he and O'Cain took in the woman's presence. O'Cain's pleasure at seeing the queen was evident, and Boyd knew that today would be Boyd's last.

CHAPTER 33

Chapter Thirty Three

Boyd observed what was happening around him, both the O'Cain and Macleod clansmen oblivious to Titania the Fae Queen who had walked among them. Boyd cringed as his friend and ally Donald Mor was sliced across the chest, falling dead at an O'Cain clansman's feet.

He turned back to Titania and narrowed his eyes on the fickle faery as she came to stand beside Dougall O'Cain.

She grinned, her eyes alight with pleasure. "And so the day arrives, finally," she said, her voice light and sweet. So sweet that it grated on Boyd's last nerve. He'd had enough of this ominous wench.

The queen leaned up, kissing Dougall O'Cain, and realization struck Boyd. They were not here to battle honorably, this was a slaughter, and he'd led his men to the O'Cains like lambs to a pack of wolves.

"What day would that be?" Boyd asked, better to know what was to occur than not.

She chuckled, and Dougall smirked. "They day you die," she replied matter-of-factly. "The day I finally rid the world of you, never to return, and never to see your precious Maya again."

Boyd swallowed and fought not to react. There had to be a way out of this. He may die, but at least he would take one of them out first. Preferably Titania if she didn't disappear into the ether.

She flicked her hand in his direction, and Boyd wrenched back. He gasped as the sensation of a blade sliced through him, within his organs, and out again with force.

He stared down at his gut, his mind unable to comprehend what had happened. He looked back to O'Cain, even he a little unnerved by the underhanded way he would win the battle. No highlander, no Scotsman wanted to be known to win a clan battle because of a woman.

Not even a woman. But a faery.

He pressed against the wound, warm blood oozing over his fingers, unstoppable. "You let a woman win for you, O'Cain. History will remember your cowardice."

Titania laughed. "No, they will not remember, for there will be no mention of my hand in this." She turned to O'Cain. "I shall return. Do not touch Macleod until you see me again."

She disappeared into thin air, and Boyd dropped to his knees, blackness swamping him, his last thought that of his lass. Maya flashed before his eyes, and he welcomed the vision. No matter what Titania said, he would see his lady again. Mayhap not in this world, but the next. The soul would travel space and time, just as Maya had to find its true love.

He could not believe it would be any different for himself.

Maya stood looking out over the ocean. Word had reached them last evening that the battle was to take place from daybreak, some hours ago now. She had not slept, nor would she again until Boyd was back home, safe and, more importantly, alive. Her stomach churned with the fear of the unknown. Was he living? Had they won? She didn't know anything, no further updates had come in, and now it was almost eight in the morning.

Surely there should be some news by now.

"Maya lass, how good to see you again."

She gasped, turned to watch as the Fae Queen floated toward her, her robes no longer white or gray as she'd seen them last, but almost ebony black as the night. It could only mean one thing. The woman had turned to darkness, her heart cruel instead of kind.

"I wish I could say the same about you, but I see you'll be joining the Unseelie Court instead of the Seelie from this day forward. How far you have fallen from grace."

The queen's eyes flashed, their silver color almost looking as if a storm were brewing within them, churning and twisting like a snake. "I have a proposition for you. One that I think will please you."

Nothing would please Maya unless this woman were dead. Removed from her and Boyd's life so they may never have to deal with her again. "What is it?" she asked anyway. Knowing that the queen would tell her in any case.

The queen reached out her hand. "Boyd needs you, and I can take you to him."

What? Boyd needed her? Did that mean he was injured? Or had they won against the O'Cains? She closed her eyes, praying it was the latter. They could not lose. She could not lose him. They had only just begun.

Maya reached out, taking her hand and gripping it until the queen winced. Good, she hoped she hurt her, even in this small way. The Fae needed to know that no matter what power she had over them, there were always repercussions that could be dealt out in return. Maybe not by her, Boyd, or the Macleod clan. Perhaps not today or for a hundred years, but one day the queen would cross someone she should not, and then she would pay for her sins.

"Take me to him," she said, lifting her chin in defiance. Not willing to cower before this being.

The queen nodded. "Of course."

Maya barely had time to blink before she found herself on a field, men battling about her, the metallic scent of blood making her eyes water. She looked down and gasped. Boyd lay only a few feet from her, clasping his stomach. O'Cain stood over him, a smile on his lips.

Maya ran to him, pushing O'Cain away from him. The man's eyes widened but then filled with interest.

"Do not touch him," she warned, pushing her hand onto Boyd's stomach, the blood seeping through his fingers spilling onto hers.

Boyd moaned, and her eyes pricked with tears. He was dying, she could see from the pallor of his skin, an awful gray color, his skin cold as if already he were gone.

"Boyd," she begged. "Boyd, darling, look at me." He did, and she sobbed, reaching for him, holding him. The weight of one of his hands reached around her shoulders, holding her. "I love you, Maya lass."

No, this wasn't happening. This wasn't supposed to befall any of them.

"There is a way to save him, Maya. I may allow one last gift from my kind."

The word *no* whispered past Boyd's lips, but Maya was already looking to the Fae Queen. She couldn't be trusted, that she knew, but she also couldn't let Boyd die. If only he were alive, he stood a chance of winning against the O'Cains. Against this faery who had turned dark.

"How?" she asked, her vision of the queen blurred through her haze of tears.

"I shall grant him life. A mortal one, of course, if you return to your time. You do not belong here. You are out of time and out of place. A mistake in time's woven tapestry. You need to return home, to your former life."

"What do you mean to return the lass to her time? She's from England," the O'Cain stated, crossing his arms and staring at the faery as if she had a screw loose.

Of course, the O'Cains did not know Maya wasn't from their time. They were foolish to trust the Fae Queen as they so obviously had. Had she helped the O'Cains gain the upper hand? From the looks of the war that fought about them, they had.

Bastards.

"There is much you do not know, O'Cain, and I'm not patient enough to explain it to you. Just know that the lass is out of time, quite literally." She gestured to Boyd, who lay still as death.

His eyes fluttered open, and Maya leaned down, kissing

his lips. "I cannot let you die, Boyd. No matter where I am, the time that separates us, know that I cannot live knowing you were gone. I need to know that you lived. That you had a life, even if it is one without me."

"No." He fought to get up, and she pushed him back down. His wound started to hemorrhage, and she ripped off some of her kirtle, trying to stem the blood. There was too much of it.

"I will go," she stated, taking in every feature of Boyd's beautiful, handsome, sweet face. His straight nose, his cutting jaw, his long eyelashes and lips that were too perfect to be a man's. Her heart ached. Her mind screamed at the unfairness of it all. She leaned down, clasping him tightly. "I love you so much," she whispered for only Boyd to hear. "When you are healed, rid the earth of them both."

She kissed him, pulled back, and read the panic in his eyes, not over what was to come once she was gone, but because she was going. "I wish we had more time."

"Maya," he gasped, his voice barely there, just as his life was barely hanging on.

"Send me back," she said, not taking her eyes off Boyd, wanting every last moment to be of him. Nothing else. Just him.

"As you wish," the queen said, and just as before, within a moment, she was gone.

Maya blinked, and she was in a different place. She was back at Druiminn Castle, except it wasn't the sixteenth-century castle she had grown to love. It was the twenty-first one.

The room was empty, the stone wall met her back, and she looked about, spying the silk tapestry that was to be hung on the wall at her back. The tables in the Great Hall, set up for display for the paying public. The room was exactly as she had left it the night she was sent back to the past.

Maya stood, staring down at her hands, realizing they were no longer bloody, her woolen kirtle also gone, replaced by her uniform. She ran to the tapestry and touched it, ran her hands over the images, and yet nothing. No time travel, nothing but the feel of the silk against her palm.

She wandered down into the kitchen, to the staff locker area. Her phone and bag were where she left them, and she checked the date and time. The same day she had left.

How could that be? She slumped into a chair at the table, unable to process what had occurred. Everything that had happened. All that she lost.

Emotion overwhelmed her, and she crumbled like a stone. Tears streamed down her face, her gasps taking her breath. She had lost him. Had left him, and no matter the reasons behind doing so, it did not change the fact that she wouldn't see Boyd again.

How was she supposed to live without him?

She knew that she could not. A sob wrenched from her, a sound that embodied nothing but pain.

Whatever she had done, she knew one thing. She could not go back.

CHAPTER 34

Chapter Thirty Four

The will to live left him at the disappearance of Maya. She was gone, thrust hundreds of years into the future. A mortal as he was now, he could not wait out his time, live the years that spanned between them so he could see her again.

He loved her, and with that declaration, his fate had been sealed.

Boyd heard what sounded to be thunder, and had it not been for the gasp from the Fae Queen, he would have kept his eyes closed, let death take him from his pain. But something about the queen's alarm pulled him from his imminent death.

The queen stood beside Dougall O'Cain, or what was left of him since his severed head was now lying at the base of his feet. The mask of shock his death shroud.

The Fae Queen, now held by two large men, told Boyd

she could not escape their bonds, not even with her powers.

"Hello, Boyd."

If he were capable of shock, he would have gasped as the queen had. Instead, all he could muster was a small lifting of his top lip. "Sorcha," he whispered. "I canna see you very well, lass."

She kneeled beside him, placing her hand over his wound. Heat licked at his skin, the pain of the injury dispelling, ebbing away with every shallow breath.

"What are you doing?" he asked, his voice stronger, even to his own ears.

"Saving you. This is not your time to die. The queen has overstepped her bounds and will not do so again."

Breathing became easier, and the vision of Sorcha cleared. He did gasp then, for she was beautiful. As beautiful as he remembered her. The years slipped away, and he sat up, staring at the scar on his stomach, now perfectly healed as if it never was.

"Saving me? Is that not too against the rules?"

"We must have balance in the world, Boyd. Your life was taken in a war that wasn't meant to be. I am giving it back to you. In time, like everyone, you will pass on. But not today. Not this fight."

Boyd looked around. His men, many of them outnumbered, fought on. It was as if the Fae, Dougall O'Cain, and himself had been hidden by a magical veil, unseen and untouchable all this time.

He stood, picking up his sword. "I must fight."

Sorcha placed her hand on his shoulder, stilling him. "I have something for you, Boyd Macleod. Something that I should have given to you a long time ago. I'm sorry I did not come back to say goodbye."

Boyd looked down at the faery who used to be his wife, a fact that was no longer true. She was different now. A powerful being, mystical and untouchable by the mortal world. The year they had together he would forever treasure, but Sorcha never belonged in the human world. It was the one thing now that he'd seen her again that he could agree with the Fae Queen.

Regret coursed through his blood. "I spent so much time lost in hate, in my self-pity that I dinna look up to see what life could gift me. Not until Maya, that was."

She smiled, her eyes flickering with liquid steel. "I like Maya."

Boyd watched as Sorcha held out her hand, a yellow silk scarf-like material with the lightest red dots clasped between her fingers. She handed it to him, closing his fingers around it.

"Magic falls upon Druiminn walls. With this flag, no harm shall come to Clan Macleod and all. Use it wisely, three times only or not at all. I gift thee to you, Boyd Macleod, and all those who sire from your loins. Forever and more."

He stared at Sorcha, unable to comprehend the gift she'd given. "How does it work?" he asked. The idea of such a magical piece of cloth did not make sense, but even so, he would not thrust it aside, not if it meant to give him protection, his clan safety. Only a fool would do such a thing.

"When the Faery Flag is raised, and your command is called, your gift will be given." She looked out over the men battling around them, his men beyond exhausted, along with the O'Cains.

Boyd raised the flag high above his head. "A wish for

an army of men within this glen to win this war against the O'Cain clan."

Just as Sorcha had said, the men battling the O'Cains multiplied, increased by hundreds if not thousands within moments. Boyd could not move, could not say a word as the O'Cains were beaten back and killed. Those who saw there was no use to continue running off as quickly as their weary feet would carry them.

Sorcha turned to him, taking his hands and squeezing them a little. "This is my thank-you, for loving me as you did, for being a tender husband all those years ago. I shall never forget you, Boyd Macleod."

Boyd pulled her into his arms, holding her tight, unable to voice how thankful he was to the woman in his arms. Maybe this magic flag may also bring his Maya back. She rubbed his back in soothing strokes.

"I can read your mind, Boyd, and I understand, but also know, the flag does not work that way. It will not bring your Maya back." She leaned back, gifting him a sad smile. "Now I must go. The queen faces the consequences of her actions. You will not be disturbed by her again. I promise you as the new Queen of the Fae."

And then they were gone. Boyd stood on the grassy field at Glendale, the war over, his men victorious. Dougall O'Cain lay dead at his feet, and clan Macleod was secure once more. Safe from his enemy and protected from the Fae.

Boyd sheathed his sword behind his back, walking over to where Donald Mor lay dead. They would bury their dead before they started back to Druiminn. He was in no rush to return home. As much as he cherished his land, Druiminn, and the people who made up his clan, there was one person who wouldn't be waiting for him at the castle. Nor would she ever again.

Boyd pushed down the knowledge, the truth that Maya was gone, that the few months he had with her was all he was going to receive. There was no way in which he could see her again. He would cherish what time they had, live with his memories until his time came to an end.

As for the future of Clan Macleod that Maya had told him survived to her time, well, he would gift any male child Jeane birthed his birthright. Clan Macleod would continue, not with his seed, but his cousin's. There was peace in that knowledge, which may be the only peace he'd ever have again.

Maya spent the next several days at her small flat in Druiminn. She couldn't bear going back to the castle to see the reminders of Boyd, the tapestry, safely behind the Perspex covering, had been too much, and she'd complained of not feeling well and went home sick.

Her excuse would not hold for much longer, and eventually she would have to return to the castle, go back to cleaning up after the many tourists and get on with her life.

She lifted her knees to her chest, curling herself into a fetal position. But not yet. She wasn't ready to come to grips with that truth. If Boyd could see her now, he would scoop her off her bed and make her busy. Get her moving again, but her self-will just wasn't there.

Her heart felt as though it were breaking into a million pieces, and there was nothing she could do to glue it back together.

Yesterday she had gained a burst of energy and had jumped online, needing to find out all she could of the battle of Glendale. There was very little written about it, and vague accounts of who won, who was injured or killed, nothing concrete. It was said that both the Macleod clan and O'Cain suffered great losses, but also that the Fae had given Clan Macleod some magical flag, and they had won.

No matter the truth, she hoped that the bastard O'Cain laird got what he had coming for him. Had died an awful death after leading his men into a battle that wasn't necessary.

Not in Maya's mind in any case. Just a waste of good lives, like most wars in history.

She cringed, swiping at the tears that wouldn't abate. Well, she supposed that wasn't quite true. Wars were important, especially when people were persecuted because of their religious beliefs or their race.

But O'Cain merely wanted the land, the wealth, to raid another clan to gain what he did not have. Those sorts of wars, well, she hoped Dougall O'Cain was burning in hell right now and regretting his choice.

Her stomach lurched, and she ran to the toilet. She needed to stop this never-ending round of pity party she was living in. To be so depressed was making her ill, quite literally, and she needed to stop.

Boyd wouldn't want her to be like that. To live that way.

She would stop. Tomorrow, she promised herself. Today she would finish crying. Punish herself for her many regrets and choices she made on the field beside Boyd. Of all the things she had said, that wasn't enough. Of not being strong enough, getting up to fight instead of doing what the queen wanted her to. Even if she had died, at least she would have done *something!*

Maya cringed. "Enough," she said to herself. "That is enough." She needed to move on, to love and remember her time with Boyd and be happy that she'd been given such a gift.

Not everyone was so fortunate to have found their soul mate, the love of their life. Maya slumped against the bathroom wall, wiping her mouth. "If only..." she sighed, "it had lasted forever."

CHAPTER 35

Chapter Thirty Five

They had lost more than half their men on the battlefield at Glendale. Thankfully, the O'Cains suffered more losses since a Fae army, gifted by Sorcha, arrived and saved them from being eradicated from Scotland.

He hoped that Sorcha could deal with the previous Fae Queen once and for all and that she would never trouble him or his clansmen ever again. He slumped down on his chair in the solar, cringing at the aches his body suffered since the war.

It would take some time before he was healed, back to his previous strength, but there was one part of him that would never be the same. His heart. Although it beat, his body aging like the rest of his clansmen, it was all pointless. Nothing was enough, not anymore. The food was tasteless, the music dull and lifeless. The sun no longer warm on his skin, the sky as blue. Life was dead to him, for he had lost what gave him joy.

Maya.

He could not even soothe his mind with the knowledge that he would wait for the centuries and see her again. Mortal once more, even that option was gone.

Boyd ran his finger over the fine silk of the flag the Fae had given him. An odd, yellow color with the tiniest red dots didn't seem like the kind of flag the Fae would have, yet it was what was gifted. He would keep it safe, and hopefully, within his lifetime, he would not need to use it again.

"Boyd?" Jeane said, pulling his attention to her. She stood at the threshold of the door, wringing her hands at her waist.

"What is it, lass?" he asked, not in the mood for conversation but also not wanting to be alone with his thoughts. His mind was too busy as it was with wallowing. Jeane would be a good distraction.

"You returned so late last evening, but then I dinna see you at breakfast." She came into the room, seating herself across from him on a chair. "You know that Maya has gone, but no one seems to know where. What has happened to her?"

Boyd leaned back in his chair, rubbing his temple with one hand. He supposed he would have to tell his cousin the truth. Not that she would like what she heard. The truth would hurt her because she would think they did not trust her enough to tell her the lay of it when Maya was here.

"'Tis a long story, Jeane. Are you sure you wish to hear it?"

"Aye, of course, I do. Maya was my friend. I need to know if harm came to her or if she is well. Please tell me."

Boyd met Jeane's eyes, read the pleading within them. "Maya wasn't from our time, Jeane. Just like I was immortal, somehow magic brought her back from the twenty-first century. Mrs. Fletcher is the only other person to know the truth. The only servant trusted with such a secret since her family has worked for mine for a century and because she found Maya the day she stumbled into our time."

Jeane's mouth gaped, worked as if to spill words, but none were forthcoming. It may have been the first time he'd ever seen his cousin lost of speech.

"The Fae Queen, the very one who cursed me, offered Maya a deal. My life, for Maya to return to her time."

"Oh, the poor lass." Jeane sniffed, scrambling in her dress for a handkerchief. "Of course, she would have picked your life. She loved you so vera much."

Boyd stared at the desk, the flag, his sword that lay over it too, still grimy with blood and flesh. "Aye, she chose my life, just as I would have chosen hers. Doona make it any easier to accept, though, does it?"

Jeane shook her head, her eyes full of pity and despair. All the things that Boyd felt culminating in his soul. How would he ever move on? Step into his future without her?

"I doona know what I'm going to do, Jeane," he said, unable to stop the cracking of his voice. His eyes felt hot, and his nose stung. He rubbed his hands over his face, ripping himself from his chair and going to the door. "Bring ale. Lots of it," he said to a maid standing to attend outside.

"Well, 'tis not good enough. We have to get Maya back. She came here once. We have to make her come back again."

Boyd walked over to where a narrow window overlooked the rocky outcrop the castle had been built upon, in the distance the trees and path that led to the heated pools.

"I doona know how we shall get her back, but she belongs here, with us, with you. You married her, and she loves you so vera much. We cannot allow this to stand."

Boyd could not have loved his cousin more at that moment. Her determined tone, her steadfast belief that Maya would one day return, making his heartache a little less. "I saw Sorcha again at the battle. No doubt you have heard that she gifted the Macleods the Faery Flag."

"I heard from Douglas as much." Jeane frowned in thought. "Do you think Sorcha could help you? Perhaps if you call her. Beg her to grant one more gift?"

Boyd had thought of doing such a thing. He had little doubt that Sorcha knew what had happened at Castle Druiminn the past hundred years, had been keeping track in the shadows without showing herself. She would hear him if he asked.

Somehow it seemed wrong to ask the woman who was once his wife to bring his new wife back. Even so, he doubted that uncomfortable fear would stop him from doing as Jeane suggested.

All that mattered was Maya. Her happiness, which he was certain coincided with his. He loved her as she loved him. He hated to imagine what she was going through right now, five hundred years into the future, alone and heartbroken.

He wanted to wrap his arms around her, hold her and kiss away her fears, her pain. That he could not made him want to roar until the walls crumbled about him.

"I will try," he said to Jeane, willing to do anything to get the love of his life back. His soul mate. "I think after everything the Fae and their queen has put the clan through, 'tis the least they could do. Doona you agree?"

Jeane nodded, hope lighting her eyes. "Aye, I do." A maid bustled in with a tankard of ale and two glasses. "Now, let us drink to winning the war against Dougall O'Cain and to getting your Maya lass back."

Boyd went over to Jeane and gave her a quick hug. His cousin's optimism gave him hope. All he needed now was for Sorcha to hear his pleas and do one last miracle before letting him be forever. His stomach knotted with the unknown, with fear that she would ignore his plea and Maya would never come back.

Maya found herself at what was left of the heated pools near Castle Druiminn the following day. The slow-flowing river still ran not far from the heated pools, that had not changed much over the years, but the pools were no longer there. All that was left was an overgrown rockery. Maya studied it, knowing that it would be deep enough to hold water once again if it was cleared of shrubbery and fallen tree limbs.

She wrapped her arms about her, staring at the place she had swum with Boyd. Heat prickled her skin, as she thought of how that wasn't all they had done in the warm waters.

So much time. Five hundred years ago. It was impossible to fathom.

Earlier that day, she had quit her job and packed up the few small things she had kept in her locker at the castle. Each time she looked up at the building, she was reminded of everything she had lost.

Of everything she would never see again, never love and cherish.

"Maya, isn't it?"

That voice... She turned, gasped when she spied the laird of the Macleods, not the sixteenth-century one, but the twenty-first. Although she'd seen him from afar before, he'd never spoken to her. Gosh, he wouldn't have known she existed, even if she had thought him handsome. Well, handsome enough, but nothing compared to Boyd. A potential distant relative, maybe.

The shape of his jaw, the arch of his brow—she was no expert in genealogy or traits that people passed down through their bloodlines—this man certainly held features of Boyd.

She swallowed the bile that rose in her throat. Had Boyd remarried after she left? Had he found love? She had been so caught up in her own heartbreak that today had been the first time she'd stepped outside. Why didn't she go to the library? Or heavens above just looked the Macleods history up on the internet, not just the battle as she had done.

Idiot.

"Yes, I'm Maya," she replied, unsure if she was trespassing now that she had quit. She dismissed the idea almost instantly. These paths around the castle were open to the public daily. She wasn't doing anything wrong.

He gestured to the rockery behind her. "You know where the old heated pools were. Not many do, you know."

She turned back, looking at the place she'd once swam. "Really? I thought I read it mentioned somewhere in the castle information guide," she lied, knowing she hadn't read it in the brochure at all. But she also didn't want to tell him how she knew of the pools. He'd think her a crazy person.

He grinned, affection lighting his eyes. He walked up to her, holding out his hand. "I'm Richard Macleod. 'Tis a pleasure to meet you, Maya Macleod."

Maya felt the blood drain from her face. She let go of his hand, having been shaking it, and stepped back. "It's Harris," she corrected him, unable to fathom how he knew she had the same surname as he did. What on earth was going on?

"Nay, 'tis Macleod. I couldn't interfere in your life before you traveled back to the sixteenth-century, but the family knew that you were due to arrive sometime this year. I recognized you as soon as I saw you, that you were the one. We share the same eyes and smile if you dinna already notice."

An overwhelming feeling of love washed through her, and she blinked back tears as the man wrapped her into his arms. "You are my grandmother, several...several times back, but you are. 'Tis lovely to meet you, Maya lass."

What? She stared up at him, unable to take in what he was saying. All that it meant. "But if I'm your grandmother, how am I here still?" Maya gasped, stumbling out of his arms and clutching at her stomach. "Does that mean that I'm pregnant?"

"We believe so. Family journals certainly point to you being ill leading up to the battle of Glendale. The Fae did you wrong, but I can repair that damage. I'll have the tapestry taken down, and you, when you're ready, can touch it. I'm certain you will be returned to my grandfather, Boyd Macleod."

Maya swallowed past the lump in her throat. She swiped at her cheeks, unable to comprehend everything

Richard, possibly her ancestor, was telling her. "But I tried to touch the tapestry again when I returned to this time. It didn't work."

"Come," he said, wrapping her hand about his arm as they started back toward the castle. "The Macleods have a long history with magic, intertwined with the Fae. You were not meant to return here, Maya. Your heart beats in another time, and I know that at this moment, as you walk in the future, a man mourns you in the past."

Boyd...

Maya studied the man stating to be her descendent, and she couldn't quite believe it. He did have the same eyes as her, a lovely almond shape, and so blue to make the sky envious. "What if the tapestry doesn't send me back?" she asked him again, fear slithering through her like a snake.

"Ach, there are other options we can try if the tapestry doona work. There is much you doona know, Maya lass. But you shall. In time."

CHAPTER 36

Chapter Thirty Six

Her grandson, who Maya had now come to think of Richard Macleod, was too lovely for words. Almost from the moment he had told her who he was, who she was to him, she knew to her very soul he spoke the truth.

He was her grandson, hundreds of years into the future, her blood was his blood. It gave her hope that she would soon see Boyd again when Richard closed the castle from the public for several days. They gowned her in a newly made kirtle and packed her a bag full to the brim with modern conveniences she may need in the coming months and years. All too soon, Maya was ready to return to Boyd, and she could not contain her excitement over the fact.

Maya sat in the Great Hall, staring at the tapestry of

Boyd the day he lost his first wife to the Fae when the door to the hall opened, and in walked two people Maya had never seen before.

She felt her mouth gape at the sight of the man and the beautiful woman who walked before him, alive, vibrant, and incandescently happy.

"Kenzie," Richard said, kissing her cheek before shaking the other man's hand.

Richard turned to her, and Maya stood, clasping her hands at her front and feeling all kinds of absurd dressed as she was. "This is Maya Macleod, the woman who won Boyd Macleod's heart." He came over to Maya, pulling her toward the couple. "This is Kenzie and Ben Ross of Clan Ross. Kenzie was a Macleod too."

Kenzie closed the space between them and hugged Maya tight. "'Tis lovely to meet you, Maya. You are the reason why the Macleod clan exists to this day, why I can do what I do. The reason why my husband, the once renowned Black Ben, Laird of Ross, is alive. I owe you everything."

Surprisingly, Maya had heard of the notorious Black Ben, a scoundrel of the seventeenth century and good friends to Clan Macleod. She looked up at the man, his ink-black hair making him still look like someone she didn't ever want to cross, even if his face was chiseled to look like an angel.

"Good day, lass," Black Ben said, making Maya's hands shake.

She swallowed. "It's lovely to meet you as well." Maya's head spun with all they were telling her. Things she still didn't understand or comprehend, she knew everything told was true. "What gifts are you talking of?" she asked Kenzie, needing to know.

"Come, we'll explain what we can," Kenzie said.

They sat at the table, and Maya listened to the story of how she came to know her now husband, Laird Ross. How she had helped Abby Cross return to Aedan Macleod to marry the man she loved. How through Maya's actions on the battlefield of Glendale, all their fates, their futures that were at a time intertwined with the past, came to be.

She lay a hand over her stomach, having thought her sickness leading up to the battle had been stress related. That the thought of losing Boyd, of him being mortal and going into battle, had spiked a fear so grave within her she'd been physically sick.

She frowned, trying to date her last period, and knew one thing. It had been a very long time since her last. Could it be true? Could she be pregnant? One thing she did know for certain was she had to return to Boyd.

"We shall have you touch the tapestry, but if it doesn't return you home, and sometimes what initially sent us into the past, doesn't always return us to our time, then I shall help you."

That was the one point she couldn't understand. How was it that Kenzie could assist?

"How?" Maya asked.

Kenzie smiled. "The female line is gifted with magic, the ability to time jump. When you return to Boyd, in time, all will be explained. But we need you to go so that can occur. If you do not return, then Richard and I will fail to exist. And I doona want to lose my life, my love," she said, glancing up at Black Ben.

They moved over to the tapestry, all of them within reach of its silky threads. "Touch the tapestry and see if you are returned to Boyd Macleod. If you are not, then I shall help you."

Maya's stomach churned in knots with fear it wouldn't work, that she'd never return home. To Boyd.

"Because of the way magic works, how the past intertwines with the future, I doona want to say too much. Our lives all hang on what happens to you next. History could change if we say too much before the time for you to know is right. So," Kenzie said, taking her hands and kissing her cheeks. "It was lovely meeting you, Maya. I wish you a wonderful life full of love, family, and happiness."

"'Twas a pleasure, no matter how fleeting," Ben Ross said, his voice deep and gravelly.

Richard came toward her, arms outstretched before he pulled her into a hug. "Thank you for loving him. Thank you for all that you surrendered to win your highland Scot."

Maya hugged Richard in return, unable to stop the stream of tears. "I suppose 'you're welcome' fits, but somehow doesn't seem to be enough. But know," she said, gathering herself and stepping out of his hold, "that I adore Boyd. He is everything to me, and I do not regret my choice. I never felt that this was my time. I always felt unwanted, even from a young age." She didn't want to place some of that blame on growing up in foster homes, but nevertheless, it was true. "I'm home when it comes to Boyd. This castle, this very room, already holds many sweet memories for me with him. My heart is light, knowing that my returning to him enables all of you to live, have happiness, and love. Do not miss me too much," she joked.

Richard chuckled, going to stand beside Kenzie and Ben. "Touch the tapestry, lass and bless you."

Maya took in the three of them, forging them like stone into her memory. "Goodbye." She reached out, touching Boyd, just as she had previously, and woke up in total blackness, no sky, no ground, nothing.

Where the hell was she now!

It only took her a moment to gain her bearings, and she realized with no small amount of relief that she was in the room she had shared with Boyd. Except it was different somehow.

The light was dimmer, the room several degrees colder than it normally was, but at least the fire was banked high and well alight, taking some of the chill air away.

Maya walked to the window and gasped. A blanket of white, crisp snow covered everything that she could see. She knew she had been gone only a week or so in her time, but what did that mean in the past? Had she missed only weeks or years?

Please don't have been years. She could withstand a month, or even a year or two, but no more. That would be too cruel for Boyd to have lived without her for so long.

She went over to a large chest Boyd had allocated to her during her stay, and she opened it, relief pouring through her that her woolen plaid shawl was still there. She picked it up, remembering before she left the room the bag slung over her shoulder with her supplies to help her live in the past. Maya went over to the bed and, kneeling, shoved it underneath. No one should find it there.

Without waiting a moment more, she left the room. She could hear voices coming from the Great Hall, not many, but one definitely Mrs. Fletcher.

Maya stepped into the hall just as Mrs. Fletcher turned to leave. The housekeeper spotted her and, with a cry of amazement, proceeded to drop to the ground, her only saving grace the rushes that broke her fall.

"Oh dear," Maya said, running to her and trying to

wake up the older woman. So far, her return had not gone well. She could only hope that Boyd's seeing her would end in a much more pleasant way.

CHAPTER 37

Chapter Thirty Seven

"What do you mean he's not here?" Maya demanded several minutes later after Mrs. Fletcher had come back to her senses. They sat before the fire in the Great Hall, a cup of wine each to soothe mostly Mrs. Fletcher's nerves other than Maya's.

"He was due to return last week, but we had several inches of snow. I would believe that is what has delayed Laird Macleod. They were finishing up some repairs on crofter's cottages. Two days' ride south of here when the blizzard blew in. I should think the laird will be back within a week or so, once the snow melts a little."

Maya shivered, hating the idea of Boyd being out in this weather. Hopefully, the cottage he was housed in was one that had been repaired and was well-equipped to keep them safe and warm until the weather broke. "What if it doesn't melt? What if this snow sticks, and he's stuck out there for months?"

Mrs. Fletcher waved her concerns aside. "Nay, lass. He'll be back. Our laird is never away from Druiminn during the winter months."

"There is always a first time," Maya grumbled, finishing her wine. She couldn't sit still. She needed to see him. To make sure he was safe and well. That the Fae Queen had indeed healed him as she promised.

"And you're sure he has no injuries from the battle?"

A shadow entered Mrs. Fletcher's eyes before she said, "Only his heart, Maya lass. He's not been the same since you left. There have been several occasions over the past two months that we've shuffled him to bed, well in his cups, and he's mumbled about the Fae and what they made you do. I doona know all of what happened at Glendale, but I do know that Clan Macleod owes you a debt of gratitude. You have given us back our laird, our men, and our homes. We couldna be more grateful."

Maya threw her a small smile. "You're welcome, but it wasn't just me." She turned back to the window, staring out at the gray afternoon, the trees hanging low with the weight of the snow. It would have to be several inches thick underfoot. However was he to return in those conditions?

"And doona go getting any ideas of traveling out to find him, Maya lass. Not in your condition."

Maya gasped, having told no one of her condition. She looked at Mrs. Fletcher. How the hell had she found out?

"Ach, lass, doona look so surprised. Ye have the sweetest pouch, something that wasn't there when you were here last, and there is a healthy glow to your skin and eyes. I can see it from a mile away that you're carrying the laird's babe." The housekeeper smiled. "I'm happy for you, lass. 'Tis a blessing indeed."

"Thank you," Maya said, happiness swamping her at the notion. "But please don't say anything to anyone. I want Boyd to hear it from me."

"Of course, lass. And you shall. I'm certain he'll be home in a day or two."

He was not. Three weeks later and Boyd still had not returned. When Douglas and Jeane returned after spending some time at Jeane's new estate after their marriage, even they were concerned, even if their excitement of seeing Maya again gave them pleasure.

Boyd's absence was too long. Something was wrong, and if the clan did not do anything about it soon, then she would.

Over the past weeks, Boyd had felt no great need to return to Druiminn. There wasn't anything there for him, and his clan was safe for the time being. Over the last weeks, no matter how severe the snowstorms had been, they had managed to fix several crofter cottages and storage barns.

He had taken the time while here to get to know his clansmen who worked his fields, bred his cattle, and kept Druiminn and Macleod land thriving.

He could tell the men he had brought here to work were ready to return to their stronghold, and so with the first break of the weather, they had started the two-day journey north back toward Druiminn.

What he would do there when he returned, he was not sure. Throw himself back into the work of keeping the castle, his clan name strong. Not that there would be future generations to enjoy it.

Not unless Jeane and Douglas, now married, happened to have children. Mayhap their wedding trip back to Jeane's estate was a successful one.

He smiled at the thought. It would be nice to have children running about Druiminn halls once again. Boyd pushed down the prick of envy that the little bairns would not be his and Maya's. That he would not get to hold a daughter in his arms, teach her to be a strong swordswoman just like her mama wished she had been.

Boyd rubbed a hand over his face, sighing. *Enough, man*, he shouted in his mind. Maya lass was gone. Had given her life here with him so that he would live. No greater sacrifice could anyone make, not when he knew how much the lass had loved him.

How much he had loved her...

He looked ahead. By this evening, they would be back at Druiminn. He would not live in pity, not anymore. His people needed him. Maya would not like to see him wallow about, and it was not who he was. Mayhap if the gods gifted him in a future life, he would reunite with Maya. Now that he was mortal, at least it was a possibility, even if an unlikely one.

"Macleod." Thomas held up his hand, halting their caravan of horses and men. "Horsemen, just beyond those trees."

Boyd narrowed his eyes, seeing the flickering of horse legs through the copse of trees ahead. The riders were heavily covered in animal furs and wool. There were several of them, mayhap five if he was counting correctly. Boyd recognized Douglas's brown gelding within a moment, and the horse's one white stocking that extended to its knee.

"'Tis Douglas. No doubt checking to see that we are well. I should imagine they expected us weeks ago."

"Aye, 'tis Douglas alright," Thomas agreed.

Boyd pushed on, lifting his plaid over his shoulders when the snow started to fall. At least it was not heavy as it had been over the past several weeks.

He watched the other riders grow ever clearer in his vision, and a prickling of awareness ran down his spine like ice-cold water. He narrowed his eyes, trying to see who the rest of the party was made up of, and couldn't quite... Blood rushed to his brain, and for a moment, he felt lightheaded.

Nay, it could not be. "Get up," he shouted, kicking his horse.

The other rider, the one his eyes would not move from, did the same, and he almost lost his seat when he knew, to his very core, that Maya was cantering toward him, a much better rider than she was the first time she'd sat upon a horse.

He kicked his horse harder, thankful they followed a well-worn path used by animals, even in this time of year, and it was reasonably clear of snow. She stopped and waited for him, and he pulled his mount up beside her, noting that his clan, both behind and afront of him, had stopped to allow them privacy.

He devoured her with his eyes, not believing that she was real. He set his horse along hers, facing her, and reached out, clasping her face. She had rosy cheeks, her nose delightfully red, and her eyes, wet with tears, had snowflakes sitting on her lashes.

"How?" he asked, baffled and overwhelmed. She could not be here. He could not be so blessed in his life.

"With the help of your several-times-removed grandson," she said, laughing. "I will explain it all to you tonight, when we're alone, in our room. In our bed."

He barked out a laugh as heat licked along his spine. He wanted to wrench her from the saddle and kiss her. Hell, he'd kiss her anyway. Boyd leaned down, taking her lips. They were chilled and yet, so perfect. He kissed her long and deep, showed her with all that he was how much he loved her.

"I've missed you, lass. I love you so much," he said between kisses to her lips, her cheeks, her eyes, everywhere he could.

She giggled, wrapping her hands about his waist. "I love and have missed you too. I didn't think I'd ever see you again. I've been waiting weeks, and you didn't return, and I couldn't wait any longer. I hope you're not mad."

Stupid fool, he cursed himself for staying away. "Nay, I could never be mad at you, lass." He kicked himself for not having returned earlier. Had he known that Maya was at Druiminn, not even a snowstorm would have kept him away.

"I dinna think there was anything to return to. Not with haste. You must know that I would never have kept away had I known you were there."

"I understand." She leaned up and kissed him again. God's blood, she maddened him. Made him want her, and he knew from this moment on, he was a slave to her every command, her every wish.

"Shall we go home?" she asked, looking up at him with hope. With love.

His heart burst, full of the same emotion. "Oh aye, let us return home. We have a life to live."

Together.

CHAPTER 38

Chapter Thirty Eight

Six months later

Maya sat at the dais in the Great Hall, watching the clan enjoy their nightly meal, the laughter, the jokes, jibes, and good-humored banter that went on about the hall, making her smile.

The clan, Druiminn, had become home from the moment she had returned to sixteenth-century Scotland, and she could not have been happier. Except for one thing. The upcoming birth of their child. Maya glanced down at her pregnant belly, rubbing a hand over it. She was too large. She was either suffering from too much fluid or having twins.

Neither of which she knew for certain, but both made

her uneasy. A twin birth could be dangerous. Statistically, one of the children could be breech. Not that Boyd had understood anything of what she was telling him when she went to him about her anxieties, but nonetheless, he tried to comfort her, but it was no use.

She was terrified something bad would happen.

Something that would take her away from the life she loved. Away from the man she loved and adored.

"You're frowning again, Maya lass." Boyd placed his hand over hers, rubbing her stomach. "Doona worry, lass. The clan has one of the finest midwives, has been birthing babes for thirty years. She'll not let anything happen to the lady of Clan Macleod."

Maya sighed, hating that she was obvious with her concerns. So much so that others were picking up on her unease. "I know. I'm just worried. What if there are two?"

Boyd shook his head. "Nay, lass. There is only one. The future Laird Macleod. Our son. He's but a big boy, strong already. That is why you've rounded so much."

Maya slapped his arm, glaring at him. "Boyd, you're not allowed to say that to me. I'm not so big," she said, looking down at her belly, which really was huge.

He grinned, downing his ale. "You are perfect to me, lass. Just as you are."

Gasps and the sound of chairs scraping the stone floor pulled Maya's attention to the hall. A light, blinding in its intensity, floated toward them until it stopped before the table. A figure appeared to be walking toward them in the light before coming to stand right in front of them.

Maya could barely believe it. It had been months since they had any trouble from the Fae, and now, here they were again, going against their rules in interfering with the clan yet again.

"Hello, Maya, Macleod."

Maya wished she could sound as pleased to see the Fae, but she was not. "Sorcha?" she said without warmth. The Fae had almost caused her to lose Boyd. She would never forgive them such evil. "What are you doing here?"

Maya felt Boyd stiffen beside her before noticing he clasped the sword that leaned against his legs. That he would protect her against a woman Maya knew he had loved for a century made her love him all the more. Let her know that he was hers as much as she was his.

"You should not be here, Sorcha."

Sorcha smiled at Boyd, her eyes warming and annoyance spiked in Maya's blood. The Fae would not want to be starting any new troubles, or Maya would use the sword in Boyd's hand against her herself.

"I promise you. This will be the last time. For all the troubles you've had with the queen, the Seelie Court believed that you should be gifted with one more gift. The queen has now been punished and will not walk the mortal world again."

"We doona need any more gifts. We have the Faery Flag."

Maya nodded, remembering everything Boyd had told her about what happened after she returned to the future. How Sorcha had made the queen face the consequences of her actions. How the clan had been gifted a flag that was supposed to hold magical powers that had allowed them to win the war.

"This is a gift from me to the clan that I loved as much as I once loved its laird. A gift to your new bride, who I know is your future, and the clan's. Allow me this one boon. Please, Boyd," Sorcha said in a tone that Maya had never heard before. It was almost human, and she felt

Boyd relax at her words, his hand moving off the hilt of his sword.

"Vera well. One more favor."

Sorcha moved closer, her eyes flickering with power. "I have gifted you the Faery Flag. This flag is to be passed down from son to son, laird to laird, to keep Clan Macleod and Druiminn safe from harm. I also gift to you, Maya and Boyd, any female children from the Macleod bloodline the gift of sight, the gift of time jumping, both into the past and future. These gifts I gift to thee."

Maya thought back to Kenzie, how Richard brought her to Druiminn to help her return to Boyd should the tapestry not work. She leaned back in her chair, understanding what Kenzie had told her of sight and that in time she would understand. That should she not return to Boyd, their future, the one Kenzie, Richard, and Black Ben held dear was in peril.

"It is all a little mechanical, Maya lass, but you're right. Kenzie had the powers you were gifted today, while also not having them because you had not been gifted them at that point. But," Sorcha shrugged, smiling at her, "when time jumping, I always find to accept what is, and not try to figure out anything more than that."

"Are you saying any female children of Macleod blood, not just our blood, but cousins, siblings, will have this gift?"

"They will. The Macleod clan in the future will need them to continue, to thrive. You were my family once too. I shall never forget your kindness, and I gift you this now to keep you always from harm."

Boyd nodded, taking Maya's hand. "I thank you, Sorcha lass."

Maya nodded, thankful too. "Thank you, Sorcha, for both gifts. We're forever grateful. Truly."

Sorcha turned and started to walk back to the light. "'Tis my pleasure," she said, her Scottish accent as thick as Boyd's. Maya smiled, knowing she spoke so to please her past love. A goodbye. A full stop to that part of her life.

Maya turned to Boyd. "I can see why you liked her so much."

Boyd laughed, pulling her onto his lap and kissing her, his arms protectively across her belly. "I love you more," he said, his eyes darkening with heat.

She clasped his face, kissing him back, knowing that he did. And that, in return, she'd adore him until her final breath.

Several days later, Maya lay in bed, her two little babes lying on either side of her asleep. Boyd on the end of the bed, lying on his back, and also passed out as if he'd done all the work. Which, she would remind him, he did not.

She glanced down at her little family. There were four of them now. All of them utterly adorable, and each of them able to break her heart should anything happen to them.

Maya would be lying if she did not fear her son's future. This was the sixteenth century. Men were warriors in this time. Clan wars still occurred for a hundred years, and so she had no doubt her little lad too would fight at some point.

But she also knew he had a future. Children of his own, and that settled her fear somewhat.

She looked down at her daughter. She had the sweetest button nose and long, dark eyelashes like her father. Her heart swelled, and she couldn't stop staring at them.

"You need to rest, lass."

Maya met Boyd's eyes across the bed, knowing what he said was true but also knowing she wanted to relish this time. All too soon, it would be gone, and they would have their own adventures, their own lives.

"I will rest, I promise. I was watching you all rest."

Boyd chuckled, slipped off the bed, and poured her a wine, bringing it over to her. She didn't tell Boyd that alcohol while breastfeeding was a no-no, and instead, she took the wine and set it down.

"Have I told you, lass how much I love you and our babes? I've never been so happy." He came and sat beside her, pulling her to lay in the crook of his arm.

Maya snuggled into him, laying her head on his chest and hearing the beat of his heart, reveling in the sound. "I'm so glad they're born and well. I was a little worried."

“I canna believe you birthed twins."

She smiled, running her hand over his chest. "Promise me you will protect them with your life."

He met her gaze, frowning a little. "Aye, always, lass. Just as I will always protect you." He paused a moment, reaching down and picking up Lily-Rose, who was sucking her thumb. "My wee lassie will be a warrior. Strong and powerful and shall have the world at her feet."

Maya picked up Samuel Harrison, kissing his sweet, chubby cheeks. "And our boy?" she asked.

"He will be a powerful, noble laird, strong and true."

"And us?" Maya asked Boyd, the babies sleeping in their arms.

"We, Maya lass, will live forever. No matter when death finally comes to call, our love shall surpass, and I will find you again. Even if it takes me a thousand years next time, I shall see you again."

Maya sniffed back the tears, unable to swallow past the lump in her throat. "I love you, thank you for us."

"Nay, it is I who is thankful," he said, leaning down and kissing her, and even merely hours after having children, her stomach fluttered at his touch.

No matter how many years passed, that feeling never changed. Not for either of them.

Not even with their final breaths.

EPILOGUE

Sixteen Years Later

"Boyd, your daughter has disappeared yet again after I told her not to. I know where she's gone, and it has to stop."

Boyd looked up from his desk at the vision of his wife, her hair askew as if she'd been running a hand through it or, more accurately, flying about the castle trying to find their daughter.

"She'll return for dinner. She always does."

"I know she's jumped into the future. I just know it."

Their son walked in after his mother and slumped into the chair before Boyd's desk, laying one leg over the arm, an apple in hand. "I think she has a suitor."

Maya all but stomped her foot, staring at them both with widened eyes. Boyd tried to stop his laughter from spilling forth, but his wife, so at a loss with their daughter's actions over the past weeks, was too amusing not to laugh at. Lily had been jumping between times, and although Boyd worried for her, he also knew she was well prepared to defend herself, and the future times from what Maya had told him seemed safer than the past. She could not get into too much trouble surely.

"Come here, lass, and stop fussing so. Lily will be back and with many grand tales to tell as always."

"She has to stop this. Just because you can time travel doesn't mean you should. She could be messing up the future or the past. What if she does something in the future and I disappear?"

Boyd frowned, disliking the notion. "I shall speak to her. We shall stop her from messing about with her power."

"I wish I had a power," Samuel said, mumbling as he ate his apple. "Laird or no, I think I should have liked to see the future."

Maya threw up her hands, coming over to Boyd and sitting on his lap. "I give up. Both our children now want to go into the future. I think your first wife did this to us on purpose. She was probably jealous of me, and this was her payback."

Boyd still stumbled with some of the terms Maya came up with. Payback? He shook his head, knowing Sorcha did not give the gift out of malice but out of love. Just as he loved and adored Maya to the point of distraction.

"I shall talk to Lily."

"Talk to me about what?" their daughter said, stepping into the room, a boy or young man at her side. Maya wrenched off his lap, striding to Lily and pulling her aside.

"What have you done?" Maya demanded, looking at the boy with fear in her eyes.

"Family, this is my friend, Caelan Bruce. He's come to stay with us for a little while."

Boyd stood, towering over his daughter, who seemed not the slightest concerned over the fact she was in trouble.

Not that Lily ever did worry. The lass had always had a way of wrapping him about her finger without nary a trouble.

"Lily, where is Caelan from?" Boyd demanded, sensing his wife already knew.

"From mother's time."

Samuel laughed. Maya's mouth gaped, and Boyd cringed, and yet, even while his daughter had defied more rules, he couldn't help but love his family and the troubles they faced every day. He wouldn't have it any other way.

AFTERWORD

To Win a Highland Scot is the third book in my Time Traveler's Highland Love series, and I hope you enjoyed the story. When writing this series, I wanted to use historical events to add adventure, action, and tragedy to the stories. The battle between the MacLeod and O'Cain clans was based on Clan MacLeod and Clan MacDonald's real-life disputes.

These clans had long disliked the other, and it is said that during the Battle of Glendale (Skye), the Faery Flag was raised, doubling MacLeod's forces tenfold, ultimately saving the clan who were losing to Clan MacDonald (O'Cain). The Faery Flag was reportedly gifted to Clan MacLeod by the Fae, where it remains to this day at Dunvegan Castle (Druiminn). Laying in wait for when the clan needs the help of the Fae once more.

Thank you for taking the time to read *To Win a Highland Scot*! I hope you enjoyed the third book in my Time-Traveler's Highland Love series.

I adore my readers, and I'm so thankful for your support with my books. If you're able, I would appreciate an honest review of *To Win a Highland Scot*. As they say, feed an author, leave a review! Alternatively, you can keep in contact with me by visiting my website or following me online. You can contact me at www.tamaragill.com or email me at tamaragillauthor@gmail.com.

If you'd like to learn about my time travel books, please read on. I have included chapter one of A Stolen Season for your reading pleasure.

Tamara Gill

A STOLEN SEASON

One small mistake in the past will change everything about her future... Archaeologist Sarah Baxter just broke one of the biggest rules of time travel: leaving a piece of 21st century equipment in 19th century Regency England. Unfortunately, when she goes back to retrieve it, she makes an even bigger mess of things—resulting in the death of an English Earl.

. . .

Now his brother is not only out for revenge, but he also has Sarah's device. Which means an entirely different approach is needed. It doesn't occur to the new Earl of Earnston that his charming acquaintance is responsible for his brother's death. He is merely swept away by a passion that threatens his very reputation. Yet he gets the distinct impression that Miss Baxter is hiding something from him.

Now Sarah must find a way to steal back her device, hide the truth about the earl's brother and—most importantly— not fall in love...

CHAPTER 1

England 1817 – Kent

Sarah shifted in the saddle, the weight of her saturated clothes heavy on her shoulders and hindering her seat. The horse's pounding hooves, as loud as a drum, echoed in her ears. She kicked her mount and urged him over a small hedgerow, her determination not to be caught overriding her common sense.

Rain streamed down her face, but she couldn't stop. The future of TimeArch depended on it. Her father's years of research. The hundreds of hours spent working on man's greatest, most sought-after ability. Sarah slowed her mount to canter through a fast moving ford, the stones causing the horse to stumble, making the short trip across painfully slow. Time was up. She had to get away. Though the horse grappled and slipped up the other side of the muddy bank to continue on, apprehension still threatened to close her throat in panic.

The mount missed a step, and Sarah clutched the saddle, cursing the weather. She flashed a glance over her shoulder and cried out her frustration into the sheeting rain at the sight of the Earl of Earnston not two horse-lengths behind.

His gaze held hers, and with fearless determination, he urged his mount beside, clutching for her reins.

"Let go." Sarah punched his hand and kicked out, trying to push him away. All in vain, as it seemed nothing could deter his resolve.

"What does it do?" he yelled, pulling on her reins.

The horses bumped hard, and Sarah fought for balance. "Let go, Lord Earnston. You'll kill us both."

He released her reins for a moment as a large bush separated them. But, at blistering speed, he drew beside her again.

"What's so important you'd risk your life?" he hollered over the storm.

Sarah shook her head. Why wouldn't he leave her alone? Damn her clumsiness in his library. Had she never knocked over the vase—had she not tripped, for that matter—the Earl would never have investigated the sound. But he had, and he'd found her hands deep in his collection of peculiars, stealing a device not of this time.

"Forget about it. Forget me," she yelled through the deluge. "Go home!"

"No," he said, spurring his horse ahead of hers.

A low-lying tree branch slapped her face. Sarah cringed at the stinging pain. The night was perfect for thievery, but not for escape at breakneck speed. If they kept up the chase, it was only a matter of time before one of them was killed.

"Stop your horse!"

Sarah shook her head and kicked her mount on. No matter the dangers, she couldn't obey him. The future, her father's business, everything she held dear hinged on her getting away. "I won't. My lord, please leave me."

He clasped her reins and jerked hard. Sarah's horse bucked at the aggressive manhandling, and she tipped awkwardly to one side. Feeling herself about to fall, she reached out and clutched at the earl. Her reins slipped from his grasp as his strong arm encircled her waist, struggling to keep her from falling between the two horses. But it was little use. Her horse veered away, and she fell hard against his lordship's mount. Her fingers, cold and wet, slipped for purchase on his saddle, but his horse shied away from her.

"Hold on, I have you." With an oath, the earl tried to pull her up, but gravity was against them.

"I'm slipping. Let me go. I'll bring you down." Sarah's feet dragged on the muddy, stone-strewn road, and she braced herself for a bruising fall. A gentleman to the last, he shook his head and tried to pull up his horse. "Please, let me go." But it was too late. His horse slipped, and they both hit the muddy track with a sickening thud.

Sarah landed on her knees and rolled. Leaf litter and mud entered her mouth, and her leg twisted, shooting a pain into her hip.

Moments later, the wet nose of her horse nuzzled her neck. She dragged herself to a sitting position and wiped mud from her face and eyes with a torn remnant of her shirt. Taking deep breaths, she waited for her body to stop shaking. The only sound was the rain slapping at the leaves through the foliage above.

Then she saw the motionless form on the muddy track. Dread clawed up her spine. Sarah crawled to where the earl lay, his head twisted at an awkward angle. She rolled him over and cursed his vacant, lifeless eyes.

"Don't be dead. Please, don't be dead." She felt along his stubbled jaw and around to the nape of his neck where a lump protruded from his skin.

Unable to accept what her eyes told her, she bent over his chest and listened for a heartbeat.

Nothing.

Sarah slumped back on her haunches and covered her face. She'd killed him. She'd killed Lord William, the blooming Earl of Earnston! "I'm so sorry," she said, tears mingling with the rain in a muddy pool at her feet. What had she done? The earl wasn't supposed to die, not yet, and certainly not by her hand. Within the space of half an hour, she'd probably wiped out a complete generation of earls. She'd stuffed up history, and she couldn't undo it.

Not even her father could.

A crack of lightning illuminated the dark forest, and Sarah quickly stood when the silhouette of a horse and man loomed from the shadows.

"Halt!"

Ignoring the warning, she grappled to mount her horse as the fired-up mare pranced. "I'm sorry," she said to the cloaked figure as he dismounted and ran to the earl's limp form sprawled on the ground.

He bent, felt for a pulse, and gasped. Her stomach rolled with nausea knowing what she'd done and what he'd discovered. A flicker of silver flashed as he stood.

"Stay where you are or I'll shoot you as dead as my brother."

Sarah turned her head, frantically searching for someone to help. Perhaps Richard, her partner, who'd warned her not to go tonight. He said the weather wasn't good for safe getaways.

And he was right.

It was the flash of lightning outside the earl's library window illuminating a menagerie of severed and stuffed animal heads that had scared the shit out of her, and she'd tripped. The earl heard the commotion, came to investigate, and caught her red handed.

Idiot.

"Please. It was an accident." She watched him cock the pistol and wondered if he'd actually shoot a woman. His voice, trembling with shock and hate, told her he would.

"Get off the horse—now."

"I can't." With shaking fingers, she grabbed the reins. "I'm sorry." She turned her horse and kicked it hard.

"Halt, I say."

She ignored the steely voice that thrummed with warning. Instead, she pushed her mount into a gallop, the horse slipping, unable to move fast enough. And then the shot, followed by searing pain, deafened her and deadened the sound of the thrashing storm to a vague rumble.

Her fingers tingled and warmth seeped along her skin. Sarah looked down, expecting to see her arm missing. He'd shot her! "Get up," she hollered to the horse, ignoring the pain and the curse from behind.

The horse gained its footing, and she peered over her shoulder, the silhouette of the man all she could see. Cold rain set goose bumps over her skin, yet she pushed on, determined to make the inn and London. The second decade of twenty-first century London to be exact.

~

With a running nose and an arm that throbbed and ached with every thud of the horse's stride, Sarah sped through the night. At last, she spied the glowing lights of the inn, a welcome beacon on this frightening journey.

Wet and bedraggled, like a beggar woman, she entered the common room and waited for the innkeeper to acknowledge her.

He walked toward her and eyed her injured arm with suspicion. "Ye have an injury there, lass. Do I need to summon the doctor for ye?"

"No. I'll be fine." She tried to pull what remained of her jacket across her wound, then gave up. She placed her sodden shawl about her shoulders, thankful she had thought to pack it in her saddlebag.

"What can I get ye then, love?" The innkeeper leaned on the counter, his fetid breath making her queasy stomach roll even more.

"Can you direct me to Mr. Alastair Lynch's room please? I believe he has a chamber set aside for a Miss Phoebe Marshall." A knowing twinkle entered his eyes, and Sarah's own narrowed in comprehension.

"Right this way, Miss Marshall."

The smell of wine, beer, and cooking meat permeated the air, making her nose twitch. She needed help and quickly. Summoning a smile, she thanked the innkeeper as he walked her to a door and nodded.

"This is ye're room, Miss. I'll send up a girl when I have one spare if ye wish for a wash."

"Ah, yes, thank you. That would be most kind." Sarah waited for his heavy footfalls to disappear down the stairs before she entered the chamber. The smell of damp wood burning and the flicker of two candles greeted her along with a pair of boots warming before the hearth.

Sarah shut the door and sagged against it. Relief poured through her veins, making her legs shake. The wound thumped, reminding her of the injury, and she pulled her shawl away to look.

Richard jumped from his seat. "Sarah, good God, you've been shot!"

"I have, but that's not the worst part. I also tripped in the Earl of Earnston's library and both brothers came to investigate. I ran." She walked over to the bed, threw her soggy shawl to the floor, and flopped onto the hard mattress. "He caught up with me when I escaped on horseback. How, I have no idea."

Richard came over and pulled her boots from her feet. "Knew the area, I suppose." He checked her wound. "It doesn't appear too bad. Just a graze by the looks of it."

Sarah glanced at the bloodied mess. "Yes. But that's not all. I killed Earnston."

Richard reeled as if slapped. "You killed the Earl… Good God! How? Why?"

She shook her head and gave him a rundown of the night's events. Sarah shut her eyes, not wanting to remember his lifeless gaze staring up at her or the horror of knowing she was the cause of his demise. "His brother came upon us and demanded I stay. Of course I ran. I had to. And…he shot me."

With one hand, she undid the first button at the front of her shirt, stood, and tried to pull the sleeve off her arm.

"Here, let me help you." Richard pulled out a knife. He cut the garment from around her arm and slid it down over the soaked chemise underneath.

Nausea pooled in her throat. "We have to go home. I need this wound seen to and…" "What?" he asked, brow furrowed.

"I don't feel well. It's not very nice being shot."

Richard chuckled, walked over to a bag in the corner

of the room, and shuffled the contents. "I should imagine not. I think I have some morphine in here and a tetanus jab, also. Should be enough until we're home tomorrow."

Morphine sounded heavenly at the moment. A knock sounded at the door, and Richard allowed a wide-eyed maid to enter. With steady hands, she placed a steaming bowl of water and linens on a side table.

"Will ye be needing my assistance, Miss?" the servant asked, her eyes stealing to Richard, then back to her.

"No. Thank you. I shall be fine on my own." Sarah smiled and waited for the door to close before walking over to the water. She soaked a small cloth, dabbed it against the wound, and washed the blood from her arm. The injury was surprisingly clean—a flesh wound that wouldn't require stitching. A small mercy this night.

"Does it hurt?" Richard flicked the morphine needle. "Yes, so hurry up and give me the shot; you know I have a low pain threshold."

Within moments, the ache faded, and a warm fuzzy feeling settled over her. Richard fussed with her arm and bandaged it. Then she collapsed before the fire and stared at the flames that produced hardly any heat. What a mess she'd made of things. How was she ever to explain to her father?

"Are you good, then? I'll see you in the morning if so." Sarah nodded. "I'll be fine. The wound's hardly bleeding, and I intend to go to bed before the morphine wears off." She paused, knowing she had one more confession this eve. "Richard, I lost the mapping device."

He frowned. "You don't have it?"

"It was in my pocket, but it must have fallen out when I fell. I have no idea where it would be now."

He came and sat across from her, two fingers pinching

the bridge of his nose. "Should we go back tomorrow and try and find it? Do you think the earl's brother knew what you'd stolen?"

"No," she said, standing and walking to the window to look out over the blackness illuminated at intervals by distant lightning. "Not yet at least. And with any luck the mud and rain has hidden the device, and all will be well. Well, at least," she said, turning back to Richard, "until my father finds out what I did and the shit hits the fan."

"Shit's right." Richard paced the room, his footfalls loud in the small space. "This could be a disaster. Now he knows the device is valuable, for whatever reason, and will keep it hidden."

"That's if he finds it." She rubbed the bandage on her arm. "Let's not worry about it now. We'll be home tomorrow, and Father will tell us what to do."

"He certainly will. And let's hope for our sakes he's in a better mood than when he sent us here the first time."

Sarah sighed and pulled back the woolen blankets and coarse linen sheets on her bed. "Don't hold your breath. My father's going to be furious. Not only have I lost a device that could blow the lid off TimeArch and all its secrets, I've changed the history of a family forever."

~

Eric, now Lord Earnston, cursed and threw his flintlock to the ground. Pain seized his chest when he glanced at his elder brother, dead at his feet. His eyes narrowed on the small female figure disappearing into the shadowy forest surrounding his family's estate.

He stumbled to his knees and allowed the rain to wash away tears shed for his closest confidant. A man of honor about to start a new chapter when he married his betrothed.

No longer. Thanks to the woman who'd snatched his future away.

He ran a hand through his hair, wondering why his brother had followed the chit at such breakneck speed.

With trembling fingers, he closed his brother's eyes, sending a prayer to God.

The woman had stolen something. But what?

He whistled for his horse, who, as if sensing death, hung his head lower with every step toward him. Eric lifted his brother, not an easy feat considering his size, and laid him over the saddle.

At the sound of crunching under his boot, Eric bent and frowned at the mud-soaked silver device beneath his feet. He rubbed it against his jacket and stared in amazement at the highly polished silver trinket.

A trinket his sibling had treasured for reasons Eric could never fathom.

With another rolling boom of thunder, he mounted his horse and turned for home to announce the death of his much-loved brother, bury him, and see justice served on the wench who took his life. Then he would find out why the object was so valuable—and why his brother and the woman would risk their lives to possess it.

LORDS OF LONDON SERIES
AVAILABLE NOW!

Dive into these charming historical romances! In this six-book series, Darcy seduces a virginal duke, Cecilia's world collides with a roguish marquess, Katherine strikes a deal with an unlucky earl and Lizzy sets out to conquer a very wicked Viscount. These stories plus more adventures in the Lords of London series! Available now through Amazon or read free with KindleUnlimited.

KISS THE WALLFLOWER SERIES AVAILABLE NOW!

If the roguish Lords of London are not for you and wallflowers are more your cup of tea, this is the series for you. My Kiss the Wallflower series, are linked through friendship and family in this four-book series. You can grab a copy on Amazon or read free through KindleUnlimited.

ALSO BY TAMARA GILL

Royal House of Atharia Series

TO DREAM OF YOU

A ROYAL PROPOSITION

FOREVER MY PRINCESS

ROYAL ATHARIA - BOOKS 1-3 BUNDLE

League of Unweddable Gentlemen Series

TEMPT ME, YOUR GRACE

HELLION AT HEART

DARE TO BE SCANDALOUS

TO BE WICKED WITH YOU

KISS ME DUKE

THE MARQUESS IS MINE

LEAGUE - BOOKS 1-3 BUNDLE

LEAGUE - BOOKS 4-6 BUNDLE

Kiss the Wallflower series

A MIDSUMMER KISS

A KISS AT MISTLETOE

A KISS IN SPRING

TO FALL FOR A KISS

A DUKE'S WILD KISS

TO KISS A HIGHLAND ROSE

KISS THE WALLFLOWER - BOOKS 1-3 BUNDLE

KISS THE WALLFLOWER - BOOKS 4-6 BUNDLE

Lords of London Series

TO BEDEVIL A DUKE

TO MADDEN A MARQUESS

TO TEMPT AN EARL

TO VEX A VISCOUNT

TO DARE A DUCHESS

TO MARRY A MARCHIONESS

LORDS OF LONDON - BOOKS 1-3 BUNDLE

LORDS OF LONDON - BOOKS 4-6 BUNDLE

To Marry a Rogue Series

ONLY AN EARL WILL DO

ONLY A DUKE WILL DO

ONLY A VISCOUNT WILL DO

ONLY A MARQUESS WILL DO

ONLY A LADY WILL DO

TO MARRY A ROGUE - BOOKS 1-5 BUNDLE

A Time Traveler's Highland Love Series

TO CONQUER A SCOT

TO SAVE A SAVAGE SCOT

TO WIN A HIGHLAND SCOT

HIGHLAND LOVE - BOOKS 1-3 BUNDLE

Time Travel Romance

DEFIANT SURRENDER

A STOLEN SEASON

Scandalous London Series

A GENTLEMAN'S PROMISE

A CAPTAIN'S ORDER

A MARRIAGE MADE IN MAYFAIR

SCANDALOUS LONDON - BOOKS 1-3 BUNDLE

High Seas & High Stakes Series

HIS LADY SMUGGLER

HER GENTLEMAN PIRATE

HIGH SEAS & HIGH STAKES - BOOKS 1-2 BUNDLE

Daughters Of The Gods Series

BANISHED-GUARDIAN-FALLEN

DAUGHTERS OF THE GODS - BOOKS 1-3 BUNDLE

Stand Alone Books

TO SIN WITH SCANDAL

OUTLAWS

ABOUT THE AUTHOR

Tamara is an Australian author who grew up in an old mining town in country South Australia, where her love of history was founded. So much so, she made her darling husband travel to the UK for their honeymoon, where she dragged him from one historical monument and castle to another.

A mother of three, her two little gentlemen in the making, a future lady (she hopes) and a part-time job keep her busy in the real world, but whenever she gets a moment's peace she loves to write romance novels in an array of genres, including regency, medieval and time travel.

www.tamaragill.com
tamaragillauthor@gmail.com

Made in the USA
Monee, IL
17 May 2021